Samantha Lee Howe began her professional writing career in 2007 and has been working as a freelance writer predominately writing horror and fantasy under the pen name Sam Stone. This body of work includes 13 novels 5 novellas, 3 collections, over 40 short stories, an audio drama and a *Doctor Who* spin-off drama that went to DVD in November 2017. *The Stranger in Our Bed* is Samantha Lee Howe's debut breakaway psychological thriller.

The Stranger In Our Bed

Samantha Lee Howe

One More Chapter
an imprint of HarperCollins*Publishers* Ltd
1 London Bridge Street
London SE1 9GF

www.harpercollins.co.uk

This paperback edition 2022
1

First published in Great Britain in ebook format
by HarperCollins*Publishers* 2020

A catalogue record for this book
is available from the British Library

ISBN: 978-0-00-852382-4

Set in Birka by
Palimpsest Book Production Limited, Falkirk, Stirlingshire

Printed and bound in the UK using 100%
renewable electricity at CPI Group (UK) Ltd

For Ayshea,
Friend, adviser and cheerleader.

Based on a true story

Thanks to
   Camilla Shestopal and Finn Cotton for their guidance
and advice,

Also thanks to
   Dr David Phillips for his sound medical advice.

Prologue

The rain fell in big fat droplets and poured down into my eyes. My hair was plastered to my head – blonde turned into dirty wet streaks that clung to my cheeks. I'd been here before, another time, another moment of betrayal and sadness. *Déjà vu.* Fear sank down into the pit of my stomach. I was drowning in the endless possibilities of 'future'. What about my daughter? So small, so helpless, so alone.

Oh God! *Melody.* She was in the house ...

I wanted to run, make sure Melody was all right, but I couldn't move. My limbs were frozen, my whole body weak. I might have been suffering from shock – and no surprise.

I ran my hand over my face, clearing the water from my eyes. And then my fingers touched the sore sticky wound on my forehead and I found myself staring at the red stain on my palm. The rain eroded the blood, as though it could wash away the evidence of my crime.

I was standing on a precipice, swaying slightly. I closed my eyes, blocking out the sight of the hole in the ground at my feet. Nothing moved. I didn't want to look down at the picture of death below, even though I was responsible for it, but the shape of the body crumpled in the void was still visible behind my eyes. I shook my head, trying to dispel the unwelcome thought along with the guilt I carried.

When did this all start? How had my life taken this terrible turn?

The shovel weighed heavy in my hand, a presence in its own right, further evidence of my guilt. Like the horror of my situation, the shovel's weight was too much to bear; I dropped it down beside the makeshift grave.

Like a guilty child whose hand is caught in the cookie jar, I wiped my soiled palm on the leg of my sodden jeans.

There was nowhere to run, and no escape from the truth.

I jumped as I heard a distant, persistent wail. Sirens approached. The screeching grew louder.

I opened my eyes and lights came on in the big house behind me. The back door stood open. My only witness was framed in the glare of the kitchen light, blurred by the slicing rainstorm.

I turned to look beyond the house, facing the rain. It blinded me, as did the flashing blue light that pierced through the trees lining the long driveway.

The sirens dropped off, but lights still flickered above two police cars. In the house, I thought I heard Melody crying. And then, my legs began to work.

Unaware of the black shape slowly getting to its feet in the pit behind me, I started to walk towards the first police car.

Chapter One

Two Years Earlier

I woke early. My husband, Tom, was still sleeping. It was 5.30 a.m. and I usually slept through until Tom's alarm went off at 7.30. I listened to the sounds of our home. There was nothing unusual, yet something had woken me. My mind was fully alert, like a light switch had been turned on. I lay on my side, watching Tom's handsome face. He looked so young when he slept. It was hard to imagine him as the CEO of the conglomerate that was Carlisle Corp.

We'd met at university, ten years earlier. We'd both been studying law at Oxford. Tom was focusing on corporate law, already preparing for the day when he would take over the family business. I'd been studying corporate law too and I had ambitions for the future, but unlike Tom I'd had to work in a bar to help fund my education, and relied heavily on my student loans and any bursaries I could apply for.

I turned over and trying not to disturb Tom I got out of bed. But as I took my first step an overwhelming bout of nausea came over me. No longer trying to be quiet I ran into the bathroom, and vomited into the toilet bowl. When the sickness subsided, I brushed my teeth and looked at the yellow pallor of my skin in the mirror. I felt terrible. Perhaps I had come down with some bug?

'Char?' said Tom from the bedroom. 'Are you all right?'

I couldn't believe my luck when he asked me out for the first time. For a while I didn't trust we could have a relationship, we were too different. But when we finished our education, Tom asked me to marry him, and the future I'd planned for myself changed.

Soon after our wedding, Tom's father, Conrad Carlisle, succumbed to the cancer that had been eating away at him for years. Tom hadn't expected me to work after that.

'I need your support, Char,' he'd said. 'I'm going to be working long hours at first. If you take a job too, then we'll never see each other. Besides, you don't need to work. I'll give you everything you need.'

It was an odd notion after all of my motivations and hard work, but the whirlwind of our life soon took away any thought of finding my own place in a law firm. I became a housewife instead.

'Char?' Tom called again.

A crushing sense of gratitude warmed by stomach. Had the upset from the previous night affected me so much that it had made me sick? Tom sounded like his usual caring self. I was relieved to hear that love and warmth back in his voice. The argument had been so ridiculous. So ... unnecessary.

'I'm fine. Maybe got a bug,' I said.

'Bug my arse,' Tom said, coming into the bathroom.

'What?' I was immediately on the defensive.

'When was your period?' he smiled.

'*Period?* No ... just because I was sick doesn't mean ...'

'Reckon we did the job on our anniversary trip ...' he said. 'I'd hoped at least! But looks like we did.'

'Well it's probably too early to know. That was only ...' It was then I realized that more than a month had passed, and my period was late. By about two weeks.

'I'll ring Mother. She'll be so happy!' Tom said.

'Darling, can't we wait a bit? Just to be sure,' I said.

'Don't be silly! We don't have to keep this a secret from Mother.'

Isadora Carlisle arrived an hour later with a small pharmacy package, which she passed to me.

'Tom called on his way to work. Let's see if he's right, shall we?' Isadora said. 'You need to hold it under the flow of your pee.'

As usual she was treating me as though I didn't have the intelligence to read instructions for myself.

I went into the bathroom, closing the door behind me, then unpacked the pregnancy test and read the instructions.

'I'm sure it's way too early to tell,' I said.

'No. These days they can tell even if you're just a few days along,' Isadora said from the hallway. 'So useful!'

She was right, of course; the test said it could work up to six days *before* your period was even due.

After peeing on the wand, I stared at the indicator. The test said one blue line meant 'no', two blue lines was 'yes'.

'Let me in,' said Isadora.

I opened the bathroom door and held out the test. 'It says ...'

'Pregnant!' Isadora grew very quiet and thoughtful. She didn't throw her arms around me, or start to congratulate me, she merely smiled. A kind of satisfied expression. As though she was just getting the answer she had expected all along.

'That's very good then,' she said.

I half-smiled, but then my mood plummeted. Was I really ready for motherhood? The thought was terrifying.

'I know what you're thinking,' Isadora said. 'You see, Charlotte dear, you remind me a lot of myself at your age.'

I sat down on the edge of the bed and stared back at her with the blankest expression I could muster. There was nothing similar about us at all. She was happy about the prospect of a future grandchild and I was a mixture of unexplainable emotions. Perhaps this self-doubt, the fear, the slight tingle of excitement was perfectly normal, I didn't know, but they were also accompanied by a consuming loss of control. And something else at the back of my mind, a name I had told myself to forget: Ewan Daniels.

'This will settle things permanently for you both,' Isadora said.

'What do you mean?'

'It's just ... it's a final commitment. Having a baby ...'

'Isadora, we are committed. We're married.'

'Oh, yes. I know. But you know what I mean ... you'll be a family now. Not just a couple. This is grown-up. This is, well, it's the future CEO of Carlisle Corp you have in there. Isn't it?'

And then she peered at me intently as though she expected me to say otherwise. I was confused by this silent enquiry.

'I hadn't thought of it that way ...'

'Well, I'll get on to finding you the best doctor and private midwife service. And of course the best hospital.'

'That's usually decided by your local GP,' I said.

'Not for people like us, dear. We have to have the best.'

And then it really sank in. I was growing tired of not being listened to. The only trouble was, I couldn't blame Isadora or Tom for any of it. I had caused this by not standing up for myself when it was too easy to just accept another person's decision.

Like the bedding I'd bought months ago that had caused such a row the night before. I couldn't make any sense of Tom's angry outburst. It was so over the top and out of character. Tom was usually so calm.

I asked Isadora to leave me, explaining that I didn't feel too well. She was sympathetic, but still took it upon herself to call Tom and confirm his suspicions. I couldn't hear everything he said to her on her mobile phone, but I heard the pleasure and excitement in his voice.

'We're so happy,' Isadora said before leaving. 'Rest up, Charlotte dear. The morning sickness won't last long. I'll get you booked in with a private doctor as soon as possible.'

'Thanks,' I said.

She let herself out and I went back to bed and lay, eyes open, staring at the ceiling. *They* would control every decision that needed to be made as they always had.

*

By the afternoon, the initial sickness abated and I got up, dressed and went out. I was sick of being predictable. I thought I ought to at least start to put things into place that I wanted to happen. This child might be a Carlisle but it was also my child and I would have a say. I don't know what came over me.

I found a note on the kitchen notice board from Tom, reminding me to return the purple satin bedding that he'd disliked so much. At least that would give me something to do. I folded the bed linen neatly, squeezing them back into the original packaging. There was no need to search out the receipt, my account would show the purchase, and so I placed all of the items into a large canvas bag.

I didn't feel like travelling on the tube with all of these things just in case the sickness returned, so I took a cab to Harrods.

'Morning Mrs Carlisle,' the store doorman said. 'Let me get someone to help you with that ...'

A few moments later two shop assistants arrived and took the bag from me.

'I'm afraid I have to return this,' I told the first assistant, a different girl to the one who had originally served me. 'My husband ... doesn't like it.'

She processed the refund without protest. I was a good customer in the store, and so was my mother-in-law. As I waited for the refund receipt, I felt the hairs prickle on the back of my neck. I turned around with a feeling of *déjà vu*. A tall man stood behind me, so close I could reach out and touch him. It was Ewan Daniels. A shiver of something like excitement ran along my spine, as if I had been waiting for him to appear.

'Charlotte,' he said, as though my presence there surprised him. 'I thought I might never see you again ...'

That was the third time I'd met Ewan by accident; it appeared it was becoming a habit.

Chapter Two

We went for coffee in a local café.

Ewan looked well, but I was sure I didn't look very good at all. I hadn't bothered with make-up or made the usual effort I made whenever I went shopping – just in case I bumped into one of the other wives, or Isadora's friends.

'I've often thought of you since our meal out,' Ewan said.

I smiled but didn't admit that I had thought about him too. More often than I should have. He was not as handsome as Tom, but Ewan had a boyish charm that was attractive. There was something very unassuming and modest about the man. His colouring was the opposite of Tom's; Ewan had sandy blond hair and blue eyes, and Tom was dark-haired with brown eyes. They couldn't have been more different in looks and personality. But I found myself liking Ewan, far more than a married woman should like another man.

For that reason, I still held a residual guilt about our previous meeting.

'How are you doing?' Ewan asked. 'Was the rest of your trip successful?'

Successful, for a holiday, was an odd thing to say but I caught his meaning.

'Yes. We had fun,' I said. 'The northern lights were lovely.'

Ewan nodded. 'And your husband enjoyed it too?'

'I think so. Tom ... finds it difficult to switch off sometimes. From work I mean. But yes, he enjoyed the trip.'

Ewan smiled. 'That's good then.'

I sipped my coffee to hide a moment of awkwardness at discussing Tom with Ewan.

'I'm glad I was able to keep you company before he arrived that day,' Ewan said.

At his words I had a flash of memory about our previous meetings.

Ewan had been in Harrods the day I found the purple satin bedding. We'd struck up a conversation and he'd bought the same bedding. A few days later I found myself in his company in Reykjavik. I'd let him take me to dinner because Tom had been delayed by a problem at work and had yet to join me in Iceland.

I'd thought it quite a coincidence meeting the man again, but he had been kind, and his behaviour offered friendship and nothing more and so I'd agreed.

I took a sip of coffee now with a shaking hand. As I caught his eye I found myself talking, my words falling out in a rush. At that moment I understood just how much I needed a friend. 'It was very nice of you,' I said. 'I was quite ... lonely.'

I burst into tears then. I couldn't believe I had admitted to a virtual stranger that I felt this way. It was unfathomable and embarrassing. Ewan, far from being surprised or shocked, took my hand and held it. He handed me a linen handkerchief from his pocket, and I mopped up the flow of tears with a sigh of utter exhaustion.

'Would you like to talk about it?' he asked when I finally fell quiet.

'It's silly. Probably hormones. You see, I just found out that I'm pregnant.'

'And this is a surprise?'

'It shouldn't be. We were, *sort of*, trying. But I didn't think it would happen so soon. I mean, it seems to take other people months.'

'That's usually the way when you aren't ready,' Ewan said.

For the first time I began to wonder about Ewan's age. He appeared to be only a few years my senior, yet spoke so wisely, more than his thirty-something years might suggest. He was right, of course, I didn't feel ready to be a mother. And, despite my protestations that this was probably just hormones, I was often lonely. I had everything I could possibly want, and yet I lacked *something*.

As we sat and talked, I felt happier than I had done in years. He talked to me as if I was his equal, someone whose opinions were important. A feeling I didn't always have in my marriage. The afternoon passed by too quickly and I realized that I needed time to get home to make dinner for Tom. He would possibly want to celebrate with champagne – though I couldn't have any now – and some form of romantic, robust dinner.

'I have to go,' I said to Ewan, 'but thank you for being so kind.'

'Take my number,' he said. 'That way, if you need a friend to talk to who isn't judgemental, you'll have one.'

I was about to refuse, but his warm smile – and his genuine compassion – made me pause. I found myself pulling my mobile out of my handbag. There was something so appealing about his offer of unconditional friendship and the way he looked at me, with an honest and open expression, which made me consider he probably was the only one in the world I could talk to. The guilt came again. I shouldn't think this about anyone other than Tom. What was wrong with me?

'Okay, what's the number?'

I sent him a text so that he could store my number as well. 'I really have to go ...'

'Goodbye for now, Charlotte,' he said. He stood as I did, and then gave me a hug and a soft kiss on the cheek.

I was a little shy about the contact, but thanked him again to cover any awkwardness, then I left the coffee shop and hurried out into the busy London streets.

It was rush hour and therefore the worst time of day to find a taxi or to travel quickly by tube. Even so, I hurried towards the nearest tube station just as it started to rain. A real summer downpour. I didn't have an umbrella with me, and my hair was soaked in seconds. The water dripped down into my eyes. I faltered a little as I joined a large group of tourists waiting for the traffic lights to change. Thoughts of Ewan leaning closer and kissing me, the warmth of his smile, all brought a shiver to my spine. The pavement was too crowded, and most of the people, as is always the case in London city centre, appeared to be in a massive hurry.

As soon as the lights changed the crowd surged forwards. The first wave of people rushed across the road.

I don't know what happened. One minute I was about to step off the pavement the next I was being jostled. I lost my footing, stumbled, and time seemed to slow down. I saw a bird fly overhead, a pigeon wheeling in the sky as though it were about to dive in a suicidal swoop towards the ground. Horns blared. I heard a female voice cry out. And then – a hand pressed into my back. As though someone had reached out to stop me, or perhaps also lost their footing, and then I fell forwards, unable to stop myself – right into the bus lane.

Chapter Three

'Charlotte?'

A rush of sound filled my ears, like air whipping through the branches of a tree. A screech of brakes. Then I heard Tom's angry voice, '*What the fuck is this, Char?*'

I opened my eyes and looked up into Isadora's concerned face.

'Tom! Quickly! She's awake!'

Tom's face came into blurred view. He had a deep frown on his normally smooth brow.

'Char. Darling ...'

'Where am I?' I croaked.

I felt as though I'd been in a serious battle with a heavy-weight boxer. I had another flash – a memory – of Tom's flustered, angry face as he had stared at the sheets in my hands. *I don't understand why you're so cross. It's just new bedding!*

'Have some water,' Isadora offered, and before I could agree or refuse a straw was pushed into my mouth. 'You're in A & E.'

I sipped the water and it did ease my throat.

'What happened?' I asked.

I was in some kind of booth with a curtain drawn around us.

'You were ... you had an accident,' Tom said. 'You *fell*. In front of a bus.'

I had another flashback then, of the double-decker tourist bus, brakes screeching, as it careered towards me. I shuddered. I didn't remember the vehicle hitting me or anything else after that moment. Just this sense of freefalling as I fell onto the road. I remember getting back up off the ground seconds before the bus hit me. I was thrown aside, cracking my head on the kerb.

'You were lucky,' said Isadora.

'*Lucky?*' said Tom. 'What on earth were you doing crossing the road like that?'

'What do you mean?' I asked.

'A witness said you just ran out. Without looking,' Tom said.

'No. That isn't what happened. I walked out, with a group of people. One of them ... jostled me. Or maybe they tripped and pushed me ...'

'You're saying someone pushed you?' asked Tom, and there was something about his expression that made me go quiet for a moment. I thought it through and decided I couldn't be sure what had actually happened and so it was best not to commit.

'No ... It was raining. I slipped, stupid high heels I guess. Then, I got up and the bus—'

'It's okay, dear,' said Isadora. 'Rest up.'

'Am I ... injured?' I asked.

'The doctor says you have concussion. You'll have to stay in overnight,' Tom said.

'But ... the baby?'

'That's all okay, dear,' Isadora said.

I closed my eyes tight. Tears leaked out of the corners anyway.

'There, there. It's all going to be okay. But you'll have to be careful for a few days,' Isadora cooed.

I drifted back to sleep as their voices floated down with me.

'You see,' said Isadora. 'What a *silly* thing to assume she did it on purpose.'

'Yes, Mother. It's just ... a witness told the police.'

I awoke in a white room, disorientated and scared. And then I realized I must have been moved from the A & E department. I looked to my left, saw the mandatory monitors. I wasn't hooked up to anything though. I raised my hand to my face; I had the headache of all headaches.

I'd hit the floor on this side and my arm had borne the brunt of my weight: it was a mass of bruises. Yes, I'd been lucky. This could have been so much worse. At least I hadn't broken anything. I put my hand on my stomach. Was the baby really okay?

I tried to sit up, but the headache brought on a bout of nausea. I looked around for a receptacle of any kind; instead I found the nurse's call button. I pressed it, swallowing back bile and gagging on it.

A nurse hurried in; she reached for a paper bowl, helped me sit and held it under my chin. I vomited until my stomach wrenched.

When the nausea passed, I flopped back down on the bed.

'It's normal in your condition,' said the nurse. 'Plus with a head injury like that ...'

My throat seized up and I couldn't talk.

'Don't worry. You're in safe hands. Your husband moved you here to recuperate. Got to look after your precious cargo after all!'

I learnt that I had been moved to a private hospital. It seemed impossible that I had been so unconscious that I hadn't realized, but it had happened and now I was being looked after with the best possible attention.

The doctor came in.

'All is well, Mrs Carlisle, with your pregnancy. But that head injury was quite severe. Hence why we are looking after you for a few days.'

'A few days?' I queried. 'The A & E doctor said I only needed an overnight stay.'

'Well, I'm a specialist in this area. I feel we need to monitor you longer.'

Like the other controlling elements in my life, the doctor shot me down with his better knowledge.

I woke up three days later and opened the window to look out on the grounds. I was stronger today, ready to return home and escape the watchful eyes of the nurse. I had barely been permitted to walk to the en suite bathroom without a nurse beside me over the past few days. But gradually the head injury had improved. I was eating better now and even the morning sickness had subsided.

The nurse had told me to eat something in the mornings before I got out of bed and it had helped.

When the doctor entered my room, I was waiting for him. 'I'm ready to go home today,' I said.

He wouldn't meet my eye. 'No,' he replied.

I frowned. 'Why? I'm perfectly well enough. The scan on my head was clear—'

'Your husband and mother-in-law would like you to remain. To make sure—'

'To make sure of what?' I asked.

The doctor smiled. 'Soon, Mrs Carlisle. We have to make sure that there have been no adverse effects on the baby.'

Five days had passed since my arrival and I was beginning to feel paranoid and suspicious. After breakfast I was alone in my room reading, wondering what Tom was doing with his day. He and Isadora had visited me regularly, but I felt distant from them. It was probably a hangover from the head injury. I resented them both, and their decision-making that never took what I wanted into consideration. I still hadn't got a sensible answer from the doctor about my condition. He often said, 'I'll explain this to your husband,' or, 'your mother-in-law would like you to rest.' It was as though I was being held prisoner – maybe until my baby was delivered safely. A ridiculous thought, but one I couldn't ignore. As I turned to the next page of the book I couldn't remember the previous pages I'd read: my mind unable to focus on the words. I put the paperback down beside me on a small table by the chair. I was frustrated and bored. I was beginning to wonder if I'd ever leave this place when there was a sharp knock at my door and the nurse entered.

'Your husband is collecting you today,' she said with a smile. 'I expect you'll be glad to go home.'

I felt a rush of relief as my phobia abated. I stood up, bumping the table and the book fell to the floor. I bent to retrieve it. My palms felt suddenly sticky, as another odd feeling took over, something akin to agoraphobia. The hospital room had become a buffer to my ordinary life. Now I'd have to return to it, and to Tom and especially to Isadora.

'Perhaps I should stay on another day ...' I said with a shaky laugh.

'Yes,' she laughed too, but it sounded forced. 'It's a bit like living in a five-star hotel this place, isn't it?'

I wasn't sure I agreed, but knew that this hospital had every luxury a private hospital could have.

Tom arrived with his chauffeur, Stefan, and I was pushed out to the limo in a wheelchair, even though I told them I was fine to walk.

'Stop being stubborn,' Tom said. 'We're looking after you. You deserve it.'

The idea of further argument exhausted me and I fell silent and let them help me into the back of the car as if I was an invalid.

'How's your head feeling?' Tom asked once we were both in the limo.

'I'm fine. Really. Please don't worry.'

He took my hand and kissed my fingers. 'I'm so glad we can finally take you home. I've been so worried about you.'

Isadora had hired a home help, a young Polish girl to help clean and do all of the cooking for me. I was not to do anything until I was fully recovered.

'And anyway,' she said, 'I never understood why you wanted to clean your own house. It ruins your fingernails and spoils your hands.'

'I like cleaning,' I said. 'It's part of my fitness regime.'

'Well, there's none of that nonsense for now,' said Isadora. 'After the baby comes ... well there will be plenty of time to get back into shape. I'll find you a trainer when the time is right.'

She didn't see me roll my eyes.

Chapter Four

I was dreaming of swimming, gliding serenely through a warm lake. The shore ahead, the aqua blue sky reflected above. Then I felt that first fatal cramp. The pain struck so deeply through my core – a white hot pain. Sheer agony, as the dream faded and changed. I was drowning now, my limbs like lead, holding me down as I sank like a heavy rock to the bottom of the ocean.

'Char ... Char, wake up!'

I opened my eyes. Tom was staring into my face with a look of concern.

'It was just a nightmare,' I said.

'You were crying out.'

He sat up, moved away, and I pulled myself into a sitting position. Then, thinking I needed the bathroom, I pushed back the covers. The white sheets glared red. The whole lower half of my body was covered in blood. I tried to calm my breathing, but the room began to spin as I realized what this macabre sight might mean.

'Oh my god!' Tom said.

I was vaguely aware of him rushing across the room and picking up his phone. Swearing as he pressed three numbers.

'I need an ambulance,' he said.

I was bundled onto a trolley after they mopped up the mess. I knew without looking that the mattress had to be ruined, just as the white bedding most certainly was. Just as my life was. It crossed my mind that the purple satin set wouldn't have shown the damage so boldly. And then it occurred to me that this was a strange moment to think of that bedding. I should instead have been thinking about my baby.

Much to the excitement of our neighbours, I was wheeled into the back of the ambulance.

'I'll follow in my car,' said Tom, as they hooked me up to an IV and placed monitors on my heart.

When they closed the doors on him, to continue their work in peace, one of the paramedics, a woman with kind eyes, said, 'It's already too late. I'm afraid the baby is gone. Normally we wouldn't take you in for that. But your husband is very concerned about you due to your accident.'

I closed my eyes and felt tears running down my face. I didn't know why. Was it sadness for the loss of this tiny, yet unformed thing inside me? Or was it relief?

'The pregnancy may not have been viable to begin with,' the doctor said. 'It happens sometimes with a first one. Like a trial run.'

'But the accident?' Tom said.

Why oh why did he keep labouring this? Didn't he realize I felt bad enough?

'I doubt it was responsible, but it's possible. Most pregnancies are robust. They can withstand all sorts of trauma. That's how the human race has survived through the worst periods of our history. Your wife will be fine. There's no reason why you shouldn't have another healthy pregnancy in a few months' time. But for now, I think she needs rest.'

I lay in the bed, Isadora holding my hand, as these two men talked about me as though I wasn't present, or capable of understanding anything. But it was only later, when I realized things had to change or else I would lose my sanity, that I looked back and remembered all of this with clarity.

Chapter Five

Tom and I had been married ten years and for most of that time I couldn't imagine my life turning out any better. I'd been orphaned when I was sixteen. It had been hard for me financially and emotionally. I'd had to be independent and strong, but all I'd ever wanted was to be safe and secure. Tom gave that to me. I was grateful, and I felt privileged too. I never wanted this amazing life he offered to change me. But it did despite my best efforts.

We never discussed the fact that I had, effectively, squandered the amazing opportunity I'd had in getting into Oxford. Nor that I had gained a first – and Tom a 2:1. For Tom, such a privilege was a given and he could have worked harder, he just didn't need to. But that wasn't the way he was with the firm. No, that was his real obsession. His life – above all else, even me – was about running the company. As for me, I didn't mind someone taking care of me for a change. Tom gave me more security than I'd had in years and it was a relief to no longer worry that I might not be able to pay the rent, or buy food that week.

You can only appreciate having money when you've truly had none. For years I'd been completely broke. And, when you've seen life from both ends of the spectrum, you also know which side your bread is buttered.

You see, I knew my life wasn't perfect, but I accepted it.

Sometimes I was bored. Oh, I didn't mean to be ungrateful, but at times I had to recognize how my intelligence had been wasted. It frustrated me. I tried to do what the other wives did: lunches, charity benefits, hair and beauty appointments and the obligatory gym membership. We, as the wives of men such as Tom, had to keep our figures and looks regardless of anything else.

I had friends of course. Some I genuinely liked, but none had carried over from the old days. When I took my certificate on graduation day and then didn't accept that all-important job offer, I dropped off everyone's radar. Instead Tom and I went on a cruise. Looking back on it now, I realized that my life was mapped out from the day I met him.

I had been lucky in many ways. The Carlisles were snobs, and they valued my education as much as my looks, thankfully, and this, I suppose, allowed them to ignore my humble beginnings. Isadora groomed me. Smoothing away any final rough edges, teaching me the ways of the corporate wife and all the duties it entailed. It was like marrying into royalty, only marginally less public.

Our wedding was featured in a top business magazine and was full of embellishments about Tom's business acumen – all important for the shareholders to see. My only embellishment was the most expensive designer dress Isadora could find. And my looks. My looks were, I think, the most important of all. The wedding took place at Isadora and Conrad's manor house in Surrey. A beautiful old and huge building that sat in several acres of land and had been passed down through generations of Carlisles.

Of course, I didn't mind Isadora's detailed planning of our special day, down to who would be bridesmaids – wives of important people in their world, because I had no sisters or cousins to fit the bill. I'd been an only child, long since orphaned, and Isadora's attentions pleased me at first. She became my surrogate mother, even though I was fully aware that everything she did was not for my sake, but for Tom's.

After the wedding, Isadora started to ask about grandchildren. We avoided it for the first few years, telling her we had to find our feet, that Tom's long working hours would mean he'd have no time for me, let alone a new baby.

When I turned 30 we ran out of excuses.

'Everyone else in your peer group has children, Charlotte dear,' Isadora had said. 'Don't you think it's time?'

She always called me 'Charlotte dear' when she wanted to manipulate me in some way. I knew what she was doing but didn't really mind. I'd learnt early on that Isadora always got her way and it sometimes wasn't worth the argument.

'It's not easy when Tom works so hard, comes back home late and tired,' I had said. 'But, I'll talk to him on our anniversary trip. Who knows, we may well start there!'

Isadora had been pleased that we were 'potentially' on the way to parenthood and I had effectively appeased my mother-in-law again. I don't know what it was, but I wasn't that concerned about having children. I enjoyed our life as it was – maybe that was selfish of me. But we had everything that money could buy and I loved to travel. I knew that babies would limit our freedom, perhaps even change our relationship. I'd seen that happen too many times with some of the other corporate wives.

'I hope you're feeling frisky. Your mother wants grandkids!' I had told Tom.

Tom had laughed, but never took it too seriously: he only wanted me to come home to and had no immediate desire to be a father. That was why it had surprised me when he told me to stop taking my contraceptives before our trip to Iceland.

I guessed, in the end, Isadora had applied enough pressure on him too.

Two months after the miscarriage my life resumed its normal pattern. Even the wives of Tom's colleagues stopped asking me how I felt. I was able now to meet them for lunch and I had resumed my gym sessions, carefully, after six weeks.

To avoid a pregnancy too soon, I had restarted my contraceptives. Tom and I fell back into our life as if nothing had happened. I didn't fall back into my usual pattern with Isadora though. I felt different about her. Perhaps I even blamed her for my current unhappiness. Our regular lunch dates stopped and I only met up with her when I had to.

Even so, I wasn't feeling myself. I couldn't put my finger on the problem, but a lot of what Isadora said or did irritated me more than usual. I had less patience and I found myself feeling sad a lot – not a usual thing for me at all. Life was boring me a little too. The days dragged on and I had no inclination to return to the way things were before. I began to feel that I couldn't really talk to Tom about my feelings. I thought he'd misunderstand, or think I was ungrateful when he had given me such a lovely life. These thoughts and feelings wouldn't shift; they continued to mutate and grow until the only thing I knew for sure was that I was lonely.

I suppose I was beginning to feel dissatisfied, despite what I had.

'Perhaps you should see someone,' Tom said one evening, observing my low mood.

'I'm fine,' I said. 'I'm just tired.'

'If it's the loss of the baby,' he said, 'I'm still feeling sad too.'

'I know. I'm sorry. But, I'm fine, darling. Really,' I lied.

Then I distracted him by changing the subject to *his* day.

While he was talking, I considered my situation. Was I sad because of the baby? *No.* Was I happy in my marriage. *Mostly.* Why did I have this overwhelming sense of isolation that made me somehow dread the future?

I nodded and smiled at Tom as he talked about Carlisle Corp, but my mind wandered.

Later when we went to bed, I let him make love to me, but my mind was still elsewhere. I found myself thinking about Ewan Daniels, wondering what he was doing. I hadn't seen him since the day of the accident and it hadn't even occurred to me to contact him.

Tom grunted and came inside me. As he rolled away, I turned over and lay with my back to him. I didn't want him to see the expression on my face – even though the light was off and the room was dark.

*

Unable to avoid her any longer, I met Isadora at her favourite restaurant in Mayfair. I arrived early, as she had asked, before the charity committee members and other wives joined us.

'I wanted to show you the menu I've selected for the benefit,' she said. 'That way you'll be informed when we discuss it.'

We sat in the bar, a glass of slimline tonic water each. She didn't ask me how I was or why I'd been unavailable the last few weeks. Instead Isadora presented me with a beautifully printed menu of fine cuisine. I read through it, finding a lot of it pretentious, but said nothing. What was the point? She would only shoot me down with her better knowledge and experience of these things. Over the years I'd learnt that my silence was the best way of keeping the peace between us.

Just then the others began to arrive.

'Charlotte, this is Clarissa May, the director of the charity, and her assistant, Barbara. Ah and here is the lovely Gillian to take notes for Carlisle Corp. She's Tom's PA and we have her on loan today.'

I'd met Gillian several times before then. Even so, I didn't enlighten Isadora. I shook hands with them all and more women arrived – all dressed to kill.

We sat at a large round table and were served beautiful food at the cost of Carlisle Corp.

'Emelia,' Isadora asked. 'You have a meeting with the florist today, don't you? You're still okay with the centre pieces?'

'Yes, of course,' said Emelia and then her phone rang. 'Sorry. Must take this.'

Emelia left the table then returned a few moments later, her face pale.

'I'm so sorry. I'll have to leave and cancel the florist,' Emelia looked flustered.

'What's happened?' asked Isadora.

'That was my son's school. He's taken ill and the nanny is off today.'

'Of course you must go,' I said. 'And please don't worry. I'll go to the florists and pick out the centre pieces. After all, I'm running this benefit, aren't I?'

I glanced at Isadora and smiled.

'Well ... of course,' said Isadora. 'If you're feeling up to—'

'I'm fine. I'll walk out with Emelia and get the florist appointment details.'

'She's not just like you in looks ...' said one of the women behind me.

'What do you mean, "in looks"?' Isadora asked.

'Well. Look at her. She could be your real daughter. She's a younger you for certain.'

I glanced back over my shoulder to see, for the first time, a very shocked expression on Isadora's face. We had often been taken for mother and daughter, and I put it down to the fact that we both had blonde hair and blue eyes.

When I returned and sat down, Isadora leaned in to me and said, 'I'll go to the florists. I know what I'm looking for.'

'Don't be silly,' I said. 'You do quite enough already. Besides, Emelia told me what was needed.'

Isadora frowned with annoyance.

Did she think I was too stupid to even chose flowers without assistance?

'Okay,' she said finally. 'But call me if you're uncertain of anything.'

'I can order some flowers without messing it up,' I said.

'Of course, you can, Charlotte dear,' said Isadora. Then she patted my hand in a placating, but patronizing way.

After lunch, I went to the florist and picked out some centre pieces.

'This is the display that Mrs Carlisle said to show you,' said the girl at the florists.

It was pale pink and white roses.

I stood still and stared at the display. I frowned to show my absolute displeasure, taking on the same unhappy expression Isadora had worn earlier.

'I've decided to change the colour scheme.'

'But—'

'I'm organizing the event, not Mrs Carlisle,' I said.

I chose purple satin ribbons and purple and white freesias: I don't know why. Perhaps it was because the brief for the centre pieces that Isadora had given wasn't to my personal taste and I've always thought pale pink to be very wishy-washy.

As I left the florist my heart was pounding. I realized I'd have to tinker with the brief for the room decor now too. It was a minor rebellion, but it was huge in my mind. I wanted some control in my life, even if I had to claw it from my mother-in-law's clutches.

I paused in front of the shop, thinking about the enormity of what I'd done. Then I saw a man loitering nearby. He met my eyes briefly then hurriedly looked away. I try not to be a snob, but he wasn't the sort to buy in this exclusive street and I wondered if he was up to no good. I was just about to return to the shop, to point him out to the assistant, when a car pulled up beside me.

It was Stefan, Tom's chauffeur. He got out and came around to open the back door for me.

'Mrs Carlisle,' he said. 'Mr Carlisle sent me to fetch you ...'

'Oh, that was kind of him!' I said and my voice sounded strange to my ears. Tom never sent the car to fetch me, unless we'd prearranged it.

'The other Mrs Carlisle wanted to know if everything went okay in the florists?'

'Yes, Stefan. It did.'

I got into the back seat of the car and then remembered the man I'd seen earlier. I started to look for him again, but he was gone. Who was he? What had he been doing near the shop? I found myself staring into the florist and saw the girl who'd helped me standing by the window looking out at me. She was talking rapidly into a mobile phone pressed to her ear. I swallowed, and my throat felt suddenly dry.

Chapter Six

It is difficult to say when the real resentment began. But looking back I can remember individual moments of annoyance, that later became anger. Anger at Isadora, anger at Tom for not defending me with her and most of all anger at myself for being so weak. But I didn't feel weak anymore. So as the charity evening approached and I fine-tuned and tweaked all of the arrangements, I was a little surprised that Isadora didn't check on my progress. It was as though she had taken a back seat after all.

I began to relax, believing that she was finally trusting me. I even bought a dress for the night that neither she nor Tom had seen and approved. It was purple velvet, sleek, and it followed the curves of my gym-toned body.

On the day of the event I did the mandatory trip to the salon. My hair was put up at the front but left down at the back in cascading curls. The hairdresser used a few purple-coloured clip-in extensions and I had diamond gems scattered in my hair.

Tom wasn't coming home before the event – he would shower and change into his tuxedo at the office and so planned to meet me there. I was relieved because my new look would be as much of a surprise to him as to Isadora. I hoped he would like it too.

As I returned to the apartment I found a dress bag lying on the bed. I unzipped it to discover a ball gown inside. It had a pink satin strapless bodice with diamantes and a fairytale tulle wide skirt.

Wear this tonight. It will look perfect with the decor and centre pieces.

Isadora

A feeling of dread hit the pit of my stomach. Did she know that I had changed everything?

I put on my purple dress and ignored the pink satin and tulle ball gown. Then I looked at myself in the mirror and I saw for the first time my own style and taste. Not the girly style that Isadora always made me wear, but the mature, grown-up I wanted to be: a woman in charge of her own life and destiny.

I left the other dress on the bed and pulled on a long black pashmina. Picking up a silver clutch bag that matched my shoes, I left the apartment and went outside to hail a taxi.

Tom's limo was parked by the kerb, with Stefan standing beside it.

'I thought you were collecting Mrs Carlisle tonight?' I said.

Stefan didn't answer, he merely opened the back door. Isadora was sitting in the back seat wearing dark pink, with a pale pink fur stole wrapped around her shoulders.

'What on earth have you done to yourself?' she said. 'Oh, Charlotte. This will never do!'

'Thank you for the dress, but I had already picked one,' I said.

I slipped in beside her.

Isadora climbed out of the back of the limo and went to talk to Stefan. He disappeared inside and, a few moments later, returned holding the bulky dress carrier – with the pale pink dress inside. He placed it carefully in the back of the boot and then we set off for the event. Isadora didn't speak to me at all until we reached the venue. But I was pleased that she had accepted my decision to wear the purple velvet. She could just return the pink ball gown anyway.

'I have a surprise for you,' I said as the car pulled up outside the Victoria and Albert Museum, the interior of which had been transformed for the evening for the event. 'You'll see why my dress is perfect for tonight.'

Isadora said nothing and walked to the entrance, early enough to check that everything was in place before the arrival of the many celebrities and executives who would be attending. I walked in behind her and saw Gillian, Tom's PA, had already arrived. There were also two other women that I didn't recognize, but who knew Isadora and she hurried to them and began a quiet discussion near the doors to the banquet room.

'Everything is ready,' said Gillian.

I thanked her, but I was surprised that she had arrived early. I hadn't asked her to.

The doors opened and we walked in. I took a breath, excited to see my colour scheme, but it turned into a gasp.

The room was filled with pink and white, the centre pieces were pale pink and white roses, with pale pink ribbons the exact colour of the dress Isadora had sent me.

'I had a feeling that you were going off the rails,' Isadora said. 'But don't worry, I've fixed everything.'

I think my jaw dropped open because Isadora told me to close it and 'straighten' my face.

'Now, I brought my hairdresser along. Those awful purple extensions will have to come out but the rest is salvageable. Susan will take you into the cloakroom where you'll change into the pink ball gown. You'll be the belle of the evening as always my dear, so don't worry.'

Although I was deeply offended by her altering my changes, I let her bulldoze me again. I was foiled and there was nothing I could do about it. The evening would be a disaster if I rebelled further, and I didn't want Tom to know that Isadora and I had almost had a major falling out. It would ruin his evening.

'I like my purple dress. I like my hair,' I said, even though I knew it was useless to argue.

'Don't be petulant. One day you'll thank me for this,' Isadora said. 'Tom doesn't like change. You know that.'

That sinking feeling was in my stomach again. I glanced at Isadora, wondering if Tom had told her about the purple satin bedding. I looked down at my sexy velvet dress – purple. Then I remembered the purple satin ribbons and flowers I had planned for the centre pieces. The banners and ribbons of purple and silver. Decadent and sexy – not really appropriate for a charity evening. Perhaps Isadora was right; maybe I was 'going off the rails'. And, if she hadn't stepped in, how would Tom have reacted?

I let Susan lead me away to the ladies' cloakroom, and there I was preened and groomed, all signs of my rebellion removed. The pink satin ball gown fit like a glove and I was ready just in time to greet the guests as they arrived.

'There you are!' said Tom as I came out of the cloakroom. 'You look amazing!'

He kissed me on the cheek and held my hands looking down at me with shining eyes as though seeing me for the first time.

'You look beautiful. So unspoilt ... So pure,' he said.

It was an effort to force a smile onto my face. I was angry with Isadora for gazumping my plans. In fact, I don't think I'd ever felt such rage in my life. But as we met Isadora by the door, and stood beside her to smile and shake hands with everyone who came in, Tom's words came back to me in a wave that made my stomach cramp again with this unnameable fear. *So unspoilt. So pure.* What an unusual thing to say.

Before the speeches and the raffle, but after the meal, I went to the ladies' room and stared at myself in the mirror for a few minutes. I looked like a fairytale princess. My other dress and my hair extensions had been bagged up and hung in the ladies' cloakroom waiting for me to collect at the end of the evening. The pink dress was me, but not me. It was an image of me that Isadora encouraged and cultivated. It was an image that Tom had come to expect, and Isadora was right, he didn't care for change.

So far the evening was a triumph. The guests were smiling and happy. The free champagne was flowing and soon they would be promising all kinds of donations to the cause.

I couldn't even remember what the cause was.

This was a night like many others I'd had for the past ten

years and they all melted into one. Nausea rolled around in my stomach and blended with the expensive Nuevo Cuisine. It wasn't the food; it was my mood.

I'd effectively hidden my anger, behaving normally with Isadora – I'd developed good skills over the years in covering up my true feelings. That evening, I told myself, was no different. It was all an act.

I'm trapped, I thought and a rising panic made the nausea feel more immediate. I turned and hurried to one of the toilet cubicles and then dry heaved for a moment into the bowl. Nothing came up. I wasn't physically sick, just emotionally upset. The thing was, I wanted freedom but was scared to insist on it.

'Charlotte?' Isadora's voice floated to me from the doorway of the ladies' toilets.

'I'm here,' I said. Then I flushed the toilet and came out of the cubicle.

'Are you all right?' she asked. Her eyes narrowed as she looked at me.

'I'm fine. I just needed a moment.'

'The auction is about to start. You need to make the introduction ...'

I looked at the ground. 'Would you do it?' I asked, knowing that she would.

'All right. Are you coming back out now?'

'I just need to wash my hands.'

Isadora nodded and went out again. A moment later I heard the music stop and Isadora speaking on the microphone. The PA didn't reach well into the bathroom and her voice was muffled but I wasn't interested in hearing what she had to say anyway.

I washed my hands and as I dried them I looked at myself once more. My eyes looked hollow, like someone haunted by some deep dark secret that is ruining their life. But there was no secret, and I had everything I could possibly want. Who needed more than a wonderful, handsome, massively wealthy husband who adored you?

My phone made a subtle peep in my small clutch bag. I opened the bag and went to turn it off. Then I saw that it was a text message.

It was from Ewan Daniels.

How are you?

I stared at the text for a long time.

Shortly after losing the baby, Ewan had texted me asking the same thing. I hadn't been in the best state of mind and so I'd merely replied I was fine. I'd been curt and I knew it. Trying to discourage any further contact. There had been no contact from Ewan since then. I had almost forgotten about him. So why was he now texting me out of the blue? I began to type a normal, non-committal response like the last time and then deleted it. Should I reply or just ignore the text?

I lost the baby.

I hit send and then instantly regretted it.

OMG! I'm sorry to hear that. How are you feeling?

I'm fine.

Somehow I don't believe that.

Outside the auction was underway which meant that Isadora was too busy to come looking for me again for the time being. Would Tom even notice I wasn't there, or that I had bailed on my duties, deferring once more to his mother?

The truth is I'm not okay. I'm miserable. My life isn't going how I wanted it to go.

I felt bad admitting this to someone other than myself, but it was also cathartic.

The mother-in-law still interfering?

I didn't reply. I stared at the screen wondering what to say. Was it just Isadora? Was it that deep down I was an emotional wreck after the miscarriage? Or was it something else? I just didn't know what I needed, what I lacked in my life. What this awful undertone to a life of perfection was. How could I explain all of this in a simple text?

You're really not okay, are you?

I read the text over and over.

No.

I guess it was a cry for help. Here was a friendly ear, willing to listen and totally nonjudgemental.

Meet me at the coffee shop?

My heart missed a beat. What was I doing?

Tomorrow? 1 pm?

I said 'Yes' before I could stop myself. Then I turned back to the mirror. The hollow, haunted expression had left my face and been replaced by a small smile.

I heard the auction come to an end and realized how long I had been in the bathroom. I turned my mobile phone off and placed it back inside my bag. There was no need to ask which coffee shop.

I left the bathroom and returned to my table just as Isadora finished giving out the auction prizes. Tom was on the stage with her, and so I was sure they had both been too busy to notice my absence.

'That went well!' I said as Tom finally returned to our table. His progress back had been impeded by the many guests who stopped him and shook his hand.

'Yes. Mother is very good at working the crowd. The final tally is much better than we'd hoped.'

'Charlotte dear,' said Isadora coming up behind Tom. 'You really must present the cheque at the end.'

I met her eyes, knowing that she hoped I would bale again. But the depression that had hung over me earlier had suddenly lifted.

'Of course!' I said.

That night Tom praised me for my help organizing the event.

'You did so well on the presentation too, darling. I think you should take more responsibility and not be so shy about taking the lead. Mother doesn't mind. She wants you to do more.'

I didn't correct him, though we both knew that Isadora loved the limelight and would not easily give it up.

We went to bed, both tired from the long day.

'I think maybe it's time for you to come off the pill again,' Tom said, as we lay in the dark.

I didn't answer, feigning sleep and so Tom turned over and I heard his soft breathing deepen into a faint snore.

I had trouble sleeping. A range of emotions were playing through my mind. I was excited, but anxious about seeing

Ewan again. I rationalized it by telling myself that this was only coffee. That it meant nothing and the man was really someone I could talk to about my frustrations. But underneath all of these silent justifications was the overwhelming guilt that deep down I was very attracted to Ewan. And just by realizing that, I was betraying Tom.

Chapter Seven

It was raining as I came out of the tube station and headed towards the coffee shop. I was wearing jeans and a tee shirt with a lightweight hooded jacket that I pulled up to cover my head. The curls from the night before had been brushed out and my hair lay in waves over my shoulders. I was a little blue under the eyes from the lack of sleep, but I had smeared concealer there and covered it with subtle day make-up to hide my tiredness. I passed Harrods and caught a glimpse of myself, looking like a normal woman, not the wife of the CEO of Carlisle Corp.

It was good to be anonymous.

Ewan was already in the coffee shop when I arrived. He had somehow managed to procure the same table by the window that we'd shared the last time I saw him there.

He stood when he saw me. It was an old-fashioned and gentlemanly thing to do. Then we exchanged an awkward hug and air kissed each other's cheek.

'I was going to order for you, but that seemed presumptuous,' he said.

I smiled as he called the waitress over to us.

'A vanilla latte please,' I said. 'I'm sorry about the woeful texts last night,' I told him when the waitress left. 'I was feeling sorry for myself.'

'You have nothing to apologize for. It's strange; I just had this *feeling* that I should contact you.'

'That's odd. We hardly know each other.'

'I know. But I have thought about you a lot since we last spoke.'

'Have you?' I blushed. 'I was in an accident after I left here.'

'My god! What happened?'

I explained my fall, the bus, the later loss of the child that I hadn't really been ready for.

'I was jostled. Perhaps I even tripped over someone's feet. It's all a bit of a blur. But I guess it's why I feel so bad now. I wasn't ready for motherhood and it was all over before it even started.'

'And are you any readier now?' he asked.

I lifted my latte to my lips and drank to give me a moment to think. 'I don't think so. I don't know what it is. It's like I have everything but really I feel empty. I shouldn't be telling you this.'

'There's a reason why you are, Charlotte. I hope that's because we aren't strangers anymore, but friends. I know you're married, and I shouldn't say this to you, but I hope that one day ... we can be *more* than friends.'

It was inevitable that I went back with him to his apartment. He lived over in Hammersmith and the place was stunning, expensive, and I knew then that Ewan was someone of substance, though probably not equal to Tom.

We didn't waste time on talking. He kissed me as soon as

he closed the apartment door and then he led me into his bedroom. The bed was made up in the purple satin bedding that he'd bought in Harrods the day we met. The thought of lying on those sheets aroused me; I didn't understand why. Maybe it was because I always knew from that very first meeting that we'd end up here.

As he stripped I noted that Ewan's body was lovely, not as perfect as Tom's and it didn't matter – his imperfections were beautiful to me.

After my final orgasm, when Ewan's sweat clung to my body and mingled with mine, I revelled in those purple satin sheets – this was the passion that they deserved. They were beautiful and decadent. They were everything that I wanted to be. In Ewan's arms that became possible.

Ewan got up and left the room. A few moments later he returned with two mugs of herbal tea.

'This is the moment when we should both spark up a cigarette and drink a shot of whiskey, isn't it?' I smiled.

'I don't smoke, and I bet you don't either,' he laughed.

I took the steaming tea from his hands and looked at the time on his bedside clock.

'I'll have to go soon,' I said.

Then I glanced at him sideways trying to see if his expression showed relief.

'And if I asked you to stay?' he said.

'You know I can't.'

He looked disappointed. Sad even.

'Can I use your shower?' I said, placing the hot tea down on the bedside table.

He showed me the way to the bathroom. Inside it was extremely tidy. There was no sign of another woman's presence. Just basic male stuff and I concluded that Ewan liked his home minimalist. He was not as metro sexual as my husband and it was another aspect I liked about him.

I dressed in the bathroom after removing all traces of his scent from my body. Though I hoped something remained from his towel as I used it to dry my body. I looked at my face in the mirror and saw my old self staring back, someone I hadn't seen for what felt like years. My hair was tousled and my lips red and a little sore from all of the kissing, but I looked as though a huge burden had been lifted from my shoulders. Was it obvious that I had just had sex with a man who wasn't my husband?

I sighed, preparing myself mentally to say goodbye to Ewan. This probably wouldn't happen again ... Ewan had had what he wanted, and this would be the end of it. I wasn't the type of woman who had affairs. *One slip. It can't happen again.*

I opened the bathroom door, and Ewan was standing there. He had put his clothes back on: he too looked flustered.

'Are you all right?' he asked.

I nodded. 'Don't worry. I think I understand how this goes. We can't see each other again ...'

'Charlotte ... Do you think you're just a one-night stand to me?'

My eyes brimmed with tears. I wasn't really as brave as I made out I was.

'I want to see you again,' he said. 'I know you're married ... but I can't help how I feel ...'

I was speechless but it didn't matter because Ewan pulled me to him and kissed me again.

'I hope you feel the same. Please say yes,' he said, holding me close.

I had once heard about another CEO's wife who had begun an affair. She fell in love and lost everything. I didn't want to be that woman. I had a lot to lose. But it was as though someone had unlocked a door and now I had seen through it; I didn't want to go back. This whole day had given me a new sense of freedom and, no matter what, I knew I had to meet Ewan again, maybe even have a full-on affair. For that was all it was and could ever be. But this intoxicating secret made me feel powerful, independent, *rebellious*. It would be a part of me that no one in our perfect world knew about. It was an element of my personality that I could have, that no one could moderate or change. There was a growing excitement in the pit of my stomach.

I rubbed my cheek against his chest and breathed in his scent. I held him close. He was as priceless to me as any perfect jewel could be to the richest of women.

'Meet me again then?' he murmured against my hair.

I didn't have to say the words: Ewan knew he had me.

Chapter Eight

I arrived home with my heart beating faster than it should. I was late and I wasn't sure what excuse for my absence I could give to Tom. As the lift opened on our floor, I took a deep breath and tried to quell my nervousness and guilt. I rushed along the corridor as the lift closed behind me and began to descend. I typed in the passcode to our front door with a shaking hand and hurried inside, closing it behind me.

'Hi darling,' I called, pulling off my jacket, and my voice sounded too loud in the silence. 'Did you have a good day?'

There was no response, which was not necessarily a good thing.

'Tom?' I said, wandering into the living room and then towards the door of his office. 'Tom?'

Tom's office was empty. Glancing at the clock I realized Tom was due home in a few minutes. He was a good time keeper, and always let me know if he was delayed, so that I could hold dinner back for him.

I left the study, walked across the living room and passed into the dining room. Confirming once and for all I was alone, I went into the kitchen and began to pull out pans and plates. I put a pan of salted water on the gas range and left it to boil. Then I dressed the dining table with cutlery and wine glasses and decanted a bottle of Tom's favourite red. It wouldn't have breathed enough by the time he poured it, but I hoped he wouldn't notice.

Usually I cook in a leisurely way, but this time I chopped and prepped the salad in a hurry and tossed it into a bowl, mixing it up with a splash of olive oil. Then I placed the bowl on the table.

I heard the keypad sing as Tom entered his code and then, as the door opened, I dropped a packet of fresh pasta into the now-boiling water. I put another pan on the range and melted some butter in it, then I took some raw king prawns from the fridge and dropped them in. I sprinkled in some chilli flakes and cooked the prawns in the chilly infused butter.

'Char?' called Tom. 'I'm home ...'

'In the kitchen,' I said. 'Dinner is almost ready.'

The pasta was done and so I drained it and added it back to the pan where I swirled in some red pesto. Then I put some on each plate and added the prawns to the top.

I turned off the gas and picked up our plates and took them into the dining room just as Tom poured the wine into both of our glasses.

'Slaving over a hot stove?' Tom said as he glanced at me.

'Huh?'

'You look flustered.'

I gave a half-hearted laugh and placed his dinner plate down on the table as Tom took his usual seat.

He looked down at his plate and smiled. 'Looks nice, darling.'

Then Tom sipped his wine. I was awkward: he was natural. I sat down and gulped a mouthful of wine.

'So how was your day?' I asked.

'The usual. How was yours. What did you do today?'

I sipped my wine forcing myself to appear unflustered and calm.

'Not much,' I said. 'Bathed in the glory of last night's fund-raiser ...'

Tom picked up his fork and took a mouthful of food. He chewed and swallowed and then said, 'I don't know how you do it, darling. This is delicious. You must have spent ages prepping dinner tonight.'

I wasn't sure if he was being sarcastic. I took a breath, glanced up at him with a smile, then looked back down at my own food. If he could tell this was a rushed meal he gave no sign of it. He ate the pasta and prawns as though it was the best meal I had ever given him. I hardly touched my food.

The evening passed with another bottle of wine being opened. I refilled Tom's glass several times, and he didn't stop me like he usually did. Instead he seemed to savour the wine and sat in his favourite chair watching the news while I bustled around clearing the table. I spent longer in the kitchen than usual. I straightened up the room and filled the dishwasher until I was standing around looking for something else to do.

'What's your plan tomorrow?' Tom asked when I finally sat down beside him.

'I don't have any at the moment,' I said.

Tom's phone beeped in his pocket. He took it out and looked at the email that had just arrived. He frowned. His eyes bore into me for a long moment.

'Work?' I said, breaking the silence.

Tom said nothing.

'Let's go to bed,' I suggested. 'I'm really tired.'

Tom put down his half-empty wine glass then looked back down at the email message, scrolling through the page.

'You go,' he said.

I was relieved to end this very awkward evening. I said goodnight and stood, forcing myself not to rush but to walk normally to the bedroom.

'Darling?' Tom said.

I stopped and turned around to look at him.

'Have you forgotten something?'

I stared at him blankly for a moment, then realized what he meant. I walked towards him and placed a small kiss on his lips.

'Goodnight,' I said.

In the en suite bathroom I looked at myself in the mirror as I brushed my teeth. I could see the guilt in my eyes and was convinced that Tom could too.

But it's not guilt, I thought. *It's fear*. I didn't regret what had taken place that day at all. No matter what happened afterwards I did not, and would not, regret those moments I'd spent with Ewan. But I was afraid of discovery. I explored this feeling: was it fear of Tom's reaction, or that discovery would mean that I could never see Ewan again?

I put away my toothbrush and then removed my clothing,

tossing them all into the wash basket. Then I put on a simple shift nightgown and went to bed.

I heard Tom opening the door of his office and closed my eyes. I wanted to be asleep before he came to bed. With any luck he would be in there for hours: we'd had many evenings like this. I imagined him typing a rapid reply to whoever was still working late at his office. Then he would browse his other emails unable to relax. In the past I had drifted off to sleep only to wake an hour or two later to discover that he was still at his desk. When that happened, I would go in search of him and encourage him to come to bed and sleep.

I began to drift off, the thoughts of Ewan and the frantic sex we'd had floated behind my eyes and chased away the tiredness I was feeling. I was excited by the memory and wanted to relive the moment. Ewan was very different from Tom, more considerate, more adventurous. All of my inhibitions had disappeared with him.

But what if it never happened again? I fretted that we hadn't made any plans to meet, despite his promise that we would.

The bedroom door opened and light spilled in from the hallway. Through the slit of my eyes I saw Tom framed in the doorway. His face was in shadow but I knew he was looking at me. Then he switched off the hall light and came into the room. I heard him removing his clothing and when he went into the bathroom, I burrowed further into the duvet, hiding my face from any further scrutiny.

Tom came out of the bathroom and stumbled around the bed in the dark, before he slipped in beside me.

I levelled my breathing feigning sleep while I listened to

my husband. He was lying on his back, one hand behind his head. He sighed and then turned over, trying to find his comfortable sleeping position. Though I couldn't see him, I knew every move he made in bed and recognized his stress and anxiety.

A good wife would ask what was wrong. But I was no longer the good wife and I was afraid to ask for fear that it was me that was wrong. Not, as was mostly likely, a problem at work. Even so, I lay awake until his breathing finally smoothed out and Tom fell into a restless sleep. Only then did I let myself rest.

Chapter Nine

Tom had already gone by the time I woke up the next day. I was shocked that I had fallen into such a deep sleep after all that had occurred. Bleary-eyed I stumbled out of bed and went to the kitchen. I put the kettle on and found a note from Tom with a list of jobs he wanted me to do: three of his suits had to go to the dry cleaners and he needed some more of his regular aftershave.

I fell into Carlisle wife mode and showered and dressed ready to do his errands.

My phone was charging beside the bed and when I switched it on I found a text from Tom with more things to add to his shopping list. I read the final text:

Meet me for lunch?

I looked in my diary, trying to find an excuse not to go, but the page was blank. I didn't answer straight away, as I thought of an appropriate response.

Anything else?

I sent back in response to his list.

Yes. Mother wants to join us for lunch.

I took this in and tried not to read into it. Isadora would

want to discuss the fundraiser. Her being there made sense. It would also be better than us being alone from my point of view.

When and where? I replied.

Tom sent Stefan to collect me because he didn't need him that day. I sat in the back of the limo with Tom's dry cleaning in the boot and his shopping list in my pocket, wondering if Stefan was keeping an eye on me. My phone pinged and I pulled it from my pocket, expecting more from Tom, but this time it was Ewan.

Slept really well. Think you wore me out yesterday xxx

My cheeks flushed and I glanced up at the glass screen between Stefan and myself, but the chauffeur's eyes were on the road. I swallowed and sat back in my seat trying to look relaxed. The phone pinged again.

When can I see you?

I glanced back at Stefan who was paying full attention to the road, and I began to type my reply to Ewan. I was smiling.

I'm free tomorrow

Good. Come to my place x

I felt a twinge of lust as I recalled the purple satin sheets wrapping around us as we rolled in Ewan's bed. Somehow knowing that we would do this again made me feel stronger. More determined.

Despite my inner bravado I was nervous as I walked into The Savoy restaurant to meet Isadora and Tom. They were both already at the table in deep conversation as I approached. Tom stood when he saw me and hugged me to him, kissing me lightly on the lips. Isadora squeezed my hand as I took my seat.

'You're such a good girl, Charlotte,' she said. 'The committee has been singing your praises.'

I smiled and relaxed. I don't know what I thought this lunch date was going to be about, but I had feared some kind of intervention.

Tom's phone rang at that moment and he excused himself to go outside to take the call.

'Tom's so proud of you,' Isadora said. 'He was just saying how you've never made him happier.'

I met Isadora's eyes and smiled. 'That's so sweet. I'm happy too!'

I realized then that I always put on some form of act with Isadora and that day was no different from any other. And if my indiscretion hadn't been discovered, then it was unlikely to be. If I was able to convince Isadora that I liked and appreciated her so well, then why couldn't I hide my affair from Tom?

One day the Ewan-thing would burn out and life would return to normal. Until then I wanted to enjoy my little secret life.

But Isadora stole away my good mood.

'I think for Tom's sake neither of us should speak of what happened *before* the fundraiser. I mean ... let him enjoy that it went well. I'd hate him to think there's a problem between us.'

The smile fell from my face.

'Tom's happiness means everything to me, Charlotte. It should also be your main priority.'

'What are you saying?' I asked.

'Just that; Tom needs to be kept content. It is the role of a Carlisle wife ...'

'I understand,' I said.

Tom returned to us, and I gave him a genuine smile. I loved him after all, that hadn't changed. I was just having a little fun. That wouldn't hurt anyone, would it?

I was composed for the rest of lunch and Tom, feeling my happiness, held my hand under the table, and stroked my knee. Isadora noticed these small brushes of affection but made no comment.

'Well, I have things to do,' she said when lunch was over.

'Me too,' I said. 'If you want, Stefan can take you both back and I'll get the tube.'

'Thank you,' said Isadora. 'But I'm okay. I'm going to do some shopping in town first.'

'I'll come home with you,' Tom said to me.

'Really?' I said.

'Yes. I think I'll take the rest of the afternoon off.'

Tom never left work early.

'You can do that?'

'Of course. I'm the boss,' he laughed.

Back at our apartment it became clear why Tom had taken the afternoon off. The kissing and groping started in the lift and continued once we were behind closed doors in our own apartment. We made it to the bed – just.

I was aroused and so went with the flow but behind my eyes I saw Ewan, not Tom. Tom's usual sexual moves were no less thrilling though and with the added memory of my transgression I enjoyed our romp very much. Tom was more vigorous and demanding than usual, as though my happiness excited him.

I was still sensitive from the energetic sex the day before and his penetration sent ripples through the pit of my stomach and up my spine. I found myself screaming with pleasure. It was unlike us as a couple and I was awkward about it later.

After he came, Tom got up and pulled on his robe. Then he went into the home office and checked in at work.

My body was aching from the exertion and so I ran a bath. While I soaked, I heard Tom on the phone. His voice carried into the bathroom.

'It's all going very well, just as I'd hoped,' he said.

I closed my eyes and dosed until the ping of my phone woke me.

I sat up in the bath and reached for the towel, drying my hand before I picked up and looked at my phone. It was a message from Ewan.

Can't wait to see you x

I glanced at the half-open bathroom door then deleted all of Ewan's messages.

What was I doing? I had a wonderful husband who knew how to satisfy me. Why did I need more?

'Char? I'm heading back into the office for a couple of hours,' Tom called. 'Something's come up. I won't be home at the usual time, so we'll just get a takeaway tonight. Okay?'

I placed the phone down at the side of the sink.

'Yes, darling.'

'I love you.'

'Love you too.'

As the words came out of my mouth I realized they no longer felt natural. They were as awkward on my lips as any lie.

Chapter Ten

I arrived at Ewan's apartment before lunchtime the next day. Several times I'd almost turned back, but couldn't. I knew this was wrong, but nothing could persuade me to stop. As before there was no one at the reception desk and I just made my way up to his floor in the lift, thankfully unobserved. I knocked on the door and Ewan answered almost immediately.

He looked a little shy as he stepped back and let me in.

'Can I get you a drink?' he asked.

I didn't know whether we should just fall into each other's arms or talk first. This was all new territory for me. It was awkward for a moment and then he smiled and started chatting about a forthcoming work trip he had to take. I found myself falling into natural conversation with him. Then he kissed me softly on the cheek.

'I'm so glad you're here.'

I turned my lips to his and pulled him into my arms. There was such warmth coming from him. Such gentleness and joy in the simple act of having me to talk to. We sat down on the sofa and cuddled for a while. The conversation led back to his work.

'So where do you have to travel to?' I asked.

'I'm going to Milan on the next trip. I'll be gone a few days.'

He told me his company provided fabrics to the fashion industry. There was a supplier in Milan that he regularly visited.

We went to bed then. It wasn't frantic or overexcited like the first time. It wasn't rough like my experiences with Tom could be. Instead Ewan was affectionate and loving. He took care of all of my needs above his own in an unselfish and leisurely way.

Afterwards, when we lay together, my head on his chest, his arm wrapped around me, we fitted together in a way that Tom and I didn't – as if I belonged there.

Weeks went by and I learnt that Ewan was very different from Tom. More sophisticated, but less stilted. He was lively and fun with a great sense of humour. Occasionally he talked about his dead wife and at these times I listened to him. I'd hold him as we lay in the bed and I'd hear his heart tumbling in his chest. I knew he needed to purge himself of her and I was helping him do that.

Sometimes he had to travel for his company and I wouldn't see him for several days, or a week. He kept in touch every day, either by text or, when he knew I was alone, he would call me and we'd talk about our days like an old married couple. Only we weren't married and this was just an affair. I knew and accepted that, believing one day it would end and I'd return to my old life. Perhaps then I'd be ready to have the baby that Tom and Isadora wanted me to have. But not for now. This time was for me. This was my last few months of freedom.

*

'I wish we could go out on a proper date,' Ewan said as he got up to make us both a drink. Over the past six months our relationship had evolved quickly. We had become an important part of each other's lives and this only compounded my guilt. We couldn't be seen in public because I had to keep Ewan a secret from everyone.

As the weeks had gone by it had become a habit for me to go to his apartment in Hammersmith whenever I could. This was a haven. A private world we could both inhabit where I was allowed to be myself. No one else could see us. It was a fantasy other life, and sometimes I made us drinks, or brought food we could eat together. I suppose we played house in many ways. Though Ewan never offered me a key to the place and I never turned up unannounced. It didn't occur to me to do that, because I knew he worked, and I had to plan our meetings carefully to avoid suspicion at home.

Tom and I were happy in a way. I had become quite good at pretending the world we shared hadn't changed, and I was sure that Tom didn't know or suspect anything and therefore he was happy in his oblivion. This made what I was doing acceptable because I convinced myself that no one was being hurt.

That afternoon, though, Ewan surprised me with his comment about a date. I thought he was happy with our trysts the way they were, understanding the need for secrecy.

'We could be seen ...' I said and the expression on his face made me realize that maybe Ewan was the person being hurt by our relationship. I hadn't thought this possible, believing he saw our liaisons as I did.

'I mean, I'd love it if we could go to dinner. Sit and talk in public, even coffee like we used to,' I said.

Ewan smiled. 'I'd like to treat you how you deserve. Spend more than just ... this sort of time together.'

His words struck a chord. I wanted this too, but hadn't allowed myself to explore the possibility. At that moment I considered our future together and saw only sexual encounters in his apartment. No joint friends to eat out with, no holidays together relaxing on a beach or taking in the sights of a European city. No meals out.

'I'm going to Milan again next week,' Ewan said. He stared into my eyes. 'Come with me.'

His invitation was spontaneous but sincere.

'I can't. I just couldn't give a good enough excuse. Tom would be suspicious.'

'Okay.'

'I've never gone away without him ...' I tried to explain.

'Right.'

I tried to distract Ewan then, to take away that downbeat mood that had just found its way into our little sanctuary.

'Don't you ever go on trips with girlfriends?' Ewan said.

I thought about it for a beat. Could I trust any of the few friends I had? I shook my head. There was nobody. It was impossible. But the idea wouldn't go away.

'It would be lovely to not have to hide. To spend all night with you instead of having to leave,' I said.

'I want that.'

Ewan went off to the kitchen and left me with my thoughts. The possibility of a trip ran around in my head like a puppy chasing its tail. I couldn't let it go and I thought it through and through but always came up with the same answer: there was just no way I could make it happen.

Tom came home that night in a mood.

'What's wrong?' I asked as I poured him a glass of wine.

'I have to go to our New York branch for a few days next week. There's a problem with one of the managers and it looks like I'll have to be on hand to make sure he's fired in the right way. Americans can be litigious and so far his line manager hasn't handled him well.'

'That's awful,' I said.

'It's the rotten part of being a CEO. I could delegate, but I'm the best person to handle it.'

'I understand,' I said. 'Want me to fly over with you?'

'I would. But the truth is you'd hardly see me. It'll be meetings night and day to make sure every conceivable problem is cut off at the knees.'

'How long will you be gone?'

'Three or four days. I'm not sure yet. Look if you want to come and do some sightseeing and shopping ...'

'Oh no. I'd really rather go with you when you have more free time,' I said.

I went into the kitchen, face flushing with exhilaration. Ewan had said he was going to Milan next week. It was only a two-hour flight and Tom would never know that I had been away.

Then I thought of all of the possible things that could go wrong. Isadora may call round and find me gone. Tom could call the landline late at night and I wouldn't answer. But – he *never* called the landline. We always communicated by mobile. As for Isadora, she wouldn't visit without prior warning. Even though she had a London flat as a base, she mostly lived on the family estate.

My heart beat faster. Ewan and I could be together for a couple of days as long as I was back before Tom. I planned it all out in my head as I carried the warm plates of food into the dining room. Tom was distracted and barely spoke as he picked at his food. I was grateful for the silence.

In the kitchen I pulled my mobile phone out of my bra. I texted Ewan, then turned the sound off so that Tom wouldn't hear a reply.

I think I can make it to Milan.

Chapter Eleven

As Tom boarded his plane to New York, I took the tube to Heathrow with my clothing and toiletries in hand luggage. I had planned my flight carefully, making sure that he would not be in the same terminal, and that I didn't need to check in until his flight was already in the air. I didn't use the priority lounges, because the visit might show on my card, and Ewan and I had decided not to meet up in the airport, just in case I bumped into someone I knew.

I saw him at passport control but we didn't talk or acknowledge each other's presence. Ewan had booked and paid for the tickets however, and he'd made sure we were sat together on the plane. We reasoned that by then we would be safe. If I saw anyone onboard that knew me, we'd pretend it was a random seat selection and that we'd only just met. I had a ridiculous story to explain my trip about a long-lost relative I'd discovered who lived in Italy, but I really hoped I wouldn't have to use it.

I went to a coffee bar near the gate and waited for the flight to be called. As we boarded I joined Ewan in the queue and after a quick glance around didn't see anyone I knew. This was a relief.

'All okay?' he asked.

'Yes. I'm excited. This is going to be wonderful.'

The flight was on time and all went well.

'Honeymoon?' asked the flight attendant as she observed us kissing and holding hands.

'Yes,' said Ewan.

I giggled when she went away and returned with two mini bottles of champagne.

What followed were three wonderful days and nights.

Ewan had to work in the day, and I was left to my own devices. I did the tourist thing, always paying with cash so that there could be no accidental paper trail. I went out to see churches and monuments and drank and ate in chic cafés.

In the evening Ewan would meet me at the hotel and we would go out to dinner together like a normal couple. I didn't fear being seen and it was relaxed and natural. I even thought it was all somewhat romantic.

The only problem was sometimes I had to take calls from Tom and pretend I was at home. Fortunately, Tom was so busy that he rarely texted or rang. When Ewan was with me during the phone calls, he would go very quiet, his body language tense.

'Let's go out to dinner now,' I suggested on the last evening.

We'd both be leaving early the next morning and I'd just heard from Tom that his plane would be landing a couple of hours after mine as he was taking the night flight home.

'This has been wonderful,' I said to Ewan.

'It has. Very. You're such easy company.' Ewan smiled and I knew he was genuinely happy. 'Maybe we can do it again.'

'I'd love that,' I said.

He took my hand and kissed it. We were silent for a while after that. We were in a nice restaurant eating traditional Italian food. Ewan had a pasta dish with seafood and I had gone for a thin crust pizza which was so much nicer than anything you could find in the UK. I'd fallen in love with Milan and I wanted so much to return.

I was reflective that night on what would happen next. Ewan always instigated where our relationship went, just as he had this time. I wasn't certain what this step now meant for us. We were having an affair, but had it become more serious? Did I want that?

The thought of going home made guilt rear its head again. Facing Tom might be difficult after such a big secret.

That night Ewan didn't make love to me. He merely held me while we slept, and his grip was comfortable but firm. I wanted to think it was a subconscious admission that he didn't want to let me go.

At the airport we learnt that our flight was delayed by an hour. I was worried but not too much. I wanted to get back to my house, stow my passport in the usual place and empty my hand luggage before Tom returned. I could still do this, because it was likely that Tom's international flight would take longer to clear than mine.

'Perhaps we should have foregone the final day and got you home earlier,' Ewan worried.

'It's all right,' I said. 'I still have plenty of time.'

Before long we were up in the air. Ewan held my hand all the way home but we didn't speak much. There wasn't anything to say. Things had changed for certain between us but expressing it was impossible without creating a further ripple in my life.

As the plane landed, he kissed me firmly on the lips and then we sat and waited while everyone else got off.

'Tomorrow?' he said, as I pulled my hand luggage from storage above our seat.

'Absolutely!' I said.

We had decided it was best to go our separate ways as soon as we passed through customs at Heathrow. But as we came through passport control, I realized I had messed up my timing. There was an hour difference between Milan time and Greenwich Mean Time: and it meant that Tom's plane was landing at that moment.

I stopped in the middle of the arrivals lounge as people milled around us, and I felt the colour drain from my face.

'I can't get back before he does,' I said. 'Stefan will be meeting him, and he always comes straight home to shower and change before heading into the office.'

It was 8 a.m. and I'd definitely hit the rush-hour traffic on the tube, which might delay me even further.

'Give me your bag,' Ewan said.

'Why?'

'Go and meet him off the plane as a surprise. Then you can both travel home together.'

It was a good suggestion.

Ewan took my bag, and I headed off quickly to Tom's terminal. I didn't kiss him or look back. It was what we'd agreed.

*

Stefan was surprised to see me as I joined him at the arrivals meeting point.

'Mrs Carlisle! I would have collected you if I'd known.'

'Don't worry,' I said. 'I decided to surprise my husband. It was a spur of the moment thing. Fortunately, the trains all fell right for me. Thought I wouldn't make it!'

Tom came through customs a few minutes later.

'Darling!' he said, throwing his arms around me. 'I didn't expect you to come and meet me ... What's that smell?'

He stepped back and peered at me.

'What smell?'

'Like ... aftershave ...'

'Oh, I was passing the time looking at perfumes.' I forced a smile, then I hugged him again to hide the guilty flush that coloured my face.

Stefan took Tom's luggage and we followed him back to the car park. Adrenaline pumped through my veins. Ewan's aftershave was clearly all over me, but Tom didn't question my explanation as he sank back into the limo's comfortable seats.

'A shower, then work?' I said.

'A shower then bed ... I didn't get any sleep at all on the plane. There was someone in business class who wouldn't stay in his seat.'

'Sorry to hear that,' I said. 'How did the firing go?'

'We did everything within the bounds of legality, but it still cost us a hefty settlement. It was worth it to get rid of the problem though.'

Tom closed his eyes and slept on the journey home.

*

70

Stefan pulled the car into the underground car park, and Tom and I went upstairs in the back lift.

On our floor I saw the apartment caretaker, Harry.

'Hope the power cut wasn't too much of an issue this morning, Mrs Carlisle,' he said.

'Power cut?' Tom said. He glanced at me. 'You didn't mention a power cut.'

'I ... What time was it, Harry?'

'Seven.'

'Oh. I'd already left by then. I wasn't aware of it,' I said.

'Yeah. Just a surge that popped a fuse. I fixed it as soon as it was reported. All back on by eight.'

'Thanks, Harry,' I said. 'Mr Carlisle has been away and he's tired, so we have to ...'

'Sure thing.'

I keyed in our passcode and Tom and I went inside. Tom went straight into the bathroom and I heard the shower running. I waited by the open front door for Stefan.

Stefan came out of the lift and brought Tom's bag inside.

'Just leave them here,' I said. 'Thanks. And ... Stefan. There's no need to tell Mr Carlisle that I didn't come to the airport with you. I don't want my surprise to be marred by the fact that it was spur of the moment. Do you know what I mean?'

'Of course, Mrs Carlisle. Does Mr Carlisle want me to wait for him?'

'I'll check.'

I left Stefan in our hallway and made my way down the corridor to our bedroom. Tom was drying himself when I entered.

'Any instructions for Stefan?' I asked.

'Tell him I'm taking the day off,' he said. 'So he is free now.'

'Okay.'

When Stefan had gone, I brought Tom's hand luggage into the bedroom. Tom had climbed into the bed naked and lay with his eyes closed.

I turned to leave but as I started to close the door Tom said, 'Char? Will you get in with me? I'm so tired but I've missed you.'

I stripped down to my pants and camisole and then got into the bed. I was tired anyway and a little rest probably wasn't a bad thing.

'Huh,' Tom said as he spooned me. 'That perfume is a bit masculine. I don't think I like the smell of it on you.'

'Don't worry. I didn't buy it.'

Tom was soon snoring, and I lay awake thinking about how much I'd changed in such a short time. I wasn't the person I used to be, but it still shocked me how easily every new lie fell from my lips. What surprised me more was how Tom, such an intelligent man, could believe anything I told him. Surely he could see right through me?

Chapter Twelve

I woke the next day realizing that I was completely in love with Ewan. Perhaps it was there as soon as we met but I had refused to acknowledge it. Maybe the few days we'd stolen away had consolidated my emotions. I didn't know how to react. We had never spoken the words to each other that my husband and I regularly expressed with ease. To say I love you to Ewan would not have been easy – I felt it with all of my heart.

Tom woke early because of jetlag and dived on me like a man who hadn't had sexual contact for years, not just a few days. I wasn't into it and found myself faking the orgasm that he expected. Then he crashed back to sleep until the dawn peeked around the edges of our curtains and forced us both to wake.

I made breakfast, all the time I wished Tom would hurry up and go to work, but he loitered around the house, unpacking his hand luggage and suitcase. It was only when he opened the bureau in the living room that I remembered I hadn't replaced my passport in the usual place there.

'Tom ... will you bring your washing to the machine for me?' I said hoping to distract him.

He opened the top drawer and dropped his passport in, closing it as he looked over his shoulder at me. When he went back to the bedroom, I pulled my passport from my handbag and quickly added it to the drawer. I was shaking with nerves when he came back into the room.

Tom walked past me, through the kitchen and into the utility room where he dropped his clothing in front of the washer.

'Thanks. Do you want eggs Benedict?' I said knowing this was his favourite breakfast.

'Sure.'

I made the eggs but managed to ruin the hollandaise.

'What's up with you today?' Tom said. 'You're all twitchy.'

'I didn't sleep well. What time are you going into work today?'

'I'm not. Thought we could spend the day together.'

'Oh.'

'Don't you like that?' Tom asked.

I caught him looking at me instead of what was now poached egg on toasted muffins because I'd given up on the hollandaise.

'Sorry about the breakfast,' I said.

I rang Ewan as soon as Tom left the apartment to get a newspaper.

'What time are you coming over?' he asked.

'I can't make it. Tom has decided he's staying home today.'

'That's unusual ... isn't it?'

'Yes. Work is the thing he cares about most ... He's back. I have to go.'

I hung up and placed my silenced phone in my bra.

'Hi. What do you want to do today then?' I said smiling.

Tom wanted us to go back to bed.

Afterwards we got a taxi and went out to lunch in London.

'I missed you,' he said. He had taken me to a champagne and oyster bar. I figured he would be after more sex later on. 'This has been a lovely day, darling. We should do this more often.'

'We should,' I said.

I tried to smile but his intense behaviour was actually making me feel quite uncomfortable. Something was different about him. Something had changed not just for me, but for him. Tom put his arm around my waist and pulled me to him. He kissed my temple.

'I did a lot of thinking while I was in New York. Don't you think we should try again?' he said. 'Char, you've had months to get over the miscarriage.'

And there was the punch line. I took a breath. It was the worst timing. No way did I want a child. Certainly not with Tom.

I avoided answering because Tom's phone rang and a company crisis took him back into the office after all. I was relieved but hid it well under a show of fake disappointment. I waited with him while Stefan came to the restaurant to collect him.

'Stefan can drop you home after he takes me to the office,' Tom said.

'That's all right. I have a little shopping to do anyway.'

Tom frowned at me and then said something very odd

indeed. 'If that is what you really want to do, then I can't stop you.'

He tried to meet my eyes as the limo pulled into the pavement. I blinked and then Tom kissed me on the cheek before he turned to leave.

I watched the car pull away. Then I took my phone out of my pocket and sent Ewan a text.

I'm on my way.

I did experience a pang of guilt, and my heart jolted with the worry that Tom was growing suspicious, but I just couldn't help myself. I had to see Ewan. I had to be with him.

After collecting my hand luggage from Ewan, I carefully returned my toiletries back to their permanent home. After that, I fell back into my wifely duties.

I didn't see Ewan again for a few days. An urgent business trip pulled him away. It was the right time for this to happen. I'd been about to tell him that we had to cool off for a while and that Tom might suspect.

With little contact with Ewan, life settled again into routine at home. The fear of Tom finding out receded and I was lulled into what I hoped wasn't a false sense of security. Even so, I found Tom's company harder to bear. I knew things had changed and not for the better. There was an undercurrent, a tension, in the room when we were together. Tom was never one to brood, but he was focusing on something. I just knew it.

I had to continue having sex with him too – it was difficult to avoid, though sometimes I managed. And he was always rough, desperate in his attempts to engage me. I had to wash afterwards every time: it was as though I were betraying Ewan, not the other way around.

'Mother spoke to your doctor today. He told her there was no reason why we couldn't start trying again now,' Tom said one evening.

'My doctor spoke to your mother about me?' I said. 'That's outrageous!'

'Don't be silly. Everyone has your best interests at heart.'

'I doubt that,' I said.

'What's the matter with you?' Tom said. 'Don't be so fractious.'

I sighed, then listened to his argument about why we needed to become parents right away. Why I *had* to stop taking my contraceptives.

'I feel like ... I'm losing you sometimes,' Tom said. 'You're not yourself right now and it's all because of the miscarriage, so why not bite the bullet?'

'I'll think about it,' I said to placate him.

'A new pregnancy will help you get over—'

'I said I'll think about it!' I snapped.

'I just want us to be happy.'

A shadow seemed to pass over Tom's face, and he stroked my arm with genuine affection and concern. Then he cuddled up to me on the sofa and kissed my face and hair and rubbed his hand over my back until I couldn't help but relax against him. For once he was trying to be soothing.

I was on a roller coaster of emotion. When Tom was like

this, I questioned my irrational feelings of claustrophobia and loneliness. It was ridiculous that the guilt had made me so paranoid that I had felt afraid of Tom. Tom had never done anything to hurt me. It was me that was at fault. How could I betray someone who had done everything for me?

Maybe it was time to end things with Ewan. Maybe I needed to recapture the relationship Tom and I had once had? Maybe the baby was the way forward.

As Tom hugged me, a new fear reared up out of the blue: the thought of never seeing Ewan again. The thought of returning to my old life was just as bad. But worst of all was the thought of continuing this dual life, full of secrets and guilt and the fear of discovery.

It was no way to live.

Chapter Thirteen

Sometimes the pressure of the situation built up so much inside me that I thought I was going to explode. I don't have a short fuse, but I was developing one. My patience was running thinner by the day and sometimes the urge to tell Tom the truth almost overcame my desire for secrecy. I believed the secret was the thrill: keeping anything from Tom was satisfying, because it gave me back control of my daily life.

What made it worse was that I had decided never to discuss our relationship with Ewan. It wasn't appropriate. Deep down I wanted Ewan to think that Tom and I somehow led separate lives, even though this wasn't strictly true. I talked about a lot of things with Ewan, but we both steered clear of this subject and it was hard for me because Ewan was my only real confidant: I told him everything else.

Weeks drifted on again. Sometimes Ewan worked away for more than a week, and even though he asked, there was no way I could find an opportunity to join him again. We'd been lucky the first time, but I knew it was unlikely to ever happen again. But we met whenever we could, and those meetings grew in intensity, so much so that being apart from him was torturous. Being with Tom in-between times became punishment.

Something had to give, but I had no strength to make the break with either man. A text from Ewan arrived one morning after Tom had left for work:

I need to see you. Today!

My mood lifted immediately. He had been away for several days and this was a nice surprise because I hadn't been expecting him back in London for a few more.

Hammersmith?

No. Come to The Savoy. I'll explain when you get there. We need to talk.

Is everything okay?

Ewan texted the room number, and I left my apartment soon afterwards and made my way to The Savoy. I was dressed well but not flashy and I wore a hat with my long blonde hair hidden underneath.

I was worried on the way there for more reasons than just being spotted in the wrong place at the wrong time. I wondered if this was it: the final moment when Ewan let me down and ended our relationship forever. The thought of it plunged me into a black hole of depression.

When I reached the hotel, I saw one of the board of directors' wives going inside with another woman. I kept my head down as they walked ahead of me, and I hung back to avoid being observed. I had a hairy moment when she glanced over her shoulder towards me. I turned away, trembling – had I been seen? Then the two women moved on towards a group of ladies gathering outside the restaurant. It was a familiar sight – a charity committee or maybe just wives doing lunch. I hadn't spent much time in recent months doing any of these things.

I hurried towards the lift before I was seen and entered it, pressing the button for the sixth floor. The doors closed and I was relieved to have made it this far without discovery.

The lift opened on the fifth floor and a rough-looking man got inside. I kept my eyes down, but noticed he was wearing battered brogues under mud-splattered jeans. As the door opened on sixth I hurried out without making eye contact.

My behaviour was suspicious, but I really didn't know how to act in this situation. Over the last few months of my affair with Ewan, I had always been able to visit him unobserved.

I reached Ewan's door and knocked. I glanced down the corridor and saw the man who had been in the lift with me standing by the door of the room next door. He opened the door and went inside without looking at me.

Ewan's door opened a second later.

'What's wrong?' I asked.

'Come inside,' he said, poking his head out of the door and looking down the corridor. 'Did anyone see you?'

I shook my head. 'Not anyone important. There was a guy in the lift. But ... why here?'

He closed the door and pulled me into his arms. I hugged him and then we were kissing. But instead of moving to the bed, Ewan pulled back and took a step away from me, arms dropping to his sides.

'Charlotte,' he said, 'perhaps you need to sit down.'

I perched on the edge of the bed and looked at him. My heart sank. This was the moment I had been dreading; the end of our affair. He didn't want to see me anymore.

I envisioned my life without him and my stomach turned. I decided to be brave and face it head on, because there was no point in doing this in an undignified way. I didn't want to ruin all of the happy memories he had given me by begging him to stay with me.

'Why aren't we at Hammersmith?' I asked. 'Didn't you want a scene at your home? Only, I'm not going to cause a scene ...'

'What are you talking about?'

'I guess this is the moment you tell me it's over.'

'Oh my god, no,' he smiled. That lovely disarming charm came out so easily. 'I don't want us to stop, Charlotte.'

A huge sigh escaped my lips as I let go of the breath I'd been holding.

'But things have changed. And I've been thinking for a while that we have to resolve our problems.'

'What do you mean?'

'I *love* you. Don't you know that?'

He had never used those words before, and I was overwhelmed with emotion. Partly it was relief from the doubts that had crept in from the moment he changed our meeting place, but also I now realized how much I wanted – no needed – to hear these words from him.

I pulled him down to sit on the edge of the bed with me.

'I hate to just say this as it sounds like an automatic response. But I'm in love with you, Ewan. And I didn't know if I should ever say it.'

He held my hand in response.

I didn't add all of those corny lines about never having felt like this before, because that was untrue. I had been in love with Tom once, though maybe it wasn't as passionate or as intense as this.

'What's going on?' I said. 'Your text said you needed to talk to me.'

'I wanted to tell you how I felt. *Feel*. I wanted you to know, no matter what happens. I love you. I *really* love you, Charlotte.'

I frowned, still waiting for some heartbreaking punch line. The blow didn't come though. Instead Ewan began to kiss me. It was serious kissing, not like the fun, relaxed warm kisses we'd shared before. It was as though he was trying to show me the depth of his feelings.

I stopped worrying about it when his hand ran over my breast and my nipple and my body responded to him. I sank into his arms letting the moment wash over me.

'I want you to leave him,' Ewan said afterwards as we lay naked in the hotel bed.

I was quiet, not sure what to respond. My imagination ran over and over this scenario in my head. I saw myself going back home and packing. I thought about Tom's reaction and Isadora's distain. Then, I thought about a life with Ewan, a life I knew little about, one that was both frightening and exhilarating.

'I'm serious,' he said when I didn't answer. 'I love you and I can't continue like this. We need to be together. You need to get away from ... *him*.'

'I hate the lies,' I said.

'Me too. And there is still so much I need to tell you.'

'Like what?'

'Now's not the time, darling. But you'll know everything once we are together permanently. Just believe me when I say, ever since we met you have been under my skin.'

His words concerned me a little. Ewan had never been this sincere or intense. But all I focused on was the idea of a future with him. The idea of the end to the lies, of making this permanent between us. I should have played harder to get but I couldn't. I wanted to be with him, and didn't want to keep hurting Tom. The decision had to be made, however spontaneous it seemed. I believed that Ewan would not be the kind of husband or partner who wouldn't have to control my every move. I couldn't help thinking what a relief it would be to be away from Carlisle control – especially Isadora.

'If we are to do this,' I said, 'I need to plan. I can't just ... leave.'

Ewan was silent then. Maybe he thought I was trying to avoid the issue by half agreement.

'I need to make plans too, get us a home first. We need to be away from here.'

'But ... Hammersmith?' I said.

'It was leased. Only short term and the owners are now back.'

I took this information in, wondering what else Ewan was going to tell me.

'But don't worry, darling. The lease was a convenience thing. I didn't want to own anywhere after my wife died and

I sold my old place – there were too many memories. You understand? But we'll find somewhere together. I'll get another lease in the meantime and then we can—'

'Why didn't you tell me before?'

'It honestly never occurred to me,' he said. 'It doesn't matter. I know we don't talk about these things, but I *can* look after you, Charlotte. You can walk away with nothing and I'll provide for you. I have money. Enough for us to start a new life. Buy our own house ... You don't need Tom.'

His words were reassuring, and I sank into him as he told me his plans.

'No more time apart. When I go away on my trips, you'll come with me. But we'll have a permanent base too. It's all going to work out. I have a few things to do first, but I don't want to drag this out. Let's say Monday. Leave him on Monday and meet me at Harrods. Then I'll take you to my new place and we'll begin our life properly together.'

I couldn't believe how things had changed from one day to the next. It was sudden, but it wasn't when you looked back and saw the development of our relationship. This was where we'd been heading from the day we first met. I realized then that I had been waiting for an escape route for a long time and I wasn't about to miss my chance.

'I have to go away for work again for a couple of days, but I've already put in an application for a new apartment which should be through by the weekend. It'll do us until we find what we want together.'

I left him then, hurrying back to what had become my 'pretend' life, knowing that I would soon have a 'real' one with no hidden secrets. The idea of being able to spend the whole night in bed with Ewan, watching television together, as we had on occasion at the Hammersmith flat, was all a dream come true.

I knew it was insane – giving up my fairytale life for someone I hardly knew – but I couldn't help it. I loved Ewan and for the first time in my life I could be the real me. Not some trophy wife. I focused on all of these thoughts even as the fear and doubts crept in. I had to make this decision for once and all. But that didn't mean it wasn't terrifying.

Chapter Fourteen

As usual Ewan kept in touch while he was away. We spoke every day and he confirmed that the flat was almost ours.

'My period came early,' I told Tom when he tried to make love to me.

I had my own bank accounts and some savings. It wasn't a lot, but it was enough until Ewan and I worked things out. Ewan hadn't mentioned marriage – but I assumed it would be on the cards as soon as I could free myself from Tom, and I decided that I would do that with as little drama as possible. I planned to meet with a lawyer to start the proceedings for a divorce as soon as I left. Until then, I didn't want to risk Tom finding out before I was able to tell him myself that it was over.

On the Sunday evening I made dinner for Tom and prepared to break the news. I poured us a drink with a shaking hand and then sat opposite him as he ate, wondering if this would be our last supper. I had made his favourite food: fillet steak, some mashed potato and grilled mushrooms smeared with garlic butter.

Ewan had texted me confirming the time we were to meet. It was real. It was happening and my marriage was over.

I remembered our happiest moments; our wedding day; St

Moritz for a perfect honeymoon; laughter on our trip to see the northern lights. With our history it was difficult to see how things had gone so wrong. But then I remembered the darker times. Tom's moody days when he was stressed about the company; Isadora's controlling behaviour; the feeling that I never had control and had to be prefect in order to please everyone.

'Tom,' I said. 'I have something to tell you.'

I picked up my wine; my trembling hands were slick with sweat. I almost dropped the glass but managed to pull it to my lips and take a long swig before placing it down on the coaster by my untouched dinner plate.

Tom sat back in his chair and studied me. His eyes narrowed. I looked away.

'I've met someone else. I'm leaving in the morning. I understand completely that I deserve nothing from you. I'll make it easy for you and will agree to being named on the papers for a quick divorce.'

Tom's face was white, his eyes suddenly dark with anger.

It was cruel, though I was trying to be honest.

'Is this some kind of sick joke?' he said.

His voice was colder, and I couldn't suppress the shudder that rippled up my back as I looked up at him, finally meeting his gaze.

'No, Tom. I'm sorry. This just ... happened. I met someone else and I love him.'

I almost said, *it's not you, it's me*, but then I stopped myself.

'I'm sorry. I know this isn't the life you wanted but ... it wasn't what I wanted either.'

'Shut up!' he said.

'Tom. I'm—'

'Don't say another word ... You fucking bitch. You've been having an affair? And just like that you're in love and you're fucking leaving?'

I didn't deny it; I deserved his hatred. What could I say? These two sentences summed up everything.

'How long?' he asked.

'It doesn't matter.'

'How long have you been fucking someone else?'

'I'll leave now,' I said. 'I wanted to be fair and honest—'

'Honest? You were sleeping around behind my back ... and then coming back to my bed. That was really honest, Charlotte—'

'You deserved the truth ...'

'Get out of my sight. I can't bear to look at you,' he said.

I knew he was right. There was nothing I could say.

I had already packed my bags and stowed them in the guest bedroom. I stood up and left the dining room, then went to the guest room and closed the door. I hadn't planned to leave until the next day. But it was obvious that I couldn't stay the night here now.

Then I heard the front door of the apartment slam shut.

I opened the guest room door and looked out into the hallway. Tom had left and I was relieved. I wasn't sure we could have 'talked anything out', even though I knew it would probably have been the best thing to do for his sake.

My phone beeped. I fished it out of my handbag to see the message.

I won't be home again tonight. Be gone before I get back. Tom

Chapter Fifteen

Where are you?

My text went unanswered the next day.

I had never yet known Ewan to arrive late. Wherever we met he was always there waiting for me.

It started to rain. I huddled under one of the window canopies outside Harrods. Then I sent Ewan a text telling him I'd wait in the coffee shop. I carried my handbag and one suitcase, containing all of my basic needs, to our meeting place and found a seat near the window.

My heart was in my mouth as I ordered my usual latte. Where was Ewan? Was there some miscommunication? I was sure he said meet at Harrods. I glanced at my phone for the hundredth time. He hadn't replied, nor had he read the last message I'd sent, though it showed as 'Delivered'.

I pulled up his contact details and pressed dial. The phone didn't ring, it merely cut off. I checked my phone signal and noted my reception was bad. Then I looked again at the last few messages on the chain. Perhaps he was on the tube and couldn't send or receive?

An hour over the agreed time, with the dregs of my cold coffee sitting before me, I was growing increasingly worried.

'Where are you?' I murmured. All kinds of scenarios went through my head. Had he been in an accident? Should I call the local hospital? What if he never came?

I dialled his number again. This time a voice mail picked up, and I was about to speak and leave a message when a female voice said, 'The number you have called is not recognized. Please check and dial again.'

I disconnected the call and stared at the screen. My stomach turned with rising panic as I opened up the server on my phone. My mouth was dry as I googled the business where Ewan told me he worked. The number came up and I pressed call. After a few rings, the call was answered.

'Bartle, Birling and Daniels,' said the telephonist.

'I'd like to speak to Mr Ewan Daniels please,' I said.

There was a moment's pause. 'I'm sorry we don't have anyone here by that name,' said the girl on the other end of the phone.

'He's one of your partners ...' My voice sounded uncertain. 'Mr Daniels.'

'Oh,' said the girl. 'There is no Mr Daniels. He passed away last year with a brain tumour.'

My blood turned cold.

'A brain tumour?' I said. 'Sorry. I must have the wrong number.'

I hung up and slumped back in my chair. I glanced around the coffee shop feeling as though everyone there knew the terrible mistake I'd made. Was it merely a coincidence that the partner in Ewan's firm had died a year ago of a brain tumour? The same thing that had supposedly killed Ewan's wife?

His voice echoed in my ears.

No matter what happens. I love you. I really love you, Charlotte.

I lurched to my feet, spilling my coffee cup onto the floor. Faces turned to stare at me as I bent to pick it up. One of the baristas came out from behind the counter, a mop and bucket in her hand.

'Are you okay?' she said.

I shook my head. Then grabbed my coat from the back of the chair. Without a word I pulled the suitcase behind me and exited the shop.

I stumbled out into the street. My mind kept going over his final words:

No matter what happens.

I took a cab over to the Hammersmith address. There was nothing else I could do. It was late afternoon and I had nowhere else to go. I had to find Ewan or at least talk to the people who had rented the flat to him. By that time, I was beginning to think this was all some scam, some figment of my overactive imagination. But I wanted to believe there was just some terrible confusion on mine or Ewan's part about the date and time we were supposed to meet. But that couldn't be true: we only spoke last night. Plus, Ewan had always answered his phone before. Now he wasn't answering. Had he lost it? Or had something serious happened to him? All these thoughts and excuses ran through my head, anything other than the possibility that he didn't want to meet me. It was difficult to digest even though it was obvious: why would someone make me believe they loved me and then just leave me like this? I couldn't reconcile the thought of such a cruel person with the man I thought I knew.

I paid the cab and let him go. Then I walked into the reception of the building that I had visited regularly two or three times a week since our affair had begun.

The reception was as I remembered, though part of me was convinced that it would be different.

On the third floor a thirty-something woman answered Ewan's door.

'I'm looking for Ewan Daniels,' I said. I was ready for anything now. Maybe this girl was his girlfriend. Maybe he had lied about being single.

'I'm sorry. You've got the wrong address.'

'He was your previous tenant? While you were away,' I said trying to remember what Ewan had told me about the owners of the flat.

'Tenant?' said the woman. 'I've never leased out my apartment.'

'But he lived here,' I said. 'I came here regularly. I can even describe your bathroom ...'

The girl took a step back. 'Look. No one has access to my apartment but me and my boyfriend.'

I took a breath and then I couldn't stop myself. 'Can I see a picture of your boyfriend?'

The girl frowned, then retrieved her phone from her pocket and showed me her screensaver. She didn't have to do it, but perhaps she suspected him of being unfaithful.

I stared at the photo. It was a man in his thirties, sporting that unshaven look that was so popular. There was something so ordinary about him that he looked vaguely familiar. The sort of person you would see loitering outside a shop and maybe not even notice.

'Is that him?' she asked.

'No. It's not.'

'You might have the wrong apartment,' she said. But glancing over her shoulder I knew I didn't: the furniture was exactly the same.

I didn't know what to do.

'Look. I don't know what's going on. But I was here.'

'I've lived here for six years and I'm telling you that's not possible.'

She closed the door and I stood there for a few moments. How had Ewan used her apartment without her knowledge? It wasn't possible. Was I mistaken?

I looked around the landing, but knew I wasn't. I had been here two or three times a week for the past six months. This was the place. The woman inside was lying. But why?

I thought about hammering on the door again. But maybe she'd call the police and I really didn't want to make a scene.

Downstairs I looked around for the caretaker but there was no one manning the building. There was no regular receptionist and I knew no one had seen me entering and leaving because I'd been careful. This was all very convenient at the time, but I wished someone had seen us now.

Could the miscarriage have disturbed my mind to such an extent that I imagined the whole thing?

I left the building, still dragging my case and handbag. I didn't know where to go and so I looked at my phone again. The number had been correct. Ewan contacted me just the night before. I'd spoken to him in the afternoon that same day. He was loving, reassuring, desperate for us to begin our new life. What had happened in the space of those few hours?

Where had he been last? The Savoy.

I googled the hotel number and called.

'Ewan Daniels please?'

There was silence as the receptionist searched her computer for anyone staying with that name.

'Mr Daniels checked out a few days ago,' she said.

'Do you have any forwarding address details?' I asked. 'It's urgent.'

'I'm afraid not, but I couldn't give them out if I did.'

I hung up without thanking her.

Not knowing what else to do, I returned to Harrods in the next black cab I saw. By then I'd covered every possible scenario that might lead to an honest misunderstanding, even down to doubting myself about the meeting time. Why hadn't I asked him to send me over the address of our new home? Why hadn't he offered it?

Then I stood in the rain, staring at my bedraggled reflection in the window as I let the water pour over me. I was desperately tired, and my mind couldn't bring up even one person I could contact for help. In fact, I'd let all of my friends slip away over the last few months. It had been easier than involving them.

My world was in tatters. The rain could drown me, and I'd

let it. Tom would never forgive me. I didn't want him to: that life was gone for me. But worst of all, the dawning realization that asserted itself in my mind. Ewan wasn't coming. He had *played* me. I was practically broke, homeless and alone and this man had done this to me for some warped and twisted reason that I couldn't fathom.

How could anyone be so cruel?

A black limousine drew into the kerb behind me.

I took a sobbing breath. It wasn't relief: it was horror at being found there, like that. At having failed to do what I said I would.

The blacked-out window in the back rolled down.

'Charlotte,' my husband's voice was muffled by the weather. 'Don't stand there like that. Someone might see you ...'

Did it matter anymore? The scandal would soon be out when the divorce papers were filed, as they would undoubtedly be, with me named 'adulteress'.

Stefan, got out of the limousine and came to me carrying an umbrella.

'Let me take your case, Mrs Carlisle,' he said, holding the umbrella over my head.

He spoke gently, as if he was trying to help an invalid cross the road. I wondered what my husband had told him. Did he know I'd ruined everything?

'Please, Mrs Carlisle,' Stefan said. 'Let me *help* you.'

I could have kept dry, waited under one of the store's canopies, but when I realized – when I knew it was over – I had stopped caring. As if the rain could help me take a slow and steady course to my final destruction.

I met Tom's eyes as I turned. How did it all come to this? What cruel, sick joke destroyed my once beautiful and happy life? Was Ewan in some hotel room, laughing about how he destroyed the life of the spoilt little rich girl? Maybe it had all been filmed and I would be the star of some sick new reality TV drama. I gave a bitter laugh.

Stefan put his hand on my elbow and encouraged me to walk towards the car.

Tom shuffled over onto the other seat as Stefan opened the door. I stared into the back, my mind blank, my soul broken. I forgot how to bend, how to move, how to climb into the car.

'Charlotte. *Get in!*' Tom snapped. 'It's a one-time offer.'

Stefan took my case and I sank into the leather seats from pure exhaustion rather than the desire to do so. Water dripped from my hair onto my already soaked coat and the expensive leather seat squelched against my legs. The wet stockings clung to my skin.

Tom dropped a towel onto my knee. 'Wipe some of that water off,' he said.

I lifted the towel to my face and rubbed away the rain and the tears. Then I blotted my hair, feeling nothing but cold and numb.

'How did you find me?' I said.

'A colleague saw you. I couldn't allow—'

'The scandal?' I said.

Tom stayed silent, though I waited for his bitter words, the recriminations I deserved.

The door slammed shut and Stefan took a moment to place my suitcase in the boot before he returned to the driver's seat.

I felt a surge of panic. This wasn't happening. I was starting a new life. Only I wasn't – it had all been a lie.

A moment later, the engine purred and the limousine pulled away into the slow-moving traffic.

I glanced out of the window at Harrods. Part of me hoped I'd see Ewan arriving in the nick of time. But he wasn't there. I sank back into the seat as all of the fight left me. This is the place it started: a fitting location for it to end.

Chapter Sixteen

I entered our apartment in silence. Stefan brought in the case and placed it in our bedroom. Just like that I knew that Tom was not planning to immediately throw me out on the streets. I didn't say anything; instead, I waited for him to talk. For him to tell me how much I'd hurt him.

When Stefan left, Tom ran me a bath.

'Get those clothes off,' he ordered.

Still in shock I dropped my clothing and climbed into the bath. The old Charlotte had left the rebel outside at Harrods and submissive-me was back in the driving seat. I regressed completely to my former mousy self. I soaked until Tom told me to get out and then he wrapped a towel around me.

I didn't deserve this much care and couldn't understand his tenderness.

'Dry yourself,' he said. 'Then lie on the bed.'

I came around a bit and looked about the room. My body was warm now, and so my freezing emotions lifted too. The white Egyptian cotton duvet was pulled back on my side of the bed as if it had been waiting for me to come home.

I lay down, and Tom peeled off my towel. He looked down

into my face, but I couldn't meet his eyes and so I closed mine. He kissed my mouth and began to make love to me. I was frozen, unable to respond, or move, or stop him. I thought of Ewan and remembered being in his arms.

Inside I was screaming 'no', but my mouth wouldn't move.

Tom's love making was leisurely, not frantic or angry, and it went on for a while. He made no attempt to get me to respond. He just took his own pleasure and then collapsed on top of me.

His weight was crushing but I was so overcome with self-loathing that I didn't object.

Tom sat up and threw the towel back over me. I lay there unmoving. Was this Tom's final revenge for my betrayal?

I wanted to die. The shame of it all bore down on me, the thought that Tom had just ... had me ... when it was obvious I was in a bad place.

Tom pulled on his robe and left the bedroom. When he returned he sat down on the edge of the bed beside me. I didn't look at him.

'Sit up,' he said.

I did.

'Here.'

I opened my eyes. He held out a glass of brandy. I took the glass and sipped.

'So he left you there? All day?'

I couldn't speak.

'Did you call him? Did he tell you he'd led you on?'

'His line was ... dead.'

'Who was he?' he asked.

'It doesn't matter ... he lied. It wasn't real. I doubt he even told me his real name.'

Tom sighed.

'You were stupid, really stupid. This guy ... how did you meet him?'

I shook my head.

'I've been looking into it and I've found something online I'd like to show you.' Tom got up and left the room.

I followed him down the corridor and to his office. There I saw Tom's computer, open on a Facebook page: it was called 'CATFISHED'.

'What's this?'

'Sit down. Read it.'

He went away, leaving me alone to read. There were posts by several women. All of whom had been 'catfished' by the same man.

I met him in a department store @Sharon1

He turned up on a weekend away. It seemed like a coincidence bumping into him again. He was always so charming and he spoke to me like I was the only thing that mattered. @Lizzy323

I would have been suspicious if he'd tried to extort money from me, but he always paid for everything. @MaggieCatLover

He begged me to leave my husband then never showed up. It was the cruellest thing anyone could have done to me. @ LonelySue

Tears rolled down my cheeks as I read the stories. It all sounded so familiar: the charmer who appeared one day and changed their life. He promised them everything and then he just disappeared.

I stopped reading when I saw that one woman mentioned the disconnected phone line, the fake job, the empty flat.

'This is so awful.' My voice broke and with it any remaining disbelief.

I closed the browser and left Tom's office. This was the ultimate proof: it was true. Ewan had really led me on.

What was it that one of the women said about his motives: he got some vile kick out of it.

I could hear Tom in the kitchen, making himself dinner – a rarity. I couldn't face him again and so I went back into my en suite bathroom.

I stared at my mascara-streaked face. I looked gaunt, ill, sick to my stomach. I thought I'd been lonely before I met Ewan, but I was never more alone than that moment. I splashed water on my face and washed away the tears.

I went into the bedroom and climbed into bed, exhausted and unable to think. Tomorrow Tom would throw me out. It was a given. But until that happened there was nothing else I could do.

Chapter Seventeen

Tom didn't throw me out the next day. He woke me up, gave me a mug of tea and ordered me to drink it. After that I collapsed again into a tortured sleep. I was incapable of moving from the bed for more than a few brief moments for trips to the bathroom. This went on for a few days until one morning Tom pulled the covers off me and made me shower and dress. Then he took me into the kitchen, sat me down at the breakfast bar and placed some buttered toast in front of me.

'Eat it,' he said.

'I can't.' Nausea rolled in my stomach at the thought of eating.

'Are you trying to kill yourself?' he said.

His blunt words shocked me.

'You're going to get seriously ill.'

'Wouldn't that be better for you?' I said. 'No scandalous divorce ...'

Tom sighed. He looked away, as if the sight of me sickened him. I couldn't blame him.

'I don't want to see you die. And I won't facilitate your self-pity. This man played you. You know that now, don't you?'

I nodded.

'He's an evil bastard. He led you on. Used you ...'

'Please ...' I said. 'I know. You don't have to—'

'I *do*. I do have to. Because I have to come to terms with what's happened. You've lied to me. You've been with another man ... how do you think I feel?'

'I'm sorry ...' I said.

I put my head down on the breakfast bar. I hated myself so much. I'd hurt Tom. Why? As I ran through the last few months, I couldn't imagine why I'd done what I'd done. But then hindsight is a wonderful thing.

'Look at me,' Tom said.

I didn't want to see the hurt I'd caused, but I lifted my head and met his eyes.

'This is the deal,' he said. 'I still love you. I know it's naive of me, after what you've done, but I'm willing to try to forgive and forget.'

My eyes were heavy with tears.

'How can you forgive me for this?' I said.

'Because you're my wife, and this is ultimately my fault.'

'I don't understand.'

'I spoke to Mother last night. She said I've neglected you, that the company has taken up too much of my time. That it's all *my* fault. I denied it at first but I've thought it through.'

Oh God! Isadora knew ...

'You've led a very sheltered life since you met me. Perhaps I was too controlling, too insistent. Perhaps I didn't listen well enough. It's obviously going to take me time to understand what you did, but Mother is helping me. She explained how women can feel like they are missing out on something. Even when they aren't. She thinks this will be good for us and we'll be stronger for it. We'll finally be able to move on and get over that hurdle that has been stopping you wanting a family.'

I looked at him, barely comprehending what he was saying. Was he insane? How could we ever get over *this*? How could I ever forget what Ewan had done to me? How could we just return to the way things were? 'What are you saying?' I said.

I was trembling and the tears began to fall. I was afraid but it didn't make sense in view of his acknowledgement of his part in this. All the feelings of isolation I'd had in my teens, after my parents died, resurfaced, along with the memories of waiting in the rain for a man who would never show.

Tom had been my rescuer back then, but he'd also been my goaler – keeping me like Rapunzel in a tower that had no doors and just had one window through which I could barely see the real world. And then the view was filtered through his, or Isadora's eyes.

Ewan had empowered me, made me strong enough to leave Tom. I'd have never done this without him.

But Ewan's love had been a lie and now I was terrified of the ridicule that would follow. It was the worst feeling of betrayal that anyone could have. He'd given me strength and then used it to completely destroy me. But I had experienced what it was like to be out on a limb again – just as I had been as an orphaned child and it had been terrifying. I had deluded myself into believe I could do anything I wanted and it was all because Ewan Daniels had used me and pretended to love me.

'You need to trust me, Char. I'm the person who'll always care for you. Now eat that toast. Today is the first day of the rest of our lives. It's not going to be easy: I'm expecting you to make a lot of effort in our marriage to make this work. We are going to forget this happened and try to move on.'

I heard these words but didn't believe them. Maybe this too would turn out to be a lie. Tomorrow I'd wake to find my bags packed and Tom would escort me to the door.

Chapter Eighteen

I passed that night in a state of quiet hysteria. I lay still in the bed beside Tom, pretending to sleep. My mind ran over everything that had happened since I met Ewan Daniels – from his first appearance, to the moment he re-entered my life in Harrods. Ewan had planned the sting all along.

I tried to see our time together with different eyes. Even when I knew I'd been fooled I still couldn't accept it had all been a lie, because every moment had been exciting and happy. It was so hard to imagine that anyone could be *that* good at lying. And his words wouldn't leave me, that awful declaration of love. *No matter what happens I love you* ... Was that his final and cruellest blow?

I had been at my happiest the instant I believed he loved me. A week later I found out it was a lie.

How he must have laughed when I left the hotel. All he had to do was string me along just a few more days, then he needn't pretend anymore. What a horrible, malicious thing to do to anyone. Even me, the unfaithful wife. What kind of man was he really? He must hate women. He must have hated me.

Covering my mouth with my hands I choked back a sob. Tom didn't stir beside me.

Part of me believed that I had deserved everything for my awful treatment of Tom, but part of me struggled to accept that too. Was I such a bad person that karma had found the best way to punish me? Did anyone deserve someone to lead them into self-destruction like that? Would I be happy and pregnant with my husband's child now if Ewan Daniels hadn't come into our lives?

Just before dawn, my exhausted mind stopped torturing me and I fell into a heavy sleep. But even as my body forced me to rest, the anguish of my situation followed me down into my dreams. I imagined that Ewan had showed up, but late, and all was well as he took me back to the apartment he promised we'd share. It was very similar to the one in Hammersmith, but as I walked around the layout and decor changed and it became the apartment I shared with Tom. Only this one had bars on the windows.

What's with the bars? I asked Ewan, but as I turned to face him, I found Tom staring at me. His face was flushed with rage.

It's to keep you in, you two-timing bitch, Tom said.

I jerked awake and tried to remember where I was. I turned my head to look over at Tom's side of the bed, but found he'd gone. I picked up my phone and glanced at it. It was 9.33 a.m. I was surprised that Tom's departure for work hadn't woken me.

Pushing back the duvet, I sat up and turned my legs over the edge of the bed. Then I dropped my head into my hands as a wave of sleep-deprived nausea swirled up into my stomach.

When the feeling subsided, I forced myself to stand and tottered into the bathroom.

I glanced down at the toilet bowl and saw a scatter of pills in the water. I looked around and then saw my contraceptive pill box and packet, empty and in the small bin under the sink.

I flushed the toilet.

In the kitchen I found a Post-it note from Tom listing today's errands. One of which was to meet Isadora for lunch in Mayfair. I scanned the note. Tom's words and phrases jumped out at me randomly and made no sense at all.

Look your best ... buy new lingerie ... the laundry needs doing ...

Surely, we could not just behave as normal? My vision blurred, and I gripped the sink to steady myself. Was there some other charity thing I was supposed to attend? Or was this the moment when I would be told Tom would be putting me out on the streets with nothing?

I looked around the apartment for my suitcase, but found it open and empty in the guest bedroom. In the utility room I found some of the clothing that I had been planning to take with me in the washing basket, even though it wasn't dirty. And in the bin, most of my underwear was shredded and thrown away.

Buy new lingerie ...

I was numb, beyond caring.

I pulled the washing out of the basket and began to stuff it into the washer. Then I found Tom's jogging trousers, mud-encrusted around the ankles, and a pair of trainers thick with muddy gunk. It was another sign of how stressed my husband was. He always went running when he was uptight and even the awful weather hadn't stopped him.

I pulled my clothing back from the machine and put Tom's in alone. Then I washed both joggers and trainers, but I wasn't sure the trainers could be saved.

I procrastinated a while until time dictated that I couldn't avoid it any longer.

The last thing I wanted to do was meet up with Isadora. I was mentally and emotionally drained. Exhaustion clung to me like stale sweat. Even so, I went back to the bathroom, brushed my teeth, showered and then pulled on the smart, CEO-wife clothing that Isadora would expect me to wear for our lunch date.

I carefully applied my make-up, trying to hide the gauntness of my cheeks and the dark circles under my eyes. Then I picked up my handbag, checked that my purse and cards were inside, and left the apartment to head to Mayfair.

It never occurred to me to refuse to go.

'Are you ready to go shopping now?' said Stefan as I left the apartment reception to find him and the limo waiting for me. 'Mr Carlisle said I was to escort you ...'

I considered telling Stefan I didn't need him, but I had no energy to stand up for myself: I needed all of my strength to face Isadora. I let him drive me to the store, and he dutifully waited outside while I shopped for new underwear. I didn't buy sexy lingerie; it was all cotton normal-day things. Part of me didn't want to invite Tom's attention and to buy such undergarments would suggest I wanted him.

I was mentally and physically sore. Every bone in my body hurt just from the exertion of daily functioning.

When I left the store, Stefan took my bags and placed them in the back of the car. Then without me asking he drove me to the restaurant in Mayfair to meet my mother-in-law.

It was raining when we reached the restaurant. I picked up my bag and gathered it in front of me like armour. It was all bravado though: I had no fight left in me. Isadora could do and say what she wanted; I deserved it.

Stefan opened the door and held an umbrella over my head as he walked me to the restaurant door, as though he expected me to try to make a run for it.

'I'll be here when you're ready to go home, Mrs Carlisle,' he said.

I met his eyes. 'Am I going home?' I said.

Stefan nodded, his eyes sympathetic. 'Yes. Mr Carlisle told me to make sure you're safe.'

A peculiar gratitude overwhelmed me.

I went inside and saw Isadora waiting at our table. I hesitated, almost turning around and then she saw me and waved. I made my way across the room as though walking to the gallows.

A waiter pulled out my chair for me and as I sat Isadora held out a drink to me.

'G and T. Strong. Thought you'd need it. Leave us to think for a while will you, Marcus?' she said to the waiter.

I placed my handbag on the floor and looked at her.

'Well. This guy did a number on you,' Isadora said, direct as ever. 'You've been very fortunate.'

111

'Fortunate?'

'My dear, he could have been a serial killer or something. How did you meet him?'

'Is this why I'm here?' I asked. 'An interrogation?'

'Charlotte you're here because I understand completely what you've been going through. You'll get over it. And you and Tom will be stronger in the end.'

My strength wasn't there, but neither was my patience. I had somehow lost the ability to be what Isadora expected.

'I'm sorry, but I'm having trouble processing this. You *understand*? And Tom and I will be *okay*? *Are you insane?*'

'No. I'm not insane and neither are you. You're broken right now and understandably. What's happened is *horrific*,' she paused, then, and glanced around the room. 'I have to tell you something. A truth that I thought I'd never need to tell you. I'm a Carlisle wife and it hasn't been easy for me. I went through a ... period, shall we say, of looking for other men's attention. I had *several* affairs, Charlotte, not just one. And Tom's father turned a blind eye. You know why? Because he loved the company more than he loved me. He didn't mind what happened after I gave him the child he wanted to be his heir.'

'Why are you telling me this?'

'I wanted you to know that life, *our life*, isn't always as straight forward as it seems. Being the wife of the CEO of Carlisle Corp is a job. It isn't an easy life though it has its financial benefits. And it can be incredibly lonely. You were an average girl when Tom met you, albeit a very intelligent one. I'm asking you to use that intelligence now and not to ruin what could still be a good thing for you. Tom still wants you and what he wants I want.'

'You and Tom say we can go back to normal, but I don't see how. I can't get over—'

The tears leaked from the corner of my eyes, and Isadora held out an embroidered pure-white handkerchief. It reminded me of the one Ewan gave me on our first visit to the coffee shop. I took the handkerchief and blotted my eyes.

'You've had your heart broken. I know,' she said, but her voice was cold. 'And I think the outcome of this little adventure is ... *worse* than anyone could have foreseen. We will *all* have to recover. But it was an adventure and now it's time to face reality: it's over, Charlotte, and your lover isn't coming back.'

I shook my head and dabbed my eyes again, staining the white cotton with black mascara.

'None of this is your fault,' Isadora said. She reached over the table and took my hand. It shocked me so much that I let her hold it, even though my instinct was to pull away.

'Of course it's my fault ...'

'We play this game of tug of war, but I want you to take up the mantle and be the support Tom needs. And everything I've ever said to you has been to help you, to guide you. Even though I think at times I may have seemed overbearing. Always my aim has been to *guide* you. Tom isn't like his father; he does love you. He tells me he can forgive you and I'm ... knowing my son, I know this can happen.'

I took in her words, not really understanding what she was saying. It was as though she were Dame Vera Lynn trying to rally the troops to go out and fight for King and Country.

Only the king was Tom and the country Carlisle Corp. But I knew this was the sincerest Isadora had ever been. And her revelations about her multiple affairs were not lost on me, even though it was difficult to imagine this prim and proper lady ever behaving that way. Would I ever become a serial adulteress? I doubted it. I couldn't imagine trusting any man again.

Isadora waved her hand and the waiter came over. I let her order for me as I sipped the gin and tonic.

'You can always talk to me,' she said when the waiter had gone. 'I know you haven't always trusted me. But Charlotte, I can help you and Tom get through this.'

I drank the gin and tonic down and another one appeared without me asking. Followed by a small calamari salad. These were favourite foods of mine, and Isadora was showing me she had been taking notice. By the end of the meal I had come to a new understanding with her, as if her hard shell had been peeled back and I was only now seeing a glimpse of her true self. I no longer felt that she was just Tom's annoying mother, but someone that perhaps I could confide in after all. How much of that I would do though, was still not certain.

When we finished she walked me to the door, where Stefan immediately jumped out of the car and came to greet me. Even though the rain had virtually stopped and the sun was trying to push aside the clouds overhead, Stefan still brought the umbrella.

'Everything will be all right,' Isadora said kissing me on the cheek. 'I promise to look out for you. I'm so sorry.'

'I should be the one apologizing.'

'It's not your fault,' she said again. 'You couldn't help it.'

Even though her words were strange I was a little less uptight as I got into the back of the car. Maybe the three gin and tonics had something to do with it.

Chapter Nineteen

I returned home and placed my new underwear neatly in my top drawer. It was 3 p.m. Out of habit I checked my phone for messages from Ewan. My heart sank. I put the phone down on top of the dresser and stared at it. Every day for months I had read and replied to several texts and spoken to him at least once a day on the phone. I had spent my life waiting to hear from him. Now there would be no more calls, texts and elicit meetings in Hammersmith. My phone had died as surely as his was disconnected.

Despite Tom's words and Isadora's promise of support, I couldn't imagine the future without Ewan. I wanted to cry but the thought of it exhausted me.

I began to make excuses for Ewan again. Maybe there had been an accident: perhaps he lay in a hospital seriously injured. I picked up my phone again and pressed redial on his number. I hung up when I heard the generic recorded message: *Please redial.*

I paced the room and thought about ways to find him. Even if it was to make him tell me the truth, to find out why he had ruined my life.

For the first time in a while I went into Tom's home office and started his laptop. I used it on occasion to look up information or to buy things online. But I hadn't wanted to go near it after Tom had shown me that awful Facebook group.

Now, I sat down and looked at the screen as it came to life. Then I went into the search engine and typed in Ewan's name.

The search threw up several men with similar names on Facebook. None of them were him.

I looked in images and all that came up were pictures of an actor called Ewan McGregor. I switched Ewan's name around and searched again and tried different spellings. Of course, it was obvious that he had lied about everything, including his name. I already knew this but still had to torture myself.

I had heard about software that could search pictures to find who they belonged to, but Ewan and I had never taken any together or of each other. It had always been too risky. That had played perfectly into his hands, I now saw. No pictures, a telephone number that was disconnected and an address that he had apparently never lived at – how he'd managed that one I didn't know. The girl who owned it had to be lying.

I considered getting a taxi back to Hammersmith to demand the girl tell me the truth. But what was the point? Ewan didn't want to be found, that was obvious, and no amount of me trying to track him down would make the slightest difference. If I did stumble on something that led me to him, what could I achieve other than bringing myself more pain?

I cleared the history on the laptop and shut it down. Then I went into the bedroom and lay on top of the bed, staring at the ceiling.

I must have dosed off because when I woke I found Tom in the room looking at me. As I opened my eyes I thought I saw a deep frown flicker across his face.

'What's for dinner?' he said.

I sat up, shocked that the room was in semi-darkness.

'I'm sorry, I fell asleep.'

'You must be pretty wrung out'. His voice was flat and the tone brought back all of my guilt in a rush.

'I'm sorry—'

'Get up.'

Tom turned away and left the room while I pulled myself off the bed.

A wave of dizziness hit me as I stood and I swayed, catching hold of the bedside cabinet for support. When it passed, I followed Tom out of the bedroom, down the corridor and into the kitchen.

He was pouring himself a glass of wine.

'There's salmon in the fridge,' I said. 'And salad.'

'Sounds good ...'

He left me to prepare the food and took his drink into the living room. I heard music coming from the stereo. Ambient, relaxing but fairly generic stuff. Sometimes he put this on to help him unwind after a difficult day.

I made the salad and laid the table, while the salmon was under the grill. Tom came in and sat down at the table. This was the first evening when we were trying to be normal again. It felt unnatural – like we were in a play and I had forgotten my lines.

We sat opposite each other. Tom had a bottle of wine beside his glass and he refilled it regularly but didn't offer me any.

'How did your lunch go?' he asked, as he pushed his empty plate aside.

'Fine. She was kind to me.'

'Mmm.'

'Tom, I—'

'Don't,' he said. 'I'm not ready to talk about it.'

'Okay.'

I stood and began to clear the table.

'Leave that.' He took another sip of his wine. 'Come to bed,' he said.

I stared at him for a long moment, not knowing what to say. Did he want sex or was he just tired?

'You go. I'll tidy up first,' I said.

'I said *leave* it.'

'Tom, I don't want—'

He took my hand roughly and pulled me out of the dining room and into the corridor. I stopped talking and didn't resist – his demeanour intimidated me.

Afterwards, Tom got back out of bed and went to his office. He left the bedroom door ajar and I could hear him opening and closing the file cabinet drawers.

When he came back and got in bed beside me, he said, 'Char?'

'Yes?'

'You're mine,' he said.

My heart lurched in my chest. I glanced over at Tom wondering what he meant. His possessive and assertive words, simple as they were, terrified me. I saw the future wide open again before me. I had always been Tom's possession, but after what I'd done, my future was sealed.

He turned in the bed to face me, leaning on his elbow, and stared at my face. The illumination from a street light bled around the curtains and gave just enough light for me to be able to see the stubborn set of his jaw. I couldn't see his eyes.

'Tell me,' he said.

'Tell you what?'

'Say that you're mine ...'

'Tom, please.'

He reached over and pulled the covers back exposing my naked skin to the cool air of the room.

'Say it.'

I started trembling when he leaned closer.

'You're mine,' he said. 'I'm never letting you go.'

Chapter Twenty

Life didn't return to normal, but became a new ordinary. My will had been broken, and in my misery, I did everything that was asked of me. I took up my role again as a Carlisle wife, though I can't say it was with much enthusiasm at first. I went to lunches with Isadora and other wives. I worked out regularly. I went to beauty appointments and I looked after myself. I did my duty as a wife in every way without complaint.

Tom was harsh and cold with me. But my self-esteem was so low I convinced myself that I deserved it.

Every evening he came home, ate and then took me to bed. It was torturously regular and sterile. I lay under him without protest, without pleasure. There wasn't even any disgust. Tom didn't hurt me. It was just his way of dealing with my betrayal but, every time it happened, I imagined myself getting up and packing my bags in protest. Even when my mind screamed at me to leave, my limbs wouldn't move, because an inner voice said, *where would you go?*

Oh, I knew that deep down I could sue for divorce and I wouldn't come away from it too badly, though Tom's lawyers would tie mine in knots for years. Tom would name me as adulteress, but was that any worse than this awful existence? Our marriage wasn't just broken, we were as smashed as Humpty Dumpty and all of the king's horses and all of the king's men couldn't put us back together again.

The future gaped like a bottomless pit and I hung on a threadbare wire, waiting for the line to snap. Sometimes I wished it would. But wasn't it the urge for freedom and change that had made me vulnerable in the first place? Whatever I had, I wanted something else. I was everything that Tom must think of me: selfish, hateful, disgusting. And I knew for sure that the proverbial grass was not greener.

How could anyone, even Ewan, ever love someone like me?

Then, one morning, when I thought the despair couldn't get any worse, I realized that I hadn't checked my phone at all for a few days. The pathetic habit had finally been broken. It shocked me to realize that I hadn't even thought about Ewan.

I was healing despite everything. Perhaps things would work out after all. And when my mood lifted, I was amazed at how much better I was. Depression had hung on me – unsurprising I suppose – but I hadn't recognized what it was because I had always been a naturally upbeat person.

Isadora came around to the apartment that day and I bustled about the kitchen prepping a beef Wellington as she drank a latte. The radio was on and I found myself humming to the tune that played.

'You look better, Charlotte dear,' said Isadora. 'How are things with Tom?'

'Fine,' I said.

'You don't need to pretend with me,' she said. 'He's been a total brute the last six weeks, hasn't he?'

'I was feeling a little happier until you said that,' I pointed out with a forced smile.

'Things will improve. It's a male ego thing. He has to assert that he owns you and you won't stray again.'

'I won't,' I said.

'Oh, I know that. But he isn't quite so secure. Yet.'

I didn't answer, but continued to wrap pastry around the beef.

'He was such an ... *intense* child. I was concerned about him sometimes, because he was so serious. It was always difficult to get him to ...' She paused, and I stopped working on dinner. 'There were a few girlfriends before you.'

I was surprised that she'd mention any old flames of Tom's – he'd always said there was no one significant.

'Oh, don't look shocked!' Isadora said. 'Of course, he had girlfriends. He's a very attractive man and the daughters of our peers all hoped to capture him. But he was never really interested. They were all ... weak. Spoilt girls. Tom needed someone better than that, so he was cold to them. Though I'm sure he had a few ... trysts with one or two. Probably that's the side of himself he's showing you now. But he doesn't mean it, not with you. He's always loved you, right from the first time he saw you.'

'You seem very sure of that.'

'I am. He called me the first day you met. In the library, wasn't it? He saw you, head down, pouring over the course study guide. He watched you go around the library, systematically searching out every book you needed.'

The hairs stood up on the back of my neck as she spoke. Tom had never told me he'd seen me in the university library. I remembered the day well, because I'd arrived on campus early and was making sure I got one of the few copies of each book available, because I couldn't afford to buy them with my pathetic student loan and bursary.

'What did he say about me?' I asked.

'Just that he'd met the most beautiful girl and she was smart too.'

I didn't correct her, even though the truth was we didn't meet until a few weeks later at a party. I hadn't wanted to go, but my roommate persuaded me.

'You're at uni, mate,' she'd said. 'You're supposed to have fun sometimes.'

'You brought him out of himself, made him appreciate things. You two laughed all the time. Do you remember that?' Isadora said.

I nodded. Yes, he had been a little intense at that party. And I'd said something glib about black sheep that made him laugh. The memory made me smile again. I told Isadora about it and she gave a small chuckle.

'Do you still laugh?' she said.

'No.'

'But you can find it again. It's about ... deciding to be happy. Accepting things again. Before all of this happened, you were happy, weren't you?'

Before Ewan, Tom made me happy. That's true, I thought. But not always.

'Perhaps you should both get some counselling.'

'I doubt Tom would want to air our dirty laundry.'

'Well, you know best, dear.'

Isadora stayed for dinner and I was glad of her presence when Tom arrived home. He had that mean look in his eyes again. When he saw Isadora the tension fell away. Maybe because he never wanted her to see this cruel, dark side of him. I sighed without realizing it and both of them looked at me.

'Welcome home,' I said to Tom and then I instigated a kiss and wrapped my arms around him.

He was surprised but returned the hug and the kiss. His shoulders relaxed. We pulled apart after an awkward moment and then Isadora and Tom went into the living room and sat and talked while I finished dinner.

I could hear his calm tones and I wished that she could be with us every evening.

Don't get me wrong, Tom never physically hurt me. He was cold with me, but I knew it was all anger and insecurity. It was an impossible thing to fix in too short a time. I was afraid of Tom because I feared his words of hatred which would hurt me more. Even so, he never said them. He never threw my crime up in my face. Perhaps it would have been better if he *had* called me the names.

There was a noticeable change that evening though. Tom relaxed around Isadora and therefore I saw the old Tom reappear. As I watched him, smiling and chatting after dinner with a brandy in his hand, I began to understand what Isadora had been trying to tell me. Once we had been good for each other. Was it inconceivable that we couldn't right our world again?

It was what Tom said he wanted after all.

'Thank you for a lovely evening,' Isadora said, rising to leave.

'It's been wonderful to see you, Mother,' said Tom.

He probably dreaded coming home to be alone with me too and Isadora's presence had given him respite, just as it had me.

I walked her to the door. A car had been arranged to take her home to her London apartment; Surrey was too far away this late at night.

'He was better tonight with you here,' I whispered into her ear as she hugged me.

'You're getting in your own way, dear,' she murmured back. 'Meet him halfway.'

I said good night and closed the door.

Alone with Tom I feared the flood of anger. I paused for a second by the door, then made my way back to the living room to face whatever was coming.

Tom was sitting on the sofa when I entered the living room.

'What a lovely evening,' he said.

He smiled at me with genuine warmth. I smiled back relieved by his mood and expression. He was still calm and relaxed.

'Yes it was. Your mother and I are finally becoming friends.'

'You have a lot in common,' he said.

I flushed then, wondering if he knew of his mother's unfaithful streak.

'Come,' he said patting the sofa beside him.

I sat down. Tom put his arm around me and pulled me into his chest. I snuggled in, forcing myself to relax and 'not get in my own way' as Isadora had suggested. For years I'd fought against her and now she was the voice of reason.

'I love you,' Tom said. 'I'm sorry. I haven't been able to show you that lately.'

I couldn't say the words back because I'd promised myself I'd never lie to him again, but I lifted my face and met his lips. I didn't want to live in fear and uncertainty anymore and I knew that the only way to stop this was to re-embrace my marriage. Perhaps I was weak and capitulation was the only course I could take, but for that moment I didn't care. I wanted – needed – to stop hurting. Just for a little while.

Tom kissed me and it was soft and patient and not the demanding pressure that had been the focus of our sex life for the last few weeks. I pulled away first and then I stood and held out my hand, inviting him to come to bed with me. His eyes widened, surprised that I was instigating contact.

We walked together hand in hand and went into the bedroom.

There was a moment of awkwardness as we stood at the bottom of the bed, but then I began to undo the buttons on Tom's shirt and I kissed a line down his chest that I hoped would go some distance to heal the hurt I'd inflicted on him. When I unzipped his trousers he was ready for me.

We made love for the first time in a long time. I gave myself back to him. It was an unspoken promise that I'd make things right. All the time I told myself, *choose to be happy*.

The doubts and fears reared a few times but I pushed them back, forced Ewan from my mind, and resolved that I would never think about him again. I was determined to improve things. I knew that if I didn't I would continue to die inside.

Chapter Twenty-One

Tom took a few days off work and we went away on an impromptu trip. It wasn't anywhere romantic like Paris or Milan; instead, we visited Isadora's country estate. She wasn't in residence in the winter much and so Tom had warned the housekeeper we were coming.

I hadn't been to the estate recently. Isadora spent a lot of time in London and it was there that we mostly saw her.

'I'd like to be alone with you,' Tom had said when he suggested the trip.

I had laughed because even when Isadora wasn't home, there was always staff present. This included a groundskeeper that everyone referred to as 'Old Freddie', a housekeeper called Mrs Tanner – who I'd always found very aloof – and a couple of girls who came in twice a week to clean.

As we drew nearer Tom turned to me with a smile. 'I don't know why Mother doesn't stay here more often,' he said.

We were in the Range Rover, a car Tom liked to use whenever we went to the estate or on visits to friends who lived outside London. He stroked my knee as he drove and when we stopped at some lights he had turned and kissed me. It was good and I was enjoying his company.

'I suppose she finds it lonely without your father,' I said.

But I thought I knew why Isadora didn't like being there. There was always an atmosphere. I'd been aware of it even on our wedding day. A kind of darkness that surrounded the house, like a distant memory of past times when something bad occurred there. It was a stupid thought, but it overshadowed the day until I made a mental note to 'stop being silly' and turned my attention back to Tom.

Our conversations were beginning to feel natural again. A night of reciprocated affection had done wonders for Tom's mood. His way of dealing with our problems was to push himself on me; mine was to try to avoid him. Now that I was making an effort, I was happier, and the anxious feeling that had constantly been in the pit of my stomach had receded. Tom's anger was gone too. He was smiling easily and appeared to be more peaceful.

We arrived after lunch because we'd taken our time getting to the house and had stopped to eat at a small village pub on the way. Mrs Tanner was waiting for us when we arrived, and our bags were ferried upstairs to Tom's room.

'So nice to see you both again,' said Mrs Tanner but her voice was cool and distant. Part of me wondered if she was really cross that we had turned up and made work for her.

I always thought about the book *Rebecca*, by Daphne du Maurier, when I visited the Manor, and the housekeeper Mrs Danvers. Isadora's house could be a smaller version of Manderley with its wings and grounds, and there was even a huge painting of Isadora on the landing at the top of the stairs that amused me. Isadora was still a handsome woman, but she had been very beautiful when she was younger.

The house itself was somewhat Gothic and for that reason I'd often found it a little creepy. I had never been used to large houses, not having come from the background Tom had. Tom loved the house though, and he was very relaxed whenever we'd visited in the past. In fact, it was difficult to imagine how he coped with living in our city centre apartment – albeit bigger and more luxurious than most, it was still small compared to the Manor.

As we entered the main entrance, I noticed that Isadora had redecorated since my last visit, which was probably more than two years ago.

'It looks nice in here,' I said admiring the eggshell blue on the walls.

'Bit traditional though?' said Tom.

'You have to be in keeping with a property like this though,' I said.

The huge hallway, with its central staircase that opened up in the centre and went in two opposite directions used to be painted in a dark, angry red that Isadora thought was 'grand'. The colour had always had a strange effect on me, making me feel stressed whenever I entered the house.

As we always did when we arrived, we walked upstairs together and along the landing, looking at the portraits of all of the company's previous CEOs. There wasn't one of Tom there yet; I guess that would come when he was older and greyer. I always thought this sort of thing was a little creepy but it didn't bother me that day at all. I was enjoying revisiting the place now, as there had been only happy times there in the past. I saw the Manor with new eyes now. This place held the history of an old and important family. Being part of it was something I had taken for granted before, but not now.

Perhaps I was finally growing up.

Tom's room was a master bedroom by anyone else's standards. There was a super king four-poster bed, with crisp white cotton bedding – the sort we had in our apartment. A walk-in wardrobe was behind two double doors on the right (the size of a regular bedroom) and on the left there was a huge en suite bathroom with a whirlpool bath, a double sink and large shower unit.

I ran the water into the bath while Tom went off to talk to Mrs Tanner. Then I unpacked our case into the wardrobe, which was otherwise totally bare except for some boxes on the top shelf. When Tom returned, he closed and locked our bedroom door.

'Come here, Mrs Carlisle,' he said.

I went to him and we kissed and Tom began to strip me.

'I forgot about the bath!' I said pulling away.

The water was almost overflowing by the time I turned the taps off. Tom came into the bathroom wearing only his robe while I let some of the water out. I turned and watched him drop the robe over a chair and then I looked at his perfect body and almost cried.

I finished undressing, my hands trembling.

'Darling?' Tom said.

I kept my head down but Tom refused to let me hide.

He lifted my chin and looked into my eyes.

'Are you okay?'

'I've been such a fool!' I said. Then I buried my head in his bare chest, forcing back the tears. I was determined I would never cry again over this.

'It's all right, Charlotte,' he said. 'I promised to always take care of you and I will.'

He held me for a while.

'Let's get in before the water cools,' he said.

We soaked in the bath, enjoying the bubbles as they pummelled our muscles, taking away the aches of the journey and some of the pain in my heart. We sat opposite each other, not touching, but Tom chattered to me about things that had happened in this house when he was a child. I'd heard the stories before about his nanny and the practical jokes he'd played on her and the previous housekeeper (long since retired) but I listened anyway. It was nice to see him animated again and I giggled at his stories as though it were the first time I'd heard them.

When the water cooled, Tom pulled me out of the bath and led me to his bed, where we continued to rebuild the bridges of our relationship.

We spent a few days wandering the grounds and eating in our room. I barely saw Mrs Tanner or the other servants and they kept discreetly out of our way. In those few days I became more and more familiar with the place. I didn't remember living so comfortably here before. Perhaps it was because it was Isadora's domain and I had always been a visitor. But as the days passed, it began to feel like home from home.

'Do you like it here?' Tom asked me.

It was a cold but sunny day and we had passed into the back garden via the kitchen.

'I love it. It's a beautiful house and it's so peaceful.'

'Of course, this place is technically ours,' he said.

'What do you mean?'

'It's mine. The will gives Mother the right to remain until death but the house is mine.'

'I'd forgotten about that,' I said. 'But this will always be your mother's house to me.'

'You'll feel differently once you're the lady of the house.'

'That won't be for many years, darling. Let's not think of it.'

'I would like us to live here one day, though,' Tom said. 'Raise that family. Would you mind that, even if Mother was still here?'

I looped my arm in his. Since we'd been here I had felt more relaxed and things had been better with Tom. There were worse places I could think of living. 'It's perfect for children.'

We walked towards the small area of forest that covered about an acre of the land. Nearer to the house was a newly dug patch of earth, a long narrow bed that ran along the edge of the woodland for about fifty yards.

'Mother has the gardener plant fresh bulbs for spring every year. Give it a month and this will be full of wild flowers,' Tom said.

'That's lovely,' I said.

Then I saw Old Freddie. He was over in the woods, carrying a cracked-open shotgun over his shoulder.

'Why's he holding it that way?' I asked.

'Safety. You're not supposed to walk around with the gun closed unless you're hunting.'

Tom took out his phone and took pictures of me leaning against one of the trees.

'New memories!' he said.

'I love it here.'

'Smile.'

I did and it wasn't forced.

'Freddie!' called Tom. 'Come over here and help us, will you?'

Old Freddie came out of the trees. I had never seen much of him on my visits; he always avoided us and he looked unhappy at being called over now.

'Mr Tom,' he nodded his head. 'What can I help you with?'

'Take a picture for me. Of Charlotte and I. Stand there, darling, and I'll join you ...'

Tom pointed to a patch of earth.

'On here?' I said.

'No, so it's in the background.'

I did as he said and Tom started to explain to Old Freddie how to use the camera on his phone.

'I'm sorry, Mr Tom, I don't hold with those contraptions,' Old Freddie said.

'I'll show you.'

'No!' said Old Freddie firmly. He stepped back, his eyes wide. 'I can't help you.' Then he turned and stomped away back into the woods.

'That was odd,' I said.

Tom laughed but it sounded forced. 'Don't worry about him. You know what the older generation can be like about technology.' He shrugged. 'I'll do a selfie instead.'

Tom took the picture.

'I want to capture some of the woods in the background ...' he said.

I looked back at the house and saw one of the girls hanging out sheets on the line.

'I think those are ours ...' I giggled. 'They've been well used the last few days.'

Tom laughed and pulled me to him.

'I love you,' he said.

It was just like our early days together, and the old Tom, before he became the CEO of Carlisle Corp, returned. There were no business calls and meetings. There was just us and the outside world didn't matter for a while.

It was, I suppose, a genuine second honeymoon.

On the last evening, I went down to the kitchen to get us a bottle of champagne. We'd indulged ourselves a lot, during the visit, something we'd have to tone down when we got home.

'What was he doing?' said a voice in the kitchen.

'Taking pictures,' Old Freddie sneered. 'One of those new phone things.'

I paused at the doorway. Why did Freddie speak about Tom in that way?

'She lets him do as he pleases,' Mrs Tanner's voice carried out to the hallway and I knew then it was her that had spoken earlier.

'The Missus always indulged him,' Old Freddie agreed. 'He's just spoilt.'

'Shhh!' said Mrs Tanner dropping her voice. 'I think someone's out there.'

I coughed then, making my presence known before I entered the kitchen.

'Good evening,' I said acknowledging them both. They were sitting at the kitchen table eating the same supper that Mrs Tanner had given us earlier.

Mrs Tanner nodded at me; her expression blank. I got the champagne and two fresh glasses, then left the kitchen, wishing them goodnight.

I made a lot of noise going back to the staircase, and then, when I thought they'd think me long gone, I made my way back to eavesdrop.

'I've worked here a long time, Freddie, too long,' Mrs Tanner said.

'We both have.'

'Sometimes I wonder why I've stayed ...'

And then Mrs Tanner's voice dropped again. I hurried away, not wanting to be caught listening to their conversation.

I was confused by what I'd heard. Mrs Tanner appeared to be less than happy working for Isadora these days and didn't care much for Tom either. Maybe in his youth he'd been difficult. It would explain Old Freddie's comment about Tom being spoilt. On some level I knew he was, but he was never rude to the staff at the Manor that I'd observed, and I'd always thought Mrs Tanner was loyal to Isadora.

I decided not to mention Mrs Tanner's dislike of Tom and

his mother as I climbed the stairs. Isadora was a very difficult woman though, and I understood why her employees might resent her. I tried to imagine what it was like working at the Manor with Isadora's overzealous attitude to cleanliness and her constant need for perfection. I really didn't blame either of them for feeling resentful. Hadn't I always disliked her too?

The next morning, I woke to hear the wind whistling around the balcony on our room. I rolled over and found Tom was absent. Sometimes he got up early and went jogging in the woods. I lay in the bed thinking about how frightening it would be staying in this big house alone. There were unfamiliar noises, creaking that sounded like footsteps on the stairs. The groaning of the heating system as it cooled down. There was the steady tick of an old grandfather clock that stood in one of the corridors, the sound echoing through the house.

I went to the balcony window and looked out on the grounds. Our room was in the wing above the kitchens and the gardens we'd explored a few days ago by the woodland. There was a figure walking the grounds and I recognized Old Freddie then, walking with the shotgun held before him as though hunting something late at night. A few seconds later he fired. I jumped even though I'd been expecting him to fire from the moment he raised the sight to his eye. I had an irrational fear as I recalled Tom's preference for running in the woods. What if Old Freddie had just shot him?

Freddie plunged into the woodland out of sight but emerged a few minutes later with a large rabbit hanging in his free hand. The shotgun was once again cracked open and over his shoulder.

Culling rabbits was such a normal thing for a groundkeeper to do, but the coldness with which Old Freddie wielded the shotgun brought a slight shiver to my spine.

Chapter Twenty-Two

'I wanted to see you first,' I said to Isadora at our weekly lunch date a month later.

'Is everything okay?' she asked.

'You were right. Things are better. And ...'

'What is it Charlotte?'

'I'm pregnant.'

'Oh my god. Tom must be thrilled!'

'I haven't told him yet,' I said.

Isadora sat back in her seat and studied me. 'Why not?'

'I'm a little nervous. After the last time, I thought I had better wait and make sure first.'

'Sensible,' said Isadora. 'But he'll want to know. He's wanted this for a long time.'

I frowned. 'I do. It's a little scary the idea of being a mother.'

'Pity me then. I'll be a grandmother!'

I laughed.

'Thank you.'

'What for?'

'You helped us. What you told me.'

'I've always wanted to help you,' she said. 'I'd do anything for Tom.'

Taking Isadora's advice again, I told Tom the news as soon as he came home.

'I think it happened in Surrey,' I said.

'You've made me so happy, Charlotte!' he said.

As Isadora predicted, Tom wanted to be involved with everything, even my first visit to the doctor. Isadora let me make my own decisions about where I would have the baby but she offered advice when asked. We were growing into a proper family that respected each other's views.

Once or twice my anxiety returned, but I shook away the feeling. There was nothing to be afraid of; our life was back on track.

Once I learnt I was pregnant I accepted everything that came with it and because of my previous miscarriage I took the medical advice seriously. This was the final step to helping us recover from the awful thing Ewan had done.

Tom's usually vigorous lovemaking became gentle and he was always concerned that he didn't put too much weight on me or hurt me.

We had the spare room turned into a nursery with a neutral colour scheme, because every time we had a scan, they could never determine the baby's sex. 'It's always got its legs crossed,' I explained to Isadora, 'so I suppose we are just going to have to be surprised.'

The final piece of furniture was in place: a padded and comfortable rocking chair, a present from Isadora.

'You'll need a good nursing chair,' she said after it was delivered.

Tom made sure he spent more time at home too, managing all but the occasional interruption during our evenings. We fell into new habits of domesticity: cooking together sometimes. I think this was the most natural we'd ever been. Tom also wanted to share the experience of shopping for the baby too. I didn't make a decision without him, or he one without me. My love for him returned. Whether that was because it had never really gone, or because of the excitement of being parents, I wasn't sure.

Chapter Twenty-Three

Even though I was pregnant I took on the running of the next Carlisle Charity Fundraiser. Isadora helped and supported, and I shared all my plans with her before the charity committee heard them, because I knew she would steer me in the right direction.

'How many people will be there?' asked the catering manager at the taster. Isadora had already left for a hair appointment, but it was an answer she would have known immediately.

'Oh,' I said. 'I'm not sure.'

I didn't want to bother Isadora. She had been encouraging me to be independent and take the lead. Then it occurred to me that Tom's PA, Gillian, had all the information on her database at the office. The invitations hadn't gone out and the fundraiser was four months away.

'I'll email you tomorrow with the predicted number,' I told the catering manager.

The caterers were not far from Carlisle Corp's offices. It was 4.30 p.m. when I finished the tasting and it made more sense to head to Tom's office than to go home. I could see his secretary and arrange for her to send the invitations urgently, and then travel home with Tom in the limo. Being almost seven months pregnant a comfortable ride home really appealed to me.

Outside I caught a black cab and gave the driver the address. The folder full of information about the fundraiser was heavy and I was tired as I leaned back in the seat and closed my eyes, letting the movement of the taxi lull me.

It was 5.05 p.m. when I reached the office. Tom left at 5.30, so I had plenty of time. I paid the taxi driver and entered the building.

'Well hello, Mrs Carlisle,' said George, the doorman, as he opened the door. I hadn't been to the office much recently and it was nice to see a friendly face. 'I'll radio up and let Mr C know you're here.'

'That's okay. I'll surprise him,' I said.

George nodded and was instantly distracted as another person came through the door. I went to the lift and pressed the call button. As the doors opened a rough-looking man passed me and headed towards the exit. I entered the lift and pressed the button to take me up to the top floor. Before the doors closed, I noted the man's shoes. They were mud-splattered brogues. I had a feeling of *déjà vu*, but the doors closed before I could get a better look at the man. My heart thudded in my chest and I felt sick. Where had I seen brogues just like that? I had a flash of memory that I just couldn't place.

'Can I help you?' said the receptionist outside of Gillian and Tom's office. 'Oh it's you, Mrs Carlisle. You're looking well!'

I smiled and thanked the girl. I didn't remember her name; it was Alice or Anna, something like that.

'I'm just going to see my husband's PA first, but can you let him know I'm here?'

'Of course!'

I turned left and walked straight into Gillian's office. A girl I didn't recognize was putting paperwork away in a filing cabinet.

'I'm here to see Gillian,' I said. 'Is she around?'

'Gillian? I'm sorry no one by that name works here. Can I help you? I'm Mr Carlisle's PA.'

Tom came into the office behind me.

'Charlotte? What are you doing here?'

I glanced over my shoulder at him and then back at the new PA. 'I thought I'd surprise you. Plus Gillian had the invitation list stored on her database ...'

Tom looked confused, 'Gillian? Oh, she left months ago.'

'What?'

'Come,' Tom said.

I followed him into his office, and he offered me a seat. I placed my handbag and the folder on his desk, then glanced around. I hadn't been here that often and it always surprised me how sparse, yet ostentatious this room was. As well as Tom's desk, which was about six feet wide, there was an area with two sofas facing each other and a low coffee table between them. To the left of the room was a row of tidy filing cabinets and to the right another door which led into Tom's private bathroom.

'You didn't mention Gillian had left,' I said.

'We've both had more important things to talk about. Darling you look tired.'

'I am. I thought I'd travel home with you tonight.'

'Wonderful idea! Why don't we stop somewhere on the way home to eat? So that you don't have to cook.'

I said it was a good idea, but my eyes kept straying to his assistant's office.

'She came into some money,' Tom said.

I looked back at him.

'Gillian. So, she took early retirement. I didn't mention it because you and I weren't on such good terms at the time.'

'She worked here for years.'

'Even before my time!' Tom laughed. 'Probably overdue to retire.'

'Can your new one help?'

'Tara's her name,' Tom said.

And even this was odd. In the months since Gillian left, he had never mentioned Tara. I would have remembered that name.

'Of course, the data will still be there. You'll probably have to tell her what file to look in though.'

Tom opened his door and told Tara to find the information for me. I went out into the office and sat down before her desk while she looked.

'I'm so sorry.' Tara looked embarrassed. 'I should have recognized you. Mr Carlisle has your picture on his desk.'

'I'm somewhat plumper than usual at the moment,' I said.

'When are you due?' she asked.

'Two months.'

Tara returned her concentration to the computer.

'I'm sorry, I just can't find it.'

'May I look? I don't know what she had it under, but I might recognize it.'

Tara stood up and we swapped places while I waded through the files on Gillian's old PC. There was nothing obvious. Then I found an extra server entitled 'Other' and browsed it.

'Can I get you a drink, Mrs Carlisle?' Tara asked.

'Some water would be nice.'

Tara went away to get me a glass of chilled water and that was when I saw the charity folder, right next to one that said, 'E Daniels'.

I had sorted through the folders looking for the charity's name. It was a small children's cancer charity, run by a man called David Danner. When I searched 'Dan' the folder came up and so did this one.

My hand froze on the mouse and then, as I was about to double-click the Daniels folder, Tom came into Tara's office. Blood rushed to my cheeks as Tom approached Tara's desk.

I clicked on the fundraiser folder and opened the spread-sheet file inside, filling Tara's screen.

Tom was beside me, placing something in the input tray.

'You've found it,' he said. 'Where's Tara?'

Tara came through the door with my water and I gave her the seat back and took the glass.

'Are you okay for a few minutes, darling, while I explain to Tara about the list?' I said.

Tom nodded and went back into his office.

'Do you have a spare pen drive?' I asked Tara.

She rooted around in the table drawer of her desk. 'There are some unused ones in here.'

Then she shook her head.

'Sorry, someone else might have taken them. Can I email it you?'

'Yes. And the one called E Daniels.'

I gave her my email address.

'*Charlotte?*' Tom said from the doorway.

I turned and looked at my husband, his face was serious and I knew he had heard my request.

'Can I speak to you?' Tom said to me. 'Tara – just send the other file. The E Daniels one is nothing to do with the fundraiser.'

'Yes Mr Carlisle,' Tara said.

Tom took a step back, holding his door open as an invitation for me to come in. I walked inside feeling like a naughty teenager who had been called into the head teacher's office.

Tom closed the door firmly behind us, blocking Tara out.

'Sit down, darling,' he said.

'What the hell's going on?' I asked. 'Why do you have a folder called "E Daniels"?'

'Please don't get upset. I was going to tell you.'

'Tell me what?' I said.

I was shaking. Seeing Ewan's name had been a huge shock but my first response to it had been to feel guilty. My face was still warm as I sank back into the chair I'd occupied a few minutes earlier.

'I had a private detective look into Daniels after what he did. I wanted to find out who he was. I didn't tell you because things came right between us and I didn't want to open old wounds.'

'How did you know his name?'

He sighed and looked at his desk. 'I had to know who he was.' He ran a hand through his hair. 'I was jealous. So I looked on your phone while you slept.'

I absorbed that information for a moment and couldn't find fault with him for doing it. Of course he would have looked at my phone. Anyone would want to know who the man was his wife had had an affair with.

'What did you find out about him?' I asked. I took a breath and forced myself to calm down, to look like I was only mildly curious.

'Not much. Except what you already know: that he was a liar using a fake name.'

'What is his real name?'

Tom sighed. 'I don't know. The paper trail just revealed "Ewan Daniels" using credit cards, registering in restaurants and so on during the time you were together and then ... nothing. He didn't exist. But he obviously had money. No one can invent a whole fake identity like that without it.'

'Of course he had money. He paid for everything when I was with him ... it wasn't what he wanted from me.'

Tom blinked. I saw the hurt in his eyes and then I changed the subject.

'Why? Why did you check into him?'

'I hoped we would be able to work things out. But at first I thought I may need to prove what an evil dick he was to you.'

'No,' I said. 'I knew that already. You would have been rubbing it in.'

Tom kneeled by the chair and he took my cold hands in

148

his. I was still trembling. I couldn't believe how upset I was just by seeing Ewan's name on a folder on Tom's secretary's computer.

'I want to see what's in that folder,' I said.

'That's not a good idea. Charlotte, this man hurt you. I love you and I would never have rubbed it in. I wanted you back. I wanted to protect you from him in the future too.'

'What do you mean?'

'I was worried. Scared he'd come back into our lives and ruin everything again.'

I didn't say anything. I felt sick and tired and cold. The only thing I knew was that Tom had never lied to me. He had been constant, even though I'd hurt him. I pulled him to me and held him against my pregnancy-swollen breasts and the bulge of my stomach.

'I love you,' I said. 'And I'm so sorry for everything.'

'Darling that's the first time you've said you love me since ...'

'I know. I couldn't, it felt ... I don't know. I didn't think you'd believe me.'

My stomach jerked as the baby kicked hard.

'Ouch!' I said. 'We may have a footballer in there!'

Tom laughed and kissed my stomach and then my lips.

'Let me take you home,' he said.

Chapter Twenty-Four

Tom took me to our favourite Italian restaurant on the way. 'We'll get a taxi back from here,' he told Stefan. 'Have the evening off and I'll see you in the morning.'

The restaurant was full, but a table was found for us immediately as the maître d', Francis, knew us well.

'My favourite couple!' Francis said.

I didn't know how he managed it, but we always got the same table, in the quietest part of the restaurant.

'He has whoever is sitting there removed when we arrive,' joked Tom.

'Removed?'

'Yes. Dragged off out the back through the kitchen.'

I laughed, but part of me wondered if it was true. The way Francis and the waiters fussed over us, made me wonder if Tom had some kind of stake in the restaurant.

'Thank you, Francis,' I said as he brought our drinks. Tom had red wine and I had water. 'I'll have a small glass of the wine too.'

When Francis left, Tom said, 'Are you sure you ought to drink, darling?'

'The doctor said one glass wouldn't hurt.'

'Okay. If you're sure.'

I felt guilty when the wine came; I took one sip, and then I gave it to Tom.

'I'll stick with water after all,' I said.

'Good girl,' Tom said.

I looked out around the restaurant, wondering if anyone we knew was there, and then I saw the man who had been at Carlisle Corp, standing outside the front window.

'Who's that?' I asked Tom.

He glanced towards where I indicated. 'Who?'

'That man. I saw him at your offices.'

'I have no idea.'

'He came out of the lift as I went in. I thought I'd seen him before but couldn't place him.'

Tom shrugged. 'Maybe he was delivering something.'

I stared at the man.

'I'm having veal,' Tom said.

I returned my attention to the menu.

'Just excuse me a minute,' Tom said. 'I just remembered I need to make a call. I promise I won't be long.'

Tom left the table and went to the front of the restaurant. The man I'd seen was gone now. Outside, Tom put his phone to his ear but whoever he was talking to didn't have his full attention: he looked up and down the street as though he were searching for someone. After a few minutes he came back inside.

I returned my attention to the menu.

'Everything okay?' I said.

'Yes,' said Tom.

I gave him a sideways glance.

I began to wonder then what secrets my husband had. I had always believed he never lied to me. But he had just then and in an obvious way.

I stroked my hand over my belly and then I found Tom looking at me. He was smiling. He appeared happy and relaxed.

'You look so beautiful, darling,' he said.

'I'm a blob right now.'

'No you aren't.'

I fought back the curiosity about the man and then told myself a story that would make me stop worrying about it. My observation of the man had brought him to Tom's attention. Maybe he just wanted to check him out further. In his position you couldn't always trust strangers. The man might have been spying on Tom after all.

When we arrived home a couple of hours later Tom went to his office. From our bedroom I heard him opening and closing the file cabinets and then the shredder was switched on.

I was curious about what he was doing and so I pulled on my robe and walked down the corridor to the office. Tom came out and closed the door behind him.

'Would you like some hot chocolate?' he said.

'That would be lovely.'

'I'll get it for you,' he said.

Dismissed, I went back into our room but I was intrigued as to what he had been doing.

A few minutes later Tom came in with two mugs of chocolate.

'Mother left a voice message,' Tom said. 'She cancelled your lunch date for tomorrow. Something came up apparently.'

'She has a busy social life,' I said. 'Was that the shredder I heard?'

'Yes. Work stuff. No longer needed.'

Chapter Twenty-Five

O ur baby was born six weeks later. It was a difficult birth, lasting eighteen hours, and when the midwife held our child out to Tom to cut the cord he said, 'Oh God. All that and it's a girl.'

I was a little out of it by then on pethidine and gas and air. I'd torn and so the midwife gave me the mask again as they sewed me up. Tom held our blanket-wrapped baby and walked around the theatre cooing to her.

I blacked out for a while and then woke to find Isadora by my side. I was in a private hospital that we'd chosen together. The perfect place to have our first baby and one often used by the royal family for the same purpose. I was back in my private room which had a huge bed and a beautiful ensuite bathroom that also had a bath as well as a shower.

'Where's the baby?' I said. Panicking I sat up too quickly and gasped with the pain.

'She's fine. She's in an incubator. They weren't sure she'd need it but it's a precaution because she's two weeks early.'

I slid back down against the pillows.

'Let me help you a little,' Isadora said.

She pressed the controls on the electric bed and the bed moved and lifted me into a more comfortable sitting position.

'Want some water?' she asked.

She helped me take a sip.

'When can I see her?' I asked.

'She's being examined by the doctor and then they'll wheel her in here. Although I thought you should have a rest. Someone else can feed and change her for a day or two at night time while you recover.'

'I can manage,' I said.

Isadora smiled.

Tom came in with a nurse wheeling the small cot.

'She's fine,' he said and then he kissed me. 'Well done, darling! You were so brave. I'm so proud of you!'

Tom looked tired but happy. He'd stayed with me all through the labour.

The nurse brought the cot closer, and Tom lifted our little girl up and held her out to me. She was beautiful and tears sprang to my eyes as I took her in my arms. I couldn't believe how small her fingers were. She looked so fragile and her little face was all red and scrunched into a frown as though this new place didn't please her at all.

'Melody Isadora Carlisle,' Tom said. 'Meet your mummy.'

'Oh!' said Isadora. 'She's blonde. She takes after you, Charlotte dear!'

I looked down at Melody and saw the soft short white blonde hair. She had already been washed and she smelt beautiful.

'How long was I out?' I said.

155

'Twelve hours dear. The doctor gave you a sedative. We thought it best.'

Isadora took Melody from me.

'You're worn out you poor thing,' she said. 'Get some more sleep. We'll all be here when you wake.'

'But doesn't she need feeding?' I said.

'Don't worry that's all taken care of,' Tom said.

'But ... I wanted to breast-feed her!'

'Darling, sometimes these things don't work out. Rest now, and don't worry about a thing.'

We went home a few days later. We had to stay longer than usual to make sure that Melody continued to thrive. My daughter was strong and it was all precautionary, but because she was so tiny the doctors had thought it best that I didn't breast-feed her. This, they said, was to make it easier for them to measure her nutritional intake. They gave me medication to wash my own milk away and talked at length about bottle feeding and sterilising. All of which I knew about but hadn't planned on needing.

'I can't wait to get out of here,' I said.

'I know it wasn't what you planned,' Isadora said, 'so I've bought the bottles and steriliser and milk in for you. The plus side of this is that Tom can feed Melody as well. You'll both bond with her the same way.'

'But isn't a mother's milk better for the baby?' I said.

'Don't worry. She'll have the best start there is.'

Back home I found everything I needed ready and waiting, and Tom took charge of Melody. He lifted her out of the carry seat and placed her in a Moses basket that had been positioned in the living room beside one of the chairs.

'Sit down, darling,' Tom said and he rushed about making bottles of milk formula and then placing them in the fridge ready for use.

'My goodness! I didn't think you'd be so hands-on,' I said.

'I have something for you.' He held out a box with a bow on top.

I untied the bow and opened the box. Inside was a silver photo frame with a 10 x 8 sized photograph of us. It was the selfie taken at the Manor. The small wood was behind us. It was a lovely natural picture and we both glowed with obvious happiness.

'The weekend she was conceived,' Tom laughed.

I giggled. 'What a lovely gift, thank you darling!'

'I have the same one on my desk now,' Tom said. 'It's my favourite picture of us.'

I placed the photograph on the coffee table where I could see it. I loved it.

The doorbell rang. Tom returned with Isadora carrying a bunch of flowers. After I received and admired them, Tom took the flowers and went away in search of a vase.

'He's being amazing,' I said. 'Taking such good care of me. He's going to be an amazing father.'

Isadora kissed my cheek and then looked at Melody who was sleeping in the Moses basket.

'I'll go and see if Tom needs any help,' she said.

I sat back in the chair. I was tired but so happy and everything was so wonderfully normal. I admired my beautiful child with her fair hair and long dark eyelashes.

'Here's a drink for—'

I looked up as Isadora gasped. The cup fell from Isadora's hand and tumbled to the floor.

'Oh my god!' she said, her face pale.

'What happened?' I said. 'Are you okay?'

'Your carpet. I've ruined your carpet,' she said, quickly bending to pick up the mug.

'Don't worry,' Tom said coming in with a tea towel. He blotted the coffee stain from the cream wool. 'We can get a cleaning company in if I can't get it out. You wouldn't believe how many times we've spilt red wine on this.'

I watched Isadora rush around trying to find something to clean the carpet.

Her behaviour was off, but I couldn't quite understand why.

Tom decided to go out to buy something to fix the stain.

'A foaming carpet cleaner,' Isadora said, surprising me that she knew anything about cleaning products, since she always had someone to do things for her.

'I'll make you another drink,' Isadora said and she went off into the kitchen as Tom left the apartment.

I followed her. 'What's wrong with you? You look like you've seen a ghost.'

'It's nothing,' she said with a half-smile. 'I'm jittery about being a grandmother.'

'Isadora … you're never jittery!'

I let her make me the drink because she insisted, and then Melody started to cry.

'She needs feeding and changing,' I said.

I went back into the living room and looked at the caramel-beige stain by the coffee table.

I lifted Melody and took her into the nursery, placed her on her changer and made her more comfortable. I warmed one of the prepared bottles of milk and returned to the living room, picked up the baby and fed her. Isadora sat opposite me watching in silence.

As I propped Melody up against my hand and winded her, I caught Isadora glancing at the photo.

'That was taken at the Manor,' I smiled. 'Isn't it a lovely gift? Tom gave it me.'

Isadora's eyes lingered on the photograph. Something flitted across her face, as if she was trying to solve some problem that only she knew of.

'It's a lovely picture of you both,' she said. She stared at the frame for a long time before she came to a decision. 'I have to go, Charlotte. I'm sorry. I have some errands to run.'

She kissed Melody on the forehead, then stroked my face in an uncharacteristic display of affection. Something about her behaviour brought a rush of concern for her.

'I'm sorry. Goodbye.'

'Don't worry about the carpet, Tom will sort it out.'

'Yes, dear,' she said.

I watched Isadora leave and glanced back at the photograph. Maybe I imagined it, but I was sure she was looking directly at the picture when the coffee cup fell from her hand. And if that was so, something in the image had troubled her. Whatever it was, it was something important: I'd never seen Isadora distressed in all the time I'd known her.

Chapter Twenty-Six

After a couple of weeks I was back working on the fundraiser. Isadora was helpful, but she had become a little distant since Melody's birth. I had thought she would want to see the little girl a lot, but she didn't appear to be too bothered. She even stopped our regular lunch date because she had 'other things to do'.

'Your mother is acting a little weird,' I said to Tom. 'She's barely seen Melody since the day we came out of hospital.'

'She probably hates the idea of being called Gran,' Tom said. 'You know she's vain.'

'I spoke to her yesterday about the fundraiser and she gave some advice, but again, seemed disinterested.'

'Ah,' said Tom. 'She's playing hard to get.'

'What?'

'She wants you to beg her to take over because you can't cope.'

'But I can cope.'

'Are you sure? I mean isn't this too much for you?' Tom asked. 'You do have enough on with Melody really, don't you?'

'Just a few more weeks and this year's fundraiser will be

finished. You know that your mother wanted me to do this one ... I'm sure she hasn't changed her mind. Anyway, Tina starts tomorrow.'

Tina was our new nanny. I had bowed to both Isadora's and Tom's suggestion and we'd hired one. Isadora had vetted references and individually interviewed the girls for us. Then we'd all interviewed the short list and settled on Tina. She was a sweet girl, in her late twenties, so not too young to be considered responsible. Even so, the idea of having a nanny was strange for me.

'Oh yes. I'd forgotten about that,' said Tom. 'That's good news, darling, and should give you a little time to yourself again.'

When Tina started, Tom took me out on a date night and it was nice, but I worried a lot about Melody. It amused Tom that I kept texting Tina to see if all was well.

'And you were so reluctant to have one!' he teased. 'Look at you now.'

Tom plied me with wine and it didn't take much to get me giddy after so long without alcohol.

When he got me home, and Tina had gone, I realized Tom had more of a motive for trying to make me relax. We hadn't had sex since Melody's birth and he wanted to remedy that.

'I'm sorry, darling,' I said. 'I haven't had my six-week check-up yet. The midwife says we have to wait until after that.'

'A week won't make much difference,' he said.

I was fairly tipsy and very pliable and so I didn't object as he led me into the bedroom.

'We'll need a condom. I'm not taking contraceptives yet,' was all I said.

Once I got used to handing Melody over to Tina, I started going to the gym again a couple of times a week. I wanted to get into shape for the fundraiser and it was nice to have my body back to myself again. And some time alone.

'She looks a lot like you,' Tina said to me one morning as she picked Melody up out of her cot. 'Bet Mr Carlisle doesn't like that much.'

'What do you mean?' I asked.

'Men love it when they see themselves in their kids. They forget that this is a girl and she's supposed to look like her mother.'

I laughed at the thought. I was dressed for the gym and so I kissed Melody and went to fetch my gym bag. But as I left Melody's room, I found Tom standing in the hallway outside, his expression dark with rage. So much so that I took a step back. The look on his face frightened me.

'Tom?' I said. 'What's wrong?'

He picked up his briefcase and stormed out of the house.

I was shaken and confused by his behaviour. I was sure he must have misheard the conversation I'd had with Tina.

I pulled my mobile phone from my gym bag and rang him.

'Are you all right?' I asked, when he eventually picked up the phone.

'She doesn't look anything like me,' he said.

'What? Tom ... that wasn't what—'

'I want a paternity test.'

'You know she's yours. You didn't let me out of your sight until I was pregnant ... So don't be so bloody ridiculous!'

Tom hung up on me. I stared at the phone, not knowing what to do. My heart pounded. Why couldn't he trust me? We were happy, weren't we? He had everything he wanted and still ...

I found Isadora's number in my phone and rang her.

'Hi,' I said, my voice was shaky. 'Are you free to talk? I just need some of your great advice again.'

'What's wrong,' she said with genuine concern.

'Tom doesn't think Melody is his.'

'How ridiculous ... Why would he think such a stupid thing?' Isadora said.

'Well, maybe because I cheated on him.'

'He knows that there is no way Melody could be ... that man's.'

'I know that but he overheard Tina say she doesn't look like him. Well that wasn't what she said but he took it that way.'

'I'll talk to him,' said Isadora.

I went to the gym and tried to carry on as normal, but that awful anxiety had returned as a big knot in my stomach. I felt sick and afraid. I really didn't want to live like this again.

Isadora called me back a few hours later. By then I was frantic with worry.

'He wouldn't take my call, so I went to his office,' Isadora said. 'He's very upset.'

'I ... what do I do?' I said.

'I told him he's being stupid. But he wouldn't listen.'

'I'm never going to live it down, am I? I said I was sorry. I'd never do it again.'

'I know,' Isadora said, her voice soothing. 'Look. Let him have this paternity test. Melody is his, isn't she?'

'Of course she is! How can you think otherwise?'

'I don't, but he's obviously been worried or one stupid comment from the nanny wouldn't have set him off like this. She was two weeks early after all and—'

'Oh my god,' I said. 'I don't believe this is happening. I thought we were through all this. If I agree, can you calm him down? I don't mind telling you he frightens me when he's like this.'

Isadora went very quiet.

'Charlotte ... you know you can tell me anything, right?'

'I'm telling the truth. Melody is his. She couldn't be Ewan's ...' I almost bit my tongue as Ewan's name came from my lips.

'I know that. I meant ... has Tom ever hit you?'

'Good grief no! But ...'

'Sometimes you've thought he might?'

'Yes,' I choked out the word.

'I won't ever let anything happen to you, or Melody. Just agree to the test and I'll calm him down.'

'I will but ... will it hurt Melody?'

'No. It's just a saliva swab.'

'Okay.'

A short time later, Isadora arrived with a doctor friend of hers. I sent Tina out on an errand so that she didn't see what was going on.

'This won't hurt her at all and we'll have the results in a few hours. I already have your husband's sample to make the comparison,' said the doctor.

I glanced at Isadora. She nodded.

I was somewhat railroaded. Maybe they both thought Melody wasn't Tom's. I let the doctor swap Melody's cheek and, although she cried in confusion, I knew it didn't harm her. Then he went away with the swab and Isadora in tow.

'I'll ring with the result as soon as possible,' she said.

I picked Melody up and rocked her, then I gave her another bottle to settle her down again. She was dozing in my arms when Tina returned.

Tom didn't come home at the usual time that night. I knew he was waiting for that conversation with the doctor before facing me again. Even though it wasn't possible, I searched Melody's little features for any sign of Ewan Daniels. I couldn't see it, but neither could I see Tom. Melody was like the few baby pictures of me that still existed and she also looked like herself.

My phone rang at 7.55 p.m. as I put Melody down after her final feed. It was Isadora.

'Tom's confirmed as the father,' she said. 'You see, I told you it would be okay.'

A few minutes later, as though he'd been waiting outside, Tom came home.

'Hi darling.' He kissed me on the cheek and then went straight to Melody's room. I followed him down the corridor. 'Look at *our* beautiful angel.'

My face was flushed with fury. I wanted to shout at him,

call him all the names under the sun and then, he was on his knees in front of me begging me to understand.

'I'm sorry. I'm an idiot. Mother already bollocked me!'

Tom wrapped his arms around my waist and buried his face in my now-flat stomach.

'I love you. I'm so afraid all the time that you'll leave me.'

My anger evaporated in a rush and was replaced by the ongoing guilt. It was my fault he felt like this. How could I blame him?

'We're both idiots,' I said stroking his hair. 'We have to stop dredging this up. I thought we were happy and then—'

'We *are* happy. Everything is fine. This was just a hurdle we had to face.'

He stood and kissed me as though that fixed everything.

'Come into the kitchen,' he said.

Then he foraged in the large fridge for cheese and pâté and pulled a pack of crackers from one of the cupboards: all of his favourite comfort foods.

I opened a bottle of wine and sat down at the breakfast bar while Tom put out plates, glasses, butter and knives.

That sinking depression returned. I hadn't felt like that since before the weekend at the Manor and I didn't like it at all.

'Cheer up,' Tom said.

I blinked and forced a smile on my lips. Tom poured me a glass of wine and I hid my continuing unhappiness by swigging some of it. My mood swung from anger to guilt and then to despondency. Tom drank his first glass and refilled it and mine in between eating crackers and pâté. I picked at some cheese but wasn't feeling particularly hungry.

It was a relief when Melody began to cry. I hurried off to take care of her, leaving Tom to finish the wine bottle on his own.

Melody cried and cried. I rocked her in my arms as I sat in the padded rocking chair.

'What's wrong with her?' asked Tom.

'Colic, I think.'

Melody let out another pain-filled yell and I massaged her stomach to help relieve her wind.

'Go to bed, I'll try and settle her,' I said.

Tom obeyed and I was glad to be alone with Melody, but she didn't calm down until around one in the morning. Then she fell fast asleep over my shoulder. I waited for another half an hour before I moved so as not to wake her.

Once she was in her cot I sat back down in the rocker and watched her.

Then I closed my eyes and nodded off in the chair.

I dreamed that Tom came in and looked at me sleeping but didn't wake me. He was looming over me, overly large, like a comic book villain. My dream self was scared: I knew he wanted to kill me. There was such rage in his eyes and his over-large fists clenched at his sides as though he could barely prevent himself from losing control. Then, dream Tom turned away. He went over to the cot and picked Melody up, looked at her face, as though he searched still for the image of another man in her features. He dangled Melody over me. I wanted to snatch her from him, afraid his big monstrous hands would crush her delicate ribs, or worse, he'd toss her aside like a rag doll. I was paralyzed with fear, unable to scream or move.

'She'd better be mine,' dream monster Tom said ...

I woke up trembling. My heart thudded painfully in my chest. The dream paralysis remained for a split second and then I leaned forward and looked into Melody's cot, only to discover she wasn't there.

I hurried out of the room and into our bedroom. Tom wasn't there and neither was our daughter. Rising panic made my heart pound. Where were they? I rushed down the corridor and into the living room.

I found Tom asleep on the sofa and Melody was safe inside the Moses basket.

'Tom? You took her while I slept,' I said, shaking him.

He groaned and sat up, rubbing his eyes. 'She was crying and I didn't want her to wake you. So, I brought her in here and gave her a bottle.'

'She's well away now,' I said.

I picked the basket up and took it into the nursery and placed it inside the cot. Then we both went to bed.

Tom was soon asleep and I envied his ability to do that. My heart was still racing, and the early panic escalated as I remembered my horrible dream. Had I been aware on some level that Tom had stood watching me and then taken Melody away? Tom was Melody's father. He loved our daughter. But I couldn't quell the fear that he was capable of hurting not only me, but Melody as well. I didn't know where this awful paranoia came from – perhaps it was natural for new mothers to have anxiety dreams about their babies.

Chapter Twenty-Seven

Like every other one before it, that year's Carlisle Charity Fundraiser was a huge success. But as the closing speeches were made and the cheque presented to the Macmillan Nurses by David Danner, I noticed how subdued Isadora was. I didn't sneak off into the bathroom to hide this time but took my place beside Tom on the stage. I tried not to think of the last fundraiser, or the texts I'd received from Ewan.

After the presentation Tom and I stood by the door to shake hands and say goodbye to everyone. There were a large number of Tom's business contemporaries at the event, and they were all patting themselves on their backs for their generosity.

'Everyone was very charitable,' I said to Tom.

'Yes. They think it makes up for what they do the rest of the time.'

'You mean not giving to charity?'

'No. I mean the wheeling and dealing and semi-legal investments that makes everyone in this room so wealthy.'

'But not you though? Or Carlisle Corp?' I said.

'We do everything legally, you know that. But not everyone does,' Tom said.

'How do you know?'

'It's my business to know. Any information I have on these people can be used to my advantage.'

I glanced at Tom, a little surprised by this revelation. He rarely discussed business with me.

'You mean ... you blackmail them?'

Tom laughed. 'Silly!'

When the last of the people had gone, I walked around the ballroom to give the staff the final instructions about the table decorations. The flowers were to be donated to the local church and care homes. Then I went to fetch my wrap from the cloakroom.

As I was searching in my bag for my ticket, I heard muffled voices coming from behind a curtain that dropped to the floor.

I recognized Tom's voice but not the other man's.

'No unusual activity?' Tom asked.

'Nothing,' said the other man.

'What about the phone?' Tom asked.

'No calls to anyone new. Just the normal.'

'Good. But keep checking.'

'Mr C, there's been nothing and there won't be anything.'

'What about the *other* one?'

'Your wife is as good as gold,' said the man. 'She showed no interest at all.'

I put my hand over my mouth as I fought the urge to cry out in shock.

'Here,' Tom said. 'It's all there. Count it if you like.'

I imagined Tom holding out an envelope stuffed with money.

'I trust you,' said the man. 'So, surveillance continues?'

'Yes.'

'For how much longer?'

'I'll tell you when to stop.'

I hurried to the cloakroom as I heard movement on the other side of the curtain. At the counter I gave the girl my ticket and she brought my wrap and Tom's overcoat.

'Ah there you are,' said Tom behind me.

I didn't say anything as we settled into the back of the limo. But I texted Tina to say that we were on our way home.

'Did you enjoy the evening?' Tom asked me.

'Yes. It was a success.'

'You did a wonderful job.'

'Thank you,' I said.

Tom put his arm around me and pulled me to him. I buried my face in his chest.

Tom kissed the top of my head and murmured that he loved me. I pretended to doze against him and stayed silent.

My mind was racing. I couldn't hide it from myself any longer: Tom still didn't trust me. The man he'd been talking to had to be a private detective. I was being monitored night and day to see if I would betray him again.

Chapter Twenty-Eight

I caught a cab to the gym the next day, choosing not to chat to the driver, even though he tried to engage me with a few friendly questions. At the gym, I attended my regular class and then went for a swim, but I avoided making eye contact with anyone, especially men. I kept glancing around, trying to assess if everyone there was a genuine member or if they were being paid to watch me.

When I left the gym I kept looking over my shoulder. Every man I saw that appeared to be hanging around was potentially the man I'd heard behind the curtain. Normally I'd have gone into a coffee shop to get lunch and a latte before heading back, but that day I went straight home.

Tina was changing Melody when I arrived back.

'Did you pick up the colic drops?' she asked when I came into Melody's room.

'Oh no! I forgot!'

'Want me to get them?' she asked.

'Yes. Thanks. I don't feel like going out again.'

Tina left me to my own devices. I found myself looking at my phone, wondering how it was being monitored.

Half an hour later Tina returned.

'These are the best ones,' she said. 'She'll need them regularly, to prevent another night of screaming. Poor thing, it's so painful having colic. I've also bought some of these new bottles with a straw inside that reduce the air getting in.'

'I should have remembered to collect them. Good idea on the bottles. I didn't know about those. I'm a terrible mother,' I said.

'Charlotte,' Tina said, 'you absolutely aren't a terrible mother! Don't be so hard on yourself. Motherhood isn't easy and you're a lot more hands-on than most women I've worked for. Some people hire a nanny because they don't want to bring up their own kids. You use me in the right way to give yourself the break you deserve. In fact, you should take advantage of me much more.'

'I might be going out a bit less,' I said.

Tina looked at me and laughed. 'You don't have to do that! You should take more breaks if anything. Otherwise you're paying me for doing very little.'

I didn't explain to her why I was feeling like I just shouldn't go anywhere. The paranoia was so strong I wondered if my home had hidden cameras and recording devices to listen in to my conversations. If Tom was spending time and money on monitoring me, surely that was the easiest way?

I placed Melody on the floor on her play mat with a mobile toy bridged over her. Then I went into the kitchen and made Tina and I lunch.

'What are you doing?' she said. 'I should do that.'

'I enjoy it,' I said, knowing Tina couldn't argue with that.

At the end of the day, as Tina left, I almost told her what was bothering me but held back. I so needed a friend, but how did I know that she wasn't also watching me and reporting my movements to Tom? After all she was among the women initially vetted by Isadora.

I took Melody out with me the next day and went for a walk to the local park. There were several mothers sitting together chatting as their children played on the swings and slide. I sat away from them, Melody's pram by my side, while I watched the other children having fun.

A year ago I wouldn't have imagined sitting like an ordinary woman in a normal park. My plans for the future had been different, and with someone else.

Even though I'd sworn to forget him, Ewan's face came back into view. I closed my eyes. The hurt surged up again inside me. I should probably talk to Tom about what I'd overheard. Perhaps there was an explanation? Maybe I'd been mistaken. But even as I tried to convince myself that this was likely my stomach turned.

'Hi!'

I opened my eyes and looked up at a very attractive businessman. He was very like Ewan – blond hair, blue eyes. And he had boyish charm oozing from him. I was too shocked to reply.

'Do you mind if I sit here?' he said. 'Lunch break ...'

I glanced at the empty bench beside me and nodded.

The man took a seat.

I leaned over Melody's pram and checked on her. The

fresh air and pram ride had sent her to sleep. I smiled as I watched her.

'First one?' the man asked.

'What?'

'First child? Yours, right?'

'Yes. She's mine. And it's my only one.'

'Hard work,' he said. 'Can be lonely when the father is out all day.'

The hairs stood up on the back of my neck and a bitter chill ran down my spine. I shuddered and then I turned my head to look at the man. He was smiling at me: secure in his good looks. I knew then that he was trying to pick me up. Did I appear to be available? Or was I being tested?

I picked up my handbag and stood.

'You leaving already?' he said.

'I'm not interested,' I said.

Then I released the brake on Melody's pram and pushed it away.

I didn't look back at the man, instead I glanced around the park and over to the street across from it. There I saw another man sitting on a low wall. He was definitely watching me. My stomach lurched.

I'm just imagining it, I thought. But I knew I wasn't. That man had been sent to talk to me. I turned Melody's pram around and wheeled towards the flat, trying to put as much distance between the businessman and us.

As I reached the end of the road, and was about to cross the street, I glanced back to see the businessman talking to the man on the wall. There was no doubt now. My instinct was right. What would these two strangers have to say to each other? This was a residential area anyway, so why would some random business-type take his lunch here? It was all too contrived. Something else occurred to me then, the ordinary – so forgettable – man sitting on the wall was a type. The type of man I'd seen before. Like the man wearing brogues. How long had I been followed?

I was trembling when I arrived home. Melody woke up as we entered the flat, and Tina took her away to feed and change. I put the kettle on, trying to appear normal, but inside I was so upset I didn't know what to do. I couldn't deny the truth no matter what I did. Not only was I being followed, but they were also trying to set me up. To try to trap me.

I couldn't take anymore. Enough was enough.

'Tina, you can go early today,' I said. 'I don't need you this afternoon.'

'Are you sure? It's only three?'

'Yes. Take the time while you can, as I may need you more another day.'

'Okay,' she said.

When she had gone I sat in the living room staring at the clock. Then I sent Tom a text.

I'm not putting up with this. You either deal with it or we are through.

I was in the kitchen making up a bottle for Melody's night feed when Tom came home. He was early. He stormed into the kitchen and dropped his briefcase down beside the breakfast bar.

'What does this mean?' he demanded. 'And why won't you answer when I'm calling you?'

His cheeks were flushed and he looked angry and stressed.

'You've been paying someone to follow me.'

'Don't be rid—'

'Don't lie to me. I heard you.'

'What did you hear?' he said.

'I heard you and some detective. At the fundraiser.'

Tom went quiet.

'And today, some guy tried to pick me up when I was in the park with Melody.'

'What did you do?'

'I told him I wasn't interested!' I yelled. 'What the *fuck* do you think I'd do?'

'I'm sorry,' he said. 'I had to be certain.'

I gave a sneering laugh. 'How long have you been having me followed?'

'A couple of weeks.'

I shook my head in disbelief.

'I feel sick,' I said. 'I just can't do this anymore. I'm walking on eggshells all the time anyway and now I'm even afraid to talk to someone innocently in case it's misconstrued. I can't live like this!'

Tom sank down into one of the breakfast bar stools.

'What would you have done if I had fancied that guy? Were you setting me up because you wanted a divorce? Is that it?' I jabbed a finger at him. 'Because if that's the case you only have to say ...'

'I've been through hell and back,' he said. He dropped his

face into his hands. 'I was afraid. That you were just like ...'
He stood up and walked to the window. The silence was
oppressive. I held my breath as I waited for him to speak.

At last he said, 'I was afraid you were like my mother.'

I breathed out, staring at him.

'When I found out about Daniels, I think I lost my mind
for a while. I went to see mother and she—'

Tom stopped. He shook his head, as though unable to go
on for a moment, and my heart went out to him despite my
anger.

'I know. You told me you saw her. She said you were to
blame.'

'What I didn't tell you was *why* we had a row. She had
another man there. At the Manor. She always has men over.
I guess these days they are paid for. He was a young guy. I
found him naked in her bed ...'

'Christ!' I said.

His hands were shaking. He reached for me but I folded
my arms and stepped back. Tom's dropped to his side. He
blinked away tears. Then he shook his head again, dashing
his fingers across his eyes. Looking away from me, he took a
deep shuddering breath before continuing.

'I saw it all the time growing up. Men came and went. She
picked up total strangers and brought them home. One time
she sent all the staff out for the day and I came home and
found her with a man.'

'I can't imagine it,' I said.

My anger deflated as Tom talked, telling me all about his
wayward mother, and I gradually began to realize how much

harm Isadora had caused him. Even so, he shouldn't have spied on me. It was such an invasion.

'I thought you'd never do that to me, Charlotte, and then ... You told me you were leaving.'

A wave of guilt squashed down the final upsurge of anger. He was right. What I'd done was wrong. I'd hurt him just as Isadora had.

'Can you forgive me?' he said when he finished his story. He eyes pleaded for understanding.

Despite how I'd behaved what Tom had done was so intrusive. Acid burned the back of my throat as bile fought its way up even as my rage disappeared. I was still jittery, even though I knew the fire of our argument had been extinguished by his explanation.

'I think, maybe, you need some help to deal with this,' I said at last. 'And to come to terms with Isadora's behaviour. No child should have to see that. I'm sorry for what I did to you. But you have to trust me or we can't go on. Forgiving you isn't the issue for me, Tom. It's believing that you have faith in me again. That's what's important.'

Tom let out a breath. 'I'll ring them and call them off,' he said. 'I promise I won't do this again.'

'And you'll talk to someone? A counsellor?'

Tom nodded. 'I promise.'

'Can I hold you?' Tom said.

I couldn't refuse this time but my nerves still felt raw. I was relieved when the landline phone rang and Tom went to answer it. A few seconds later he came back into the living room.

Tom's face was completely white. He wore the same harried expression as the night when I told him I was leaving him.

'What's happened?' I said.

'Isadora,' he said. 'She's sick … It … It's serious.'

Chapter Twenty-Nine

'She's been ill for a while,' the doctor explained. 'Pancreatic cancer.'

'Then we have to get her the best care,' I said.

Tom was struck dumb by the doctor's answer and so I took and held his hand. I knew this couldn't be easy for him. We sat in the doctor's office at a private medical clinic in Mayfair. It was difficult to take it in because we hadn't seen Isadora yet.

After the phone call, I'd rung Tina and asked her to come back and stay with Melody while we went to the hospital.

'She asked me not to call you, but I felt I had to,' the doctor said. 'The truth is, she hasn't got long. Days, weeks if you're lucky. Pancreatic is difficult to treat anyway, but it was left. She refused treatment and now it's too late to even consider putting her through it.'

My stomach churned as the doctor revealed that Isadora had been diagnosed almost a year ago but had refused all help and insisted that her family didn't know. She had carried on as though life was normal, telling us nothing, and she had hidden her illness so well. Was this because Tom and I were having our own troubles?

The doctor was called away to take a phone call and Tom and I were left alone in his sterile office.

'I should have known,' Tom said. 'I had noticed the weight loss but thought she'd been dieting.'

'I did too. We both should have realized. She was uncharacteristically distant.'

'I'd put that down to the row we'd had,' Tom said. 'She has been weird with me since then, but I thought we'd both get over it. Especially after Melody was born.'

The doctor came back in then.

'You can see your mother now. I've told her you're here.'

We followed him to Isadora's private room. An NHS bed was just not suitable for a Carlisle: it was five stars all the way, even to the end.

Isadora was lying in the bed. Without her make-up I could see the dark circles and tiredness around her eyes. But as soon as she saw us, she pulled herself up into a sitting position and rallied. I had to admire her strength.

I leaned over and gave her a kiss on the cheek.

'Why didn't you tell us?' I asked.

Isadora was so stubborn, even then.

'I'm fine. The doctor shouldn't have called you,' she said.

'Mother, of course he should! If anything had happened to you, I'd have sued him for not contacting me. Now look, we are going to fight this!'

Isadora shook her head. 'He's told you the prognosis. There's nothing we can do. I want to continue for as normal as possible until ...'

Tears filled my eyes and I blinked them away trying to be brave. In the face of Isadora's courage I couldn't let myself fall apart before her.

'I'm just going to get some water,' I said. 'Do you want anything?'

'No, dear. I'm fine.' Isadora met my eyes and I couldn't imagine this durable woman failing due to anything, especially illness. In all the years I'd known her she had never been sick. She still didn't even look that ill and yet I knew she was dying. It was tempting to deny it, just as she was trying to do.

I left the room and went in search of a vending machine which was quite a way from the private rooms. When I returned I heard Tom and Isadora shouting at each other.

'What *happened* to you?' Isadora said. 'I can't believe my son is capable of—'

'You know why I did it, Mother. She was going to leave me. I couldn't allow that.'

'But whose fault was it in the first place? *What were you thinking?* You brought this all on yourself.'

'What's done is done.'

'I can't believe I've covered for you ...' Isadora said.

'I appreciate what you did—'

'I had no choice!' Isadora said and her voice pitched up and carried out into the corridor.

'Be quiet. Someone will hear you.'

'If you ever ...' Isadora's voice faded down and both voices dropped to a whisper. I stood by the door unseen, but couldn't hear anything more. I didn't know what to do.

'What's taking her so long?' I heard Tom say and then his footsteps approached the door. I hurriedly walked away then turned around again and jogged to the door as he came through.

'There you are.'

'Vending machine was miles away!' I said. 'Now, Isadora. I'm not taking no for an answer. We have to try some form of treatment.'

I didn't know what I'd overheard, and with Isadora's illness, I couldn't bring myself to broach the subject with either of them. I had to deal with my paranoia and stop worrying about every overheard fragment as Tom had to cope with the prospect of losing his mother. The only thing I could do right then was be as supportive to them both as possible. Our marital problems would have to be resolved at another time.

The next day Isadora came out of the hospital and returned to the Surrey house with a team of privately paid medical people. I travelled over to see her with Melody and we stayed overnight in Tom's room.

'Why didn't you tell us?' I asked her again when I took Melody into her room. 'We should have been supporting you all this time.'

'You have enough to deal with,' Isadora said. 'I'm sorry I won't be around to watch Melody grow.'

'Let's not—'

'I've made arrangements and everything's taken care of. Promise me you'll make sure my wishes are met?'

'Yes of course, but—'

'I know you don't want to talk about it, but this is the thing. I have a few weeks left at most. I *have* to talk.'

'Okay,' I said. 'I'm listening.'

I took her instructions and offered to stay permanently. I didn't say 'until the end', though we both knew that was what I meant. But, stubborn as ever, Isadora wouldn't let me.

After that I went back and forth alone, travelling over every few days. I saw Isadora deteriorate. Now that we knew, and she was accepting this was it, she just went downhill. It was as if she didn't have the strength anymore to fight the inevitable.

'Charlotte,' she said to me on one of her last days, 'I won't let anything happen to you and Melody.'

'Yes, Isadora, I know,' I said indulging her. She was hooked up to a morphine drip and wasn't always lucid.

I patted her hand then. 'We're all fine. Everyone is safe.'

'I've taken care of everything ...' she said again.

'I know. I promise I'll do as you asked.'

Tom stayed away. I think it was because he didn't want to see his mother fading but also it was guilt. He knew he'd been hard on her and didn't know how to reconcile their issues.

'You need to see her before it's too late,' I told him after a couple of weeks. 'You have to say your goodbyes.'

Tom was as stubborn as his mother but I eventually made him agree.

'We'll go tomorrow,' he said.

The landline phone rang and we both looked at each other. The last time the landline rang it had been the hospital. I had a knot in my stomach. Tom didn't move from his seat. I got up and answered it.

'Mrs Carlisle?' asked the voice on the other end.

'Yes.'

'It's Rosa Meldrew, I'm your mother-in-law's nurse. I'm afraid I have sad news. Isadora is no longer with us.'

'But, I only saw her yesterday,' I said.

'I'm sorry. It was very sudden. We weren't expecting things to escalate quite yet. The doctor has been and confirmed the time of death. It was her wish that we didn't try to revive her. Her body has been moved, per her instructions, to the appointed funeral directors.'

'She appointed someone?' I was surprised, because I'd taken her instructions and we were supposed to do it after she passed.

'Yes. She had.'

When Rosa finished giving me all the details, I put the phone down and turned to Tom. He was sitting on the sofa looking at me, his face like stone. I didn't have to tell him she was gone. Then I sat next to him and put my arms around him. He cried and so did I. Isadora was dead and there was nothing either of us could do.

It was the end of an era. I was now the only Mrs Carlisle.

Chapter Thirty

As Rosa had said, Isadora had made her own arrangements. It was her wish that she be cremated and she had insisted on a closed coffin.

Tom had an argument with the funeral director about this, but he wouldn't budge on it. Isadora had been insistent that she didn't want anyone to see her or remember her in that way.

'She made me promise, Mr Carlisle,' the man said. 'And I can't go back on a promise made to a dying woman.'

'She was so vain,' Tom said. 'But it's typically selfish of her too. I wanted to see her one last time.'

'Maybe it's for the best,' I said. 'Now you can remember her as you last saw her instead.'

'That's somehow worse,' Tom said. 'For weeks I couldn't bring myself to see her. But I still thought I had time. And it was all so stupid. You see, in the hospital, we had another row when you went to get water ...'

I tried to look surprised. 'What about?'

'You. She was blaming me for not being a good husband. She said I'm just like my father and that I only care about the company.'

'I'm sorry. That's awful, and untrue. You're a wonderful husband and father.'

'Thank God I have you, Char,' he said.

He hugged me to him. I was glad then that I hadn't questioned him about the argument before. It was so much better that he'd volunteered the information. I was still surprised that I had never picked up on how difficult a relationship Tom had had with Isadora until recently. He had always deferred to her and at times it had bothered me how much. She in her turn had been totally devoted to him. Or appeared to be. It had been the case that what Tom wanted always came before anything else. Family secrets were a terrible thing and I wanted to make sure that we never had any between us again.

The funeral was attended by many of Isadora's friends and lots of Tom's business associates. As Isadora wished, the coffin remained closed and after the tributes and tears and smiles as people remembered her quirks, Isadora's coffin rolled away to its fiery destination.

The funeral wake took place at the Manor in Surrey, and I'd arranged caterers to feed the two hundred people who were invited to the house.

When we arrived back at the Manor, Tina was there with Melody and Mrs Tanner greeted us with tears in her eyes. It was the first time I'd ever seen the woman show any emotion. But she had worked for Isadora for a long time and it was sad for all of the housekeeping staff as well as friends and family that this formidable woman was dead.

'You must join the guests at the wake, Mrs Tanner,' I said.

But she found it difficult to switch off, and I caught her giving instructions to the catering staff and making sure that everyone in the house was fed and happy. Like Isadora, Mrs Tanner was indeed a strong and unique personality. I liked her, I always had, even though she was difficult to get to know.

Tom and I had arranged to stay over at the Manor for a few days to put things in order, and so Tina had prepped Tom's former nursery with Melody's bedding and she slept in the adjoining nanny's room to keep her eye on the baby through the night and give us both a rest after the funeral.

'I don't feel ready to wade through her personal things yet,' said Tom after everyone had left and the housekeeping staff was clearing up. 'Can we leave that for the time being?'

We sat in the lounge. The large fire wasn't lit but had so much character that it was comforting being near it.

'Of course. She left the paperwork we'll need in the office, and the solicitor comes tomorrow to read the will.'

'The house is already mine,' he reminded me. 'We don't need anything else.'

'I know,' I said.

'Maybe this isn't the right time to suggest it, but perhaps we need to move in here.'

'*Live here?*' I said.

'Eventually.'

I looked around the lounge with its expensive furnishings, and old paintings. I couldn't imagine using this much space all the time after our much smaller flat in London.

'I know we discussed this once but, isn't it a bit big for us,' I said.

'We'd grow into it. And it would be better for Melody.'

'I'll think on it. There's no rush though, right?'

The Manor could be a fresh start for us. I wouldn't miss the wives who did nothing but lunch and beauty appointments that much. It was quiet and I had been considering a move anyway when Melody had grown. Despite the sadness we experienced following the funeral, we had spent many happy hours there too. It was a lovely home, and it would be a wonderful place to bring Melody up. Even though I'd always known at some point Tom would own this place, I'd never given living here a serious thought. There was a lot to consider if we made this move. Tom would have to stay in London mid-week and we'd only see him at weekends. There was also the aspect of running and living in a home of this nature, where you had to have others living and working there too. You were never really alone. It was a way of living that I wasn't used to.

Any decision to move in was forced the next day however, when Isadora's solicitor came and read the will.

The house reverted, as Tom said, completely to him, and there was a substantial amount of money put in trust for Melody. Isadora had also given a large sum to Mrs Tanner, and, on hearing the news, the woman announced that she wished to retire.

'It just won't be the same for me without Mrs C,' Mrs Tanner said.

'We completely understand,' Tom said. 'Will you stay until we find a suitable replacement and help them learn the ropes?'

'I can give you a month,' Mrs Tanner said. 'After that I'd like to be free to go.'

We couldn't really argue; if we didn't find a suitable replacement for Mrs Tanner in that time, we'd have to close the house up until we could.

What surprised me the most was the money Isadora left to me. I hadn't expected anything, but her remaining assets were to pass into my name. That was a few million pounds and the penthouse flat she owned in London.

'But why has she left these to *me*?' I said to the solicitor.

'It wasn't my place to ask,' the man replied.

Tom didn't make any comment about it; he had enough money and wealth of his own and I suppose it didn't matter which of us inherited Isadora's money because we were married and owned half of what the other had anyway.

We went back to London after a few days and advertised for a housekeeper in *The Lady*.

'Darling, I don't like the idea of having to close the Manor down,' Tom said a few days later. 'I know it isn't ideal, but what if you move up there with Melody and Tina? At least then the other help can remain and we can replace Mrs Tanner with the right person without rushing into anything.'

'But. We'd be apart a lot.'

'Initially, but I can limit how often I go into the office once things are settled. I can work from the Manor. My father did that sometimes. We can keep the flat as my base when I'm here.'

'I don't know,' I said.

'It would help me a great deal if you do this,' Tom said. 'You know the Manor means a lot to the family. It's never been closed up before. I'm not sure from a security point of view how good an idea that would be. I also spoke to the insurance company and if the property is empty for a long period then we wouldn't be insured.'

'Can't they change the policy?'

'No insurance company will cover a permanently empty property.'

'I'll ask Tina if she's willing to move and live-in with us,' I said. 'If she isn't, we may have to find a nanny from Surrey instead.'

'Wonderful!'

Once Tom had his answer, he began to make immediate arrangements for me to move to the house.

'We have a month,' I said. 'So, no immediate rush.'

'Let's go up there this weekend anyway. I think I'm feeling strong enough to tackle Mother's personal things now.'

Chapter Thirty-One

We travelled to the Manor as planned, and Tina came with us to look after Melody so that we could be free to sort out Isadora's personal effects.

'I ordered some boxes,' Mrs Tanner said. 'Are you sure you're up to doing this?'

'Yes. I have to,' said Tom.

Mrs Tanner gave him a sideways look. She had been even more distant since the funeral. Maybe she felt awkward because she was leaving us and just wanted to go as soon as possible.

Mrs Tanner was showing Tom the accounts on the computer and they were going through all of Isadora's paperwork to make sure that the solicitor had everything he needed for probate. Tom reached over Mrs Tanner to pick up a stapler and the woman visibly jumped.

Tom exchanged a look with her then that I couldn't interpret. It threw me to see the expression that crossed Mrs Tanner's face as Tom stared at her. His face was blank and guarded. She looked ... upset.

'Everything all right?' I asked. The strange exchange

between them ended as Mrs Tanner appeared to gather herself with an indifferent shrug.

'Erm ... yes. I think you have everything you need now,' she said.

Later that day the boxes arrived flattened and Mrs Tanner left a roll of brown tape in the bedroom with them. She had stripped Isadora's bed, a massive white four-poster that imposed itself far into the room even though it was against the back wall.

'Her favourite sheets have been washed. I put them in that box over there for you,' Mrs Tanner said.

'Thanks,' I said.

Mrs Tanner hurried away. We started with Isadora's jewellery because it had been left to Melody in the will. It was all there and after we did the inventory, I placed the valuables safely back into their individual boxes and we stacked them up on Isadora's dresser. As Isadora's executor, Tom was obliged to list anything of value, this included the jewellery left to Melody. It would all be dealt with during probate.

Clearing her clothing was easy. We kept a few favourite items but everything else was packed in boxes to go to the charity shops.

Tom coped well. He stopped at one point when he found his mother's engagement ring. His expression was ... confusing. Cold, almost. I think he was trying to put on a brave face. He opened the box and looked at it for a long time, then he handed it to me.

'Some time ago Mother said she wanted you to have this. I suppose she already knew she was ill.'

It was a huge diamond surrounded by emeralds in an expensive white gold setting. I took the ring.

'I'll keep it for Melody,' I said. I didn't want to wear Isadora's ostentatious ring. It wasn't me, but it had to stay in the family.

I placed it with the other things that we had for our daughter.

'She said to tell you, you were like a daughter to her,' Tom said.

My eyes watered. Isadora had her faults but I'd rather she was alive and with us. I rubbed the tears from my eyes and continued packing clothing into a box.

One minute we were working together and sorting everything out in a calm manner and the next moment everything changed.

Tom opened the box of bedding and stared inside. 'We'll burn this,' he said.

'Why?' I said.

Then I saw Isadora's 'favourite' bedding. It was purple satin not dissimilar to the set I'd bought in Harrods. I felt my face flush with the memory. Not of buying the bedding but of everything I'd done afterwards and the memory of making love to Ewan was firmly in my mind.

I winced. I tried to hide my face from him, but it was too late, Tom had seen the expression of pain that crossed my face and guessed what it meant. His hand shot out, connecting with my cheek, and I found myself on my back in the centre of Isadora's room. White hot pain radiated through my face and eye. My hand pressed against it as I lay there stunned.

Tom towered over me. As imposing as he'd been in that

awful dream I'd had. In one hand he grasped the purple satin bedding while his other hand clenched into a fist.

For the first time in almost twelve years of marriage I saw an expression on my husband's face that made me truly believe he wanted to kill me.

I tried to scream but no sound would come out. But my primal instincts kicked in and I struggled up into a sitting position and back-pedalled on my bottom until the door of Isadora's bedroom was pressed against my spine.

Tom didn't move but he watched me with a predatory expression. It was cruel, as though he enjoyed seeing me afraid. I'd never seen such a horrible expression on his face before.

Then Tom's face changed. He glanced down at the bedding in his hand and dropped it to the floor as though it was something so repugnant he couldn't bear to touch it. He looked back at me and gave a mortified cry. He fell to his knees and crawled towards me, tears pouring down his face.

'Oh my god; Oh my god ...' he said over and over again.

'Don't touch me!' I said. I pulled myself to my feet.

Tom reached me as he crawled still on all fours and threw his arms around my waist and held onto me, even though I struggled to free myself. 'I'm so sorry!'

'You hit me,' I gasped. 'Let go of me, Tom, *I'm scared*!'

'I didn't mean to!' he said. 'She used to, used to put this on the bed ... whenever she ... had a lover coming. I saw the bedding and I ... lost it.'

'I said, let go, Tom!' I said. 'If you don't, I'll scream!'

Tom climbed to his feet and backed away from me. He

held his hands out in a placating manner that was supposed to reassure me.

'I'm sorry, Charlotte. I don't know what came over me!'

I reached behind me and turned the door handle, but I couldn't pull it open without looking away from Tom.

'I won't hurt you. Oh God, I'm so sorry—'

'You hit me!' I said. 'You *hurt* me you bastard!'

He took a step towards me.

'Stay away from me!' I shouted.

'Shhh! Charlotte, Mrs Tanner is out there.'

'Then stay away!'

My throat was dry as I struggled to open the door with weak and trembling hands. My legs felt weak under me and I was on the point of collapse. I'd never been struck by anyone and the shock of it brought rushes of hot and cold into my face and neck. All I wanted to do was get Melody and leave.

Then Tom crumpled to the floor again. He buried his head in Isadora's plush carpet and cried like a baby.

The wind went out of my sails as I watched him. Not big and scary now but a man who had suffered a terrible trauma.

'Charlotte ...'

I moved back into the room and towards him, but I was ready to flee at any moment if his mood switched again.

'You've no idea what it was like growing up in this house,' he said, his voice barely a whisper. 'But ... I loved my mother.'

It sickened my heart to hear his words. It was too awful to contemplate, and I just couldn't reconcile the woman he'd described with the one I thought I knew. I found myself sitting down on the floor with him and wrapping my arms around his broad shoulders. I was shaking still, but I told myself that his reaction had everything to do with the recent loss of his mother. He hadn't meant to hurt me. How many women justified their husband's violent behaviour in the same way, I wondered? But I wasn't an abused wife. This had never happened before: I wouldn't let it happen again.

Who knew what harm Isadora had done him throughout the years without realizing? She was so controlling, and Tom had been so dependent on her. Until recently he had been under her thumb – we both had – and by the end the cracks were beginning to show. Seeing Tom fall apart like this made me realize how bad things must have been for him growing up with an absent father and a mother who had multiple affairs. It explained a lot about their relationship.

'I never got a chance to tell her what I really thought of her,' he said.

The tears were drying now, but Tom was trembling, shaken by his own overreaction. A dam of grief had burst inside him, making him lose his sanity for a short time.

He looked up at me and gasped. 'I've bruised you!'

He wiped his face with the back of his hand. 'I'll go and get some ice ...'

He went into Isadora's bathroom and swilled his face; by the time he came out he didn't look like a man who had just admitted his mother had abused him. Or had cried so hard that I thought he'd never stop. He looked – normal. Composed.

A jolt of fear burrowed up inside me again.

'Wait here,' he said. 'I'll get ice and try and take the swelling down before it gets worse.'

I was emotionally raw and so I didn't object. I sat at Isadora's dressing table and looked at the damage while he was gone. He'd managed to hit me right on the cheekbone. Not only was it swelling and bruising but my eye was blossoming into a fierce blue-black shiner.

Tom came back in with a tea towel wrapped around ice cubes. He pressed it to my cheek.

'Ouch!'

I took hold of it because his hands were still shaking.

Tom sat down on the edge of Isadora's bed. 'I'm going to redecorate this room,' he said.

I looked at him and frowned, unsure why he'd even bother.

'We'll move into it then. I couldn't possibly sleep in here while it reminds me of her so much.'

I stared at Tom and resisted the urge to shake my head. He couldn't be thinking straight. Why would he ever want to be in this room after all that Isadora had done in here?

He continued to talk while I was still trying to reconcile his violent outburst with his complete breakdown, followed by this cold calm. He needed help and if I was any kind of decent wife, I'd make sure he got it.

Tom stood then and continued to clear Isadora's personal things into a box. He found her passport and looked at the picture inside, then he tossed it on top of the boxes of jewellery.

It was as if nothing unusual had happened.

Chapter Thirty-Two

In the days that followed, I hid my bruised eye and cheek as best as I could under make-up and told Mrs Tanner and Tina that I'd slipped from the dressing stool. Tina accepted this information and offered advice on how to reduce the bruising, but Mrs Tanner studied me for a while and then shook her head, as though she didn't believe the explanation.

All of Isadora's possessions, except the jewellery and her passport, were sent out in boxes to the charity shops. The purple satin bedding, however, remained. Tom stuffed it back in a box and took it to store somewhere else in the house. I never wanted to see it again.

'When Mrs Tanner leaves,' he said, 'we'll burn it on the garden fire.'

I tried to understand his erratic behaviour. What had happened to him was private and Tom had to now come to terms with his admission to me. He promised again that he would get counselling and because of this I chose to forgive him for hitting me. That wasn't the same as forgetting. It was an effort not to flinch if he made any sudden movements. Learning to trust him after something like that would not be easy.

Tom went back to London on the Monday morning – it was a relief to have time away from him after everything. I was exhausted and my emotions ran riot as I replayed what Tom had done.

I made the excuse to stay behind with Tina and Melody, because I needed to spend some time with Mrs Tanner. She was going to show me all of the Manor books, the staff wage records and all of the expenses that were relevant to running the house. The plan was that I would take over everything until we found a reliable housekeeper. By the end of the week, when Tom returned, my cheek and eye were mostly healed and I had a good handle on the daily running of the Manor.

'Mrs Carlisle is very capable of doing this now,' Mrs Tanner said. 'And I'm happy to take phone calls if you have any concerns. I'd like to leave sooner if you don't mind.'

Her request was abrupt, but Tom immediately said she could leave as soon as she wished. They exchanged a look again, one that told me that Mrs Tanner knew some of the family secrets that Tom had shared with me. Maybe that was why the housekeeper always appeared on edge around him: it was guilt. She probably knew that she should have helped protect him from the knowledge of his mother's affairs.

We agreed that she would end her employment the following weekend, after I'd completed everything under her supervision.

'I don't understand why she's so desperate to get away,' Tom said. 'Her sister calls her a lot. She's going to live with her for the time being. I suspect the sister is in poor health, but don't like to ask.'

'You're probably right.'

Tom took my hand then. He hadn't been very affectionate since he returned from London, and I skipped around him like a nervous cat that had gone partially feral.

'I've hired a decorator,' he told me. 'He'll be here Monday to start the renovations on Mother's ... the master bedroom. I want to make it ours before we move in permanently.'

'Darling, I'm happy in your old room.'

'I started seeing someone. A therapist.'

'That's great news!'

'She said I need to exorcise my demons. So please indulge me, Char.'

'Okay. Whatever you think best. I want you to get better.'

'I'm not sick!'

'Of course you aren't.'

'It's learning to put some things behind me ... that's all.'

I didn't ask Tom about his therapy. I guessed he would be going over my infidelity and experiencing moments of resurfacing anger. Opening up those old wounds would hurt, I knew that, and so I resolved to let him have his way and try and keep our home life calm for the moment.

Any sign of Isadora was systematically removed from the Manor's master bedroom in preparation for the redecoration, but when I suggested that we pull down the painting at the top of the stairs, Tom declined.

'It would look odd,' he said, 'to the remaining staff.'

'I need to come to the flat to pack up more of our personal things,' I said. 'I'd prefer to do that before Mrs Tanner leaves.'

'How about you come back after she's left? We'll have the decorators in by then and one of the housemaids can be here.

There'll be upheaval and it won't be much fun for you during that time anyway.'

'But it's only the master bedroom?' I said.

'No. I'm thinking we need to do more than that. This is our home now and we need to put our stamp on it. You can look at colour schemes this week, then we'll go back to the flat and sort things out properly.'

'Oh. I didn't expect that,' I said.

'You didn't tell me, is Tina happy to make the permanent move?'

'Yes. But she needs a week to sort out her own flat. Her roommate has found someone to take over her side of the tenancy, so at least she won't have to give a long notice.'

We settled down in the house for the weekend and walked around discussing what needed to change and what Tom was happy to leave. By the time we returned to London it was decided that the lounge, nursery, nanny's suite of rooms and the master were priorities. Anything else could be done once we were in permanently.

'I'll switch priority from the master to the nursery and Tina's rooms,' Tom said then he went off to discuss with Tina how she'd like her suite decorating.

I looked around the living room, and thought about all the changes we had discussed. Yes, the Manor would feel more like ours afterwards, and we would have gone a long way to exorcizing the ghost of Isadora. I told myself it would all work out and I was quite excited about the changes and managing the decorating. It was a big project and Tom was happy for me to make most of the decisions. It would be fun to do as well as being a challenge that would take my mind off things.

Chapter Thirty-Three

Back in London I kept myself busy packing up all of Melody's toys. The cot and a few essentials would remain for times when we came back with Tom.

'I don't have that much stuff,' she said. 'My friend's flat was furnished.'

I took a list of things she needed and Tom and I ordered them. The decorators had started in Tina's room by then and they were also fitting both the nursery and Tina's bedroom with built-in units. This would thoroughly modernize it for Melody and Tina's comfort. Plus, Tina had her own small kitchen, sitting room and en suite bathroom. Also, we'd arranged that she could use Isadora's London flat for the two days a week that she was off. I wanted to make sure she didn't miss out on anything. That way, she wouldn't want to leave us anytime soon.

As this was going to be a semi-permanent move and I wouldn't see that much of my friends in the future, I decided to make the effort to meet up with a few people before we left. I had been quite friendly with the wife of Tom's FEO. Her name was Valentina and she was Russian. Tom sometimes joked that

Valentina had been a 'mail-order bride' because her husband, Rufus, was a little intense and geeky and couldn't get a girl. I always thought this was a little cruel. Valentina was a lovely girl, the closest to a real friend I had among the other wives, and she was good for Rufus, who was ultimately very shy.

I hadn't seen Valentina much at all in the last year or so as I had stopped doing lunch when I met Ewan. And, when I took up my role as Tom's wife again, I had avoided being alone with any of the other wives and had only met them in groups, at parties and charity lunches, and of course the big fundraiser.

I took Melody with me to meet Valentina for lunch in a Covent Garden restaurant. This was the first time any of the wives had seen her, even though they had all sent expensive gifts. I hadn't felt up to receiving people straight after the birth, then I'd been busy with the fundraiser and after that we'd been dealing with Isadora's death. Melody was almost two months old and I hadn't introduced her to anyone.

'Charlotte! It's been too long,' Valentina said. She kissed me on the cheek and then bent over the pram to look at Melody.

'I know, Val. It's been a busy year for me.'

'Oh, she's so beautiful!' Valentina said. 'Is she a good baby?'

'Yes. Except when she's screaming the place down at two in the morning!'

'You look well,' Valentina said. 'I was so sorry to hear about Isadora. Sorry I couldn't make the funeral. I was visiting my family in Moscow.'

'It's all right, Rufus explained.'

We ordered lunch.

'I don't know if Tom told Rufus, but we are taking up residence in the Manor.'

'Really? I'm surprised to hear about the move. Rufus told me Tom hated the place.'

I frowned wondering why Rufus would even think that.

'No, he doesn't. He loves it there.'

Valentina smiled. 'I probably misunderstood. I sometimes get English meanings confused.'

I told her about the renovations.

'I wanted to see you and apologize for not being around a lot in the last year or so,' I continued. 'I won't be in London that much from now on. And I thought you'd like to see Melody.'

'Of course! And I'm delighted to see the baby. Look, I'm saying this as a friend ...'

'What is it Val?'

'There have been rumours. About you two. Look ... I don't want to pry, but I hope everything is okay?'

I blushed, wondering what Valentina had heard.

'What ... rumours?' I said.

'That you were ... One of the other wives says she saw you. In a coffee shop with some man.'

'*What?*'

'It was a while ago. Over eighteen months ago.' Valentina stopped talking and looked me in the eyes. 'I'm sorry. I can't help being direct. Rufus says I have no filter.'

'I don't know what to say ... She must have been mistaken.'

'When you stopped seeing everyone, it looked suspicious. You know?'

'Yes, I can see how these things can blow up.'

'Then you were pregnant.'

'What are you saying?'

Valentina studied Melody for a moment. The little girl was playing with her hands and kicking her legs in the pram beside the table.

'Rufus said Tom commented that Melody didn't look much like him. But I think she does.'

I was struck dumb by Valentina's words and couldn't find it in myself to admit or deny anything. Melody was Tom's, he'd made me prove it, but I couldn't tell Valentina that without revealing that Tom had doubts about me in the first place. I just frowned and smiled and shook my head in an *I don't know what you're saying but none of it is true* sort of way.

'This move sounds like a good idea. A fresh start,' she said. 'I have an idea, why don't we go into the office and surprise the men after lunch?'

'They'll be busy ...'

'Probably, but you get to show Melody off to everyone,' Valentina said. 'And they'll all see it.'

'See what?'

'She's only tiny but already you can see she has Carlisle eyes.'

I looked down at Melody and could see what Valentina meant. Although it hadn't been obvious initially, Melody did bear a strong resemblance to Tom. Her eyes, blue at birth, had turned dark and she was looking less like me as the days went on.

'So, what do you think?' Valentina said. 'We go to the office and stop all those wagging tongues?'

I flushed again but nodded.

Chapter Thirty-Four

I guess I should have known that someone had seen me. I didn't ask Valentina where or when this had occurred and perhaps it was even one of the innocent chats I had with Ewan in the beginning, when I had no reason to hide because I wasn't guilty of anything. Later, though I know we'd been careful, it was still possible that someone saw us together. Maybe I was recognized at The Savoy on our last meeting? Either way it didn't matter and if Valentina suspected the rumours were true, it didn't show. What came over instead was her wish to help me and to be a friend when I needed it.

I fought the desire to confide in her. But I just couldn't bring myself to tell anyone what Ewan had done to me. Plus, I was sure that Valentina would tell Rufus.

After lunch we caught a taxi over to the Carlisle Corp offices and we went up to Tom's office.

'Mr Carlisle is in a meeting at the moment,' the receptionist on the top floor said, 'but I'll get a message to him right away.'

Tom came out of the meeting ten minutes later.

'Darling,' he said kissing me. 'Oh, Valentina! How nice to see you!'

Tom kissed Valentina on the cheek.

'I'm so in love with your daughter,' she said. 'I insisted we bring her in to show everyone!'

'What a wonderful idea,' Tom said. 'Lisa, please get Mrs Carlisle and Mrs Gardener a drink. I'll take Melody to visit the other offices.'

'I'll come with you,' Valentina said.

Lisa took me into Tom's office and I sat with a coffee. I could have gone with them but this was Valentina's plan all along. I knew she would be pointing out the Carlisle eyes to anyone interested in listening, and if rumours had been bouncing around, no wonder Tom had been stressed about Melody's paternity. And I couldn't deny it was all my fault. Everything came back to the bad decision I'd made in getting involved with Ewan in the first place.

As I sat alone in the room, I worried about how everything had fallen apart in the last eighteen months. I wished I had never met Ewan Daniels. The man had made a good attempt at ruining our lives. If it wasn't for the fact that Tom wanted to put it behind us, we wouldn't be together and Melody would never have been born. I couldn't imagine life without Melody now.

The phone on Tom's desk rang. I looked at it and then over at the door. No one came in to answer the call so I stood and went outside. Tara and Lisa weren't at their desks.

I went back into Tom's office. The phone had stopped ringing. I shrugged and was about to sit down again when the phone started to ring once more. It rang twice before I answered it.

'Erm ... Mr Carlisle's office.'

'Is Mr Carlisle there please?'

'I'm sorry he isn't. Can I take a message?'

'Yes. Can you ask him to call the finance office – Bill Pattern.'

Bill Pattern hung up and then I realized I didn't have a pen or paper to leave Tom the note. The top of Tom's desk was neat and clear. As pristine as he liked things to be. There was a pen, but no notepad. I walked around the table and opened the top drawer.

I froze.

There was a bulky brown folder lying on top of Tom's notepad. On the front, in black marker, was written: DANIELS/ CHARLOTTE.

I went to open the folder and noticed that a photograph had slipped out. My fingers were trembling when I picked it up. It was a shot of Ewan Daniels walking towards me in Harrods.

I took a sharp breath. I opened the cover and saw a stack of other photographs, some of Ewan alone, some of him with me. Then I heard voices outside. Tom and Valentina were approaching. I stuffed the picture back into the file. Then closed the drawer and returned to my chair.

I had to process what I'd seen: Tom had *lied* to me about how much he knew about Ewan. This was not the first time I'd caught him out and it made me begin to question every-thing he'd said in the last few months.

I had to get a proper look at that file without him knowing. I took several breaths before the door opened and then I presented an outwardly calm expression as Tom and Valentina entered with Melody.

'Here's Mummy,' said Tom to Melody. 'She didn't like being swamped by so many people and got a bit cranky.'

I took Melody from him and cuddled her. Holding her made it easier for me to appear normal and to keep my emotions in check.

'She's tired,' I said. 'Oh, and someone called Bill Pattern called you. The phone kept ringing so I thought I had better answer it.'

'I'll call him back. Darling if you wait around, we can ride home together.'

I left him to make his call and went outside to say goodbye to Valentina.

'It's been observed by all,' she whispered as she hugged me. 'Happy life in your new home. Tom makes a great dad, doesn't he?'

I glanced back at Tom's open door. 'He sure does. You and Rufus will come and visit, won't you?'

'Of course! I'd love to see your renovations when they're all done.'

Valentina left and then Tom's new secretary Tara turned up. She admired Melody and I let her hold her. On the desk in front of Tara I saw the planner open and noted that Tom had a long meeting out of the office the next day – a lunch meeting.

I glanced back at Tom's office. Tom had told me he hired a detective to research Ewan after our affair. But if this was so, then how did he have a file with pictures of Ewan and me together? How was it even possible that someone had taken a photograph of our very first meeting? I had thought that Tom didn't know about my affair until I told him I was leaving. But had he known all along and just faked being angry and shocked? I couldn't imagine that Tom would be such a good actor, or that he'd ignore me having an affair if he'd known. Why would any husband do that? It didn't make sense.

Perhaps I was mistaken about the picture I'd seen? Maybe it was taken at a much later date than the first meeting as I'd thought. But I needed time to study it to be certain. I had to get back into Tom's office and get hold of that file.

Tom put down the phone and came out into Tara's office. 'I'm done for the day,' he said.

I went back into his office and changed Melody on one of the sofas. Tom stayed in the room and I had no opportunity to look again in the drawer. I tried to maintain a calm exterior but inside I was shaking.

As we left the office, I wished I had at least held on to the first photograph.

I was quiet in the car on the way back home. Tom chattered on about how everyone had fawned over Melody.

'I'm so proud of her,' he said. 'It's wonderful being a father.'

I smiled at him. He held my hand and kissed my fingers.

'You make me so happy, Char. Do you know Valentina said that Melody has my eyes? I hadn't noticed till then that they had changed from blue to brown.'

I forced a laugh, 'She's a Carlisle for sure.'

Valentina's plan had paid off. He was in such a good mood that he went into the kitchen and opened a bottle of champagne.

'I've been meaning to do this. We need to celebrate our new home, our baby and our future.'

I didn't feel like celebrating but went along with it and remained calm. Every scenario I could imagine was going through my head. What other information did the file contain? Did it reveal who Ewan Daniels really was? Why, if Tom had forgiven me, did he still have a file with photos and information about me and Ewan? It didn't make sense that he would torture himself like that.

We went to bed early. Tom cuddled up to me.

'I think we should have more children,' he murmured.

'Eventually,' I half-laughed. 'I'm just recovering from this one!'

'I know but they say it's best to have them together.'

'Who says?'

'Everyone.'

Melody was on my mind as I drifted off to sleep. I experienced a confusing anxiety whenever I thought about her. If nothing else my daughter had to always be safe, and she was, so why was I so afraid for her all of a sudden?

Chapter Thirty-Five

'Hello ... Tina?'

'Charlotte? Is everything all right?'

'Yes. Look, I know you're busy sorting your move, but do you have a few hours today? I'd like to surprise Tom and meet him for lunch.'

'What a lovely idea!' Tina said. 'Of course I can. I'm almost done anyway and could do with a change of scene.'

I was dressed up when Tina arrived. I had made a real effort because if it all went wrong, Tom at least would believe that I had come to surprise him.

'Thanks for doing this. We could do with some "us time" at the moment.'

'I know,' Tina said. 'And it's important that you do.'

I kissed Melody and then left the apartment.

Outside on the street I took a deep shuddering breath. I'd been holding myself in check since the day before, and it was difficult to sustain. I glanced up and down the street, worried that Tom still had someone spying on me. I began to experience that paranoia again. Instead of scolding myself about it I accepted that I did have every right to feel like this.

There was no one loitering outside though, so I headed off to the tube station and made my way across London to Tom's office.

When I arrived, I went into a coffee shop opposite the office to avoid being seen by the doorman and I bought myself a latte. Then I watched the entrance. At 11.45 a.m., Stefan pulled the limo up in front of the building and Tom came out, briefcase in hand and got in. The limo drove off. After that I finished my coffee and strolled across to Carlisle Corp.

'Hello Mrs C,' said the doorman. 'Mr C left a few minutes ago.'

'Really? Oh, never mind, I'll find out how long he's going to be from Tara and perhaps wait for his return.'

Upstairs Tara explained Tom was at a lunch meeting.

'He'll probably be gone all afternoon,' she said.

'What a shame!' I said. 'I wanted to surprise him.'

I turned and was about to leave, then I pretended to get an idea.

'Do you have a pen? Paper?'

Tara looked at me.

'I'll leave him a nice note on his desk. At least he'll know I was thinking about him. I should have asked what his plans were but thought he'd guess and it would ruin my surprise.'

'Sure.'

Tara gave me the pen and paper and then I walked into Tom's office and closed the door behind me. Once inside I took a breath and then hurried over to Tom's desk. I sat on his chair. Breathed again, and opened the top drawer.

The folder was gone.

I closed the drawer and then I searched the next one and the next. The folder was nowhere to be found.

'Damn it!'

My eyes fell on the filing cabinet by the door. The file I had seen would be the sort you hang inside one of those cabinets. He had to be keeping it there. I was just about to leave the desk and go and check the filing cabinet, when Tara knocked and came into the office.

'Can I get you anything?' she asked.

I stared at the blank paper.

'A coffee would be nice. I'm just thinking what to say. Trying to be romantic,' I said smiling.

Tara smiled back. 'Is Mr Carlisle the romantic sort?'

'Oh yes. Very.'

'That's nice,' Tara said.

Tara appeared to be on the verge of asking more about Tom.

'He's pretty soppy with me, actually,' I said, watching her reaction.

I don't know what I expected to see there. Jealousy perhaps? Tom is a very attractive man and I could see a young PA possibly having designs on him. But Tara gave no indication that she had any feelings for Tom other than a vague curiosity.

'That's so nice to hear,' she said. 'Obviously, we only see one side of Mr Carlisle here.'

'What's he like at work?' I asked.

'Very ... professional,' Tara said.

'Maybe it would be better if I left him a note on his computer screen. So that when he opens it ...'

'What a great idea! I'll log you in.'

Tara switched on Tom's computer and logged into it with Tom's name and password. I noted the password: MELDORA.

'He changed it after your baby was born,' Tara said. 'I thought it was sweet. I have to have access, so he told me what it was.'

'Oh yes. Of course,' I said.

Tara left to go and fetch me coffee. I browsed Tom's computer, doing a search on 'E Daniels', but the folder I'd seen on the network previously was no longer there. I searched wider, looking just for 'EWAN'. I typed in 'DAN' to see what came up and was rewarded with a Word file called 'Daniel Evans'. The name was similar, but it could have no bearing on Ewan Daniels. Even so, I had an odd premonition that it was connected.

I stared at the screen.

I didn't want to open the folder up on Tom's computer as it would show on Word's history.

I waited for Tara to bring me in the coffee. Once she'd gone, I copied the file over to a pen stick I'd brought just in case. Then I searched for any other files of the same name, but there weren't any. I took the pen stick out of the computer and put it in my jacket pocket.

I penned a note for Tom on the piece of paper and made it very gushing and a little provocative. Then I stood up and glanced through the glass panel of the door to see Tara engrossed in her computer. With Tara occupied, I tried the filing cabinet. The drawers were locked and the key wasn't anywhere obvious. I wondered how I could ask Tara for it without raising questions and decided I couldn't think of a reasonable excuse. I returned to Tom's desk and was about to shut the computer back down when it occurred to me to check his emails.

I opened up the business mail server and searched for Daniels, Daniel, Ewan and Evans. Nothing came up. I cleared the search history and then shut the computer down.

Tara came in again then.

'I decided to just write the note in the end,' I said. 'I shut the computer down. If I were you, I wouldn't mention you shared the password. Although I'm his wife he might not like it. I'd hate to see you get into trouble.'

Tara blushed, 'I didn't think he'd mind because it's you!'

'I know. And probably he wouldn't. But just in case.'

I placed the note on Tom's desk, adding a flurry of kisses. Then I picked up my handbag and left.

'Thank you so much for the coffee and all your help,' I said to Tara.

Standing waiting for the lift, my mind was racing over what might be on the computer file. There was a *ting* and the lift doors opened.

I was face to face with Tom.

'What are you doing here?' he asked.

'I came to surprise you,' I said, relieved that I had thought my story through. 'I thought we'd have lunch together, but Tara told me you were in a meeting.'

'Well, darling, you're in luck. My meeting cancelled when I was halfway there.'

Tom called Stefan on his mobile and the driver returned.

*

He took me to a seafood restaurant in Canary Wharf.

'I've been meaning to bring you here,' Tom said. 'But I don't suppose we will have much opportunity in the future. Although there are some lovely restaurants in Surrey and I'm sure we'll work our way through them all.'

Tom ordered Chablis Premier Cru and oysters. The bottle came perfectly chilled at 10.5 degrees, and the oysters were fragrant and fresh.

'You haven't read my note,' I said. 'These oysters might be quite apt.'

'Yes?' he leaned into the table, glass in one hand and smiled at me in a flirty way.

'You'll have to wait and see when you get back to the office,' I said.

Tom laughed. 'I was planning on playing truant after this.'

Tom was an incredibly handsome man and it was impossible not to respond with a similar expression when he smiled at me this way. I was torn between wanting to know what was in the file and wanting to just forget all about it. Perhaps I should have taken the pen stick and thrown it into the nearest bin. I knew I probably should have just walked away and stopped worrying – but I couldn't. Despite the fact that this was constantly ruining my peace of mind, I had to know who Ewan Daniels really was and what Tom knew about him.

The thought occurred to me that it probably didn't matter why Tom had suspected me. In the end he had been right. I had betrayed him. Reflecting on my guilt made it easier for me to kiss and canoodle with him. I even made myself forget about the pen stick still in my pocket. Not thinking was the only solution sometimes. It made a lot of things more palatable. After all I didn't want to jump in without knowing what was really going on. Once I knew what was in that file, I could talk to Tom about it. Part of me hoped, for the sake of peace, that Tom would have a perfectly reasonable explanation.

Chapter Thirty-Six

We spent a lovely day and evening together because I was able to stall my mind and stop overanalysing everything. I had felt calm, but the next day I woke with the pen stick, and its contents, on my mind.

I was agitated as I fed Melody while he took his time getting ready. He wasn't in a hurry that day – which was typical – and so I had to hide my eagerness when he finally put his suit jacket on, kissed Melody and then me, and said goodbye.

As soon as he left, I brought Melody into the office and switched on the computer.

I had left the pen stick in my jacket pocket and so, while the computer warmed up, I collected it. Part of me expected it to be gone from my pocket, and I felt a rush of fear as I searched for it. But it was there: Tom didn't have any reason to suspect I had been in his work computer after all.

I plugged the pen stick in and opened the Daniel Evans document. I hesitated for a moment before double-clicking the curser with a trembling hand. It was a Word document, but embedded in it were several pictures of Ewan. They looked like professional headshots. The filename on each of them held the name Daniel Evans. I looked at the pictures for a long time, recognizing the expressions he wore. It was Ewan, though now I knew his real name.

There was nothing else on the Word document and all I could conclude was that Tom had found out who Ewan really was, but had chosen not to tell me.

I closed the file down and deleted the Word history, but stared at the screen for a long time. Then I opened up Tom's personal email handler.

There was a password on it. I tried a few obvious ones and then remembered MELDORA. I typed it in, and Tom's email dashboard opened on the screen. I found myself mentally thanking Tara for her trusting nature. She had no idea that she had given me access to more than Tom's work computer.

Tom's personal email was full of spam. I kept glancing out of the window, checking that I was alone, as I waded through a few emails then marked them back unread before searching under the name 'Daniel'.

I found one email in the deleted box. It was from Daniel Evans to Tom.

My heart was in my mouth as I opened the file.

Mr Carlisle,

Your wife is sweet. She went to dinner with me in Reykjavik, but she was naturally cautious. I ordered champagne as you suggested. She did not flirt with me and it was all very proper.

I think you have nothing to worry about.
Take my advice and don't pursue this further.
Daniel Evans

Nausea rose in my throat: Tom had pictures of my first meeting
with Ewan because he'd set it up. I thought I was going to
vomit with revulsion.

'Oh God!' I said.

Melody started to cry as though she were sensing my
distress. I took a deep breath, calming myself for Melody's
sake and I cooed and soothed her until she was happy again.

I didn't have to be a genius to recognize that the email
was evidence that Tom had somehow *engaged* Daniel Evans
to try to seduce me.

I'd been set up and played all right – not just by Daniel
Evans but by my husband as well.

I didn't know what to do. My instinct was to take Melody
and leave Tom immediately, but I had to plan such a move
carefully for my daughter's sake. I didn't have anywhere to go
for one thing. And then I remembered Isadora's flat. I could go
there. I shook my head. No. If I left, that would be the obvious
place for Tom to look for us. I'd have to think of somewhere else.

I read the email over and over again.

What did this prove? That Tom knew Daniel and that he
persuaded him to try his luck with me. But what happened
afterwards?

No matter what happens, I love you Charlotte … I have
loads to tell you.

I forwarded the email to myself, then deleted the trail.

I logged off Tom's email and opened my own. Mine was permanently logged in but I changed my password and settings. It wasn't likely that Tom would check on my emails, but just in case, I wanted to make sure he didn't find this one.

I copied the email address into a new email and stared at it. What could I say to the man who had been hired to set me up?

I put 'Why?' in the subject line and then I quickly typed in the email body: 'How much did he pay you to do what you did to me?'

I signed it 'Charlotte' and pressed send before I could change my mind.

I picked up Melody and hugged her to me. She protested sleepily and so I returned her to her cot and let her sleep. I was sure that was the best thing because I knew she could sense my continuing distress. Then I went into the kitchen to make a drink, but I kept worrying about the email. Would he reply? And if so, what would he say? Then it occurred to me that Daniel Evans might just forward the email onto Tom. I began to regret my impulsive actions. How would Tom react if he learnt I knew the truth?

Well, there would be one hell of an argument wouldn't there? But this time it would be me yelling at him.

I was growing angrier as the day went on. I think I was bolstering myself from a possible onslaught of accusations. If Daniel Evans did contact him, he'd know I'd somehow discovered his secret and he'd probably be preparing to turn it all back on me. But I wasn't going to let him.

I was ready for the fight when Tom came home, but as he walked into the kitchen, I knew Daniel hadn't contacted him because Tom was in a very good mood.

'What a lovely note you left me!' he said. 'It made me smile all day. And darling I love and desire you too. You know that.'

My shoulders were stiff from holding myself still as I forced myself to appear calm and normal – something I was becoming very good at. Fortunately, he was tired and not too demanding of my company that night. He also didn't make any moves to have sex with me, which I was very glad of. I didn't want any intimacy with him. Not until I got to the bottom of what he'd done or how he'd lied to me. I was determined to find a way. It just meant biding my time.

Chapter Thirty-Seven

The next morning there was an unread message in my inbox. It was from Daniel Evans's email address and it asked who I was.

'Is that Daniel Evans? AKA Ewan Daniels?' I replied. 'Because if it is, you know exactly who I am, and I demand you tell me why you did this to me?'

A few moments later I received an email with a phone number. I stared at it, reading it over and over. It wasn't Ewan's number – I'd committed that one to memory and couldn't forget it no matter how hard I tried. I'd even deleted it from my phone as an effort to erase it from my mind.

I keyed in 141 to block my own number, just in case this wasn't who I thought it was, then I dialled the number. My heart was in my mouth as it started to ring.

'Hello?' I said.

'Hi, I'm Daniel's sister, Becki. What does your email mean?'

'Is he too scared to talk to me?' I said.

'He doesn't know I'm talking to you.'

'I don't understand. You're his sister? You haven't told him I emailed?'

'Ewan Daniels was a professional name Daniel used some-times. Look, I'm reaching out to you because ... my brother is missing.'

I paused before asking, 'How long has he been missing?'

'Eighteen months,' she said.

'When did you last see him?' I said.

It turned out Daniel had been with Becki the night before we were supposed to start our lives together.

'When did *you* last see him?' she asked me.

'I spoke to him that night. Then nothing since.'

'I think I know who you are,' she said. 'Daniel told me about you.'

'Will you meet me?' I asked. 'I don't want to talk on the phone. I've taken a risk already by calling you.'

Becki went quiet for a moment, then she said, 'All right.'

I arranged to meet her the next day because she wasn't working. I hadn't told her anything about my relationship with her brother, but I hadn't denied her suspicions that I was someone Daniel had spoken to her about.

The rest of that day I was nervous and uneasy. So many questions ran through my head. Not least the one major concern I still had – what if Tom was still having me moni-tored? He might already know I'd spoken to Daniel's sister. I worried that I may still be being watched or followed.

The landline rang and I jumped. I was in the kitchen and so I picked up the wireless phone that stood in the corner of one of my worktops nearest the range cooker.

'Mrs Carlisle? It's Kitchen Supremacy here. We have had

a delay on your units. I'm afraid the first batch that arrived was damaged so had to be returned.'

'Oh. Right. That's okay,' I said not really listening.

'Obviously, the work won't be finished in time for your nanny to move into her suite.'

'When will it be done?' I asked.

There was a pen and Post-it pad near the phone. Instead of writing with the biro I started to tap it on the worksurface. When would this call end?

'It'll be a week before we'll get the replacements. Fitting time should take no more than two days. We'll have all of the electrics rewired in advance. The tiles of course can't be done until the kitchen is in. That'll take another day. Look to be in and complete by the end of the month.'

'So ten to fourteen days? I'll talk to my nanny and my husband. Just do what you can to speed it up.'

I hung up and sent Tom a text about the units and the delay. 'What should we do?' he replied. 'Tina has to be out of her place by the end of the week, doesn't she?'

'I'll move her into your mother's flat until it's finished,' I said.

I decided that the delay played into my hands. It was an unexpected reprieve. I didn't want to find myself in the Manor alone and away from everyone This gave me time also to find out what had happened to Daniel Evans. I had to know the answer to this question now that I knew he had disappeared. When I had all of this information I could decide what to do about my relationship with Tom.

I rang Tina to explain the delay. Then I arranged for her to watch Melody while I went out to meet Becki.

'I'll give you a set of keys for the other flat, and we'll rear-range your removals to go there initially and then onto Surrey when everything is ready.'

'That's fine. These things never go to plan,' she said, ever practical and matter of fact. 'Where are you off to tomorrow then?'

'Oh, just seeing a girlfriend for lunch as this may be the last time.'

As always Tina approved of me having some free time.

'Well you enjoy yourself and don't rush back,' she said.

Chapter Thirty-Eight

I experienced a range of emotions as I walked into the coffee shop. The last time I was there, I'd been waiting for Ewan. Being there again brought me a great deal of anxiety that made me want to leave and never return. Even so, I forced myself forward and into the busy café.

There was a young woman sitting at the table I'd suggested to Becki, by the window. I didn't tell her that it had been the one I always shared with her brother.

'Becki?' I said but I knew already it was her. 'I'm Charlotte.'

We shook hands and I sat down and studied her face. It was difficult to not see Daniel in her. Becki was a brunette, but otherwise they were very alike.

I had printed off one of the pictures of Daniel Evans and I placed it on the table in front of her.

'Is this your brother?'

'Yes,' Becki said.

'Tell me about him,' I said.

She studied me for a moment, and I suspected all that she wanted to do was insist on knowing who I was and how I'd known Daniel. Then she blinked, as though she'd made some internal decision to play nice.

'He is an actor and model,' she said. 'That's one of his professional shots ... How do you know him?'

'Daniel came into my life almost two years ago. He told me his name was Ewan Daniels.'

Becki frowned. 'He was using that name. For a job he said.'

'A job?'

'An acting role. He told me it was going to be his most challenging role ever.'

'Who hired him?'

'I've no idea.'

I sat back, deflated. Somehow her words confirmed that Daniel was paid to seduce me. As if I didn't already know that anyway. It was awful. The feeling of betrayal I'd felt when he had abandoned me resurged and I experienced a crushing depression.

'Tell me more,' I said.

'I don't *know* much, but I've deduced quite a few things during my search for him.'

'Such as?'

'That week, Daniel rang me early on Saturday morning to ask a favour. He said the keys to the new flat were available, but he wouldn't be home until the Sunday evening because the shoot he was on had run over. He asked me to let his removals guys in on Sunday morning.

'I said I couldn't wait to see his new place and he told me then this wasn't a permanent move. "I have the lease for six months and then I'll be buying somewhere again."

'I asked him how he could afford it. He said he'd been busy the last five months and that the insurance company had finally paid out on his wife's death.'

'So it was true? He was widowed,' I said.

Becki nodded. 'Daniel wasn't very security conscious and he had all of his passwords saved on his laptop. The payout from the insurance was a million pounds. I saw it in his bank account.'

Becki revealed she had collected the keys from the letting agent and met the removals company the next day.

'I had the movers put up his bed and I found the bedding box and made it for him. I even cleaned the kitchen. I didn't want him to have to worry when he arrived home. When he did arrive, he was carrying a large bunch of flowers and a bottle of champagne, which he put in the fridge.

'Then he laughed at me. "You cleaned in here, didn't you?" he asked. I said, "Of course I did! I couldn't have my little brother living anywhere dirty."

'We went into the living room. Daniel moved the sofas around to where he wanted them and pushed back a stack of boxes. He mentioned that he didn't have time to unpack before tomorrow morning, and so it would all have to do. When I asked him what was happening tomorrow, he just laughed. I asked if he had a girlfriend and he messed around a bit, but then admitted that he'd met a "wonderful woman" and she was the best thing that had happened to him. He said he was in love.'

My cheeks flushed on hearing this. Becky didn't notice.

'I was surprised. I didn't think he wanted to have a

relationship again after all he'd been through. But I was really pleased for him as well. Then he said, "Anyway, this place is just a stop gap. She deserves better."

'Dan promised that I'd meet her in the next few days. Then he opened a bottle of wine and we sat down in his new lounge to celebrate. When he received a text a few minutes later, his whole face lit up. I'd never seen him so happy. I guess that must have been his girl and Dan told me all was well for the next day. He then said he had planned to meet her at Harrods in the morning and he'd be bringing her straight to this apartment.

'I was so pleased for him,' Becki continued. 'We drank wine and he told me bits and pieces about how he met her at Harrods and that she was married. I queried him on this. I'm a bit of a prude, I suppose, but it didn't seem right that he was having an affair with another man's wife, no matter how he felt about her. "Believe me, he really doesn't deserve her," he said.

'We drank our wine and then Daniel received a phone call. I think I heard a woman's voice on the other end, and so I assumed it was this woman. Then he went into the kitchen to talk in private.'

'What happened then,' I asked.

'Daniel was flustered when he came back in the room,' Becki said. 'I asked what was wrong, but he brushed off my questions and said he had to leave. I knew there was something he wasn't telling me but refused to talk about it. He promised he'd tell me everything the next day. When he didn't phone, I thought it was because he was busy with his new girl. Then after a few days I rang him, but he didn't answer. I had a spare set of keys still and so I went over to the flat. I found it just as he'd left it. Our two empty wine glasses were still on his kitchen worktop next to his mobile phone. That's when I went to the police.'

'What did they say?' I asked.

'They weren't very helpful at first. They said he had to be missing for twenty-four hours; I had to insist they took it seriously. By then I hadn't seen him for several days. But I didn't have anything I could tell them. Dan never told me his lover's name, but ... it's you, isn't it?'

I crumpled in my seat, tears filling my eyes.

'If he had given me your name, I'd have tried to find you,' Becki said. 'But he was very reluctant to tell me much after I reacted about the affair. I wish I'd been more open-minded.'

'He was supposed to meet me and bring me to the new flat, but he never showed,' I said.

'And the email you sent? You thought he'd played you. But why wait so long to email him and ask?'

I didn't know what to say without revealing that somehow I believed Tom had hired Daniel.

'I didn't have his email address until recently. We always texted or spoke on the phone. Besides I only just learnt his real name.'

'What else?' Becki said astutely.

'I don't know. I'm thinking it through. Daniel's phone was disconnected the day he disappeared. I rang it and it was cut off. I thought it was deliberate because he got a kick out of destroying my life.'

'No,' Becki said. 'Dan would never do that. Besides, his phone wasn't disconnected. It's still working. It was the number I gave you. When I noticed he'd left it behind in his flat, I thought he must have been back at some point, even though he hadn't stayed the night. I kept paying the contract, just in case someone rang who could help me find him.'

'That's not the number I had ... he must have had *two* phones,' I said.

She was quiet and thoughtful for a moment. I think she was processing everything and didn't know what to respond.

'Maybe he had a third one?' I said. 'And he's hiding from us both.'

'I'd probably think that, except there is still all this money in his bank account. He hasn't touched it in the last eighteen months, or his credit cards. Remember I have access to his account. If he voluntarily disappeared, he couldn't live on fresh air.'

'I agree,' I said. My heart sank. Was Daniel dead? And if so, how had he died?

'Did you try the hospitals?' I asked.

'Yes. No one was brought in fitting his description. Alive or ... dead.'

'I loved him. You've no idea how awful it was. Thinking he'd abandoned me.'

And then there was the Facebook page about the catfish that Tom had shown me. I didn't mention this to Becki then. I intended to search it out again and perhaps send her the link at a later date. But it seemed unlikely that this was Daniel these women were talking about – probably an unpleasant coincidence that had played into Tom's hands when he wanted to poison my memory of Daniel.

Becki was quiet and I felt bad because she must be hurting too. Her brother was missing and from her description of him he appeared to be the caring man I once thought he was.

'Did Daniel ever mention trips away to you?' I asked breaking the silence.

'He was always going somewhere ...'

'Reykjavik? Milan?'

'He went to Milan a lot. Lots of modelling work there I think.'

I told her about how we'd met and all that followed afterwards. Including our dinner in Reykjavik and the trip I'd taken to Milan with him.

'He went out every day looking like a businessman. You see, despite what you've told me I'm still trying to reconcile the lies with the truth.'

'He hadn't told me about any of this. I just don't know what to say.'

'You have access to his emails,' I said. 'Can I search through them?'

'I've searched for clues but haven't found anything. But I don't see any harm in you looking. His laptop is at my place. I had to get removals into his new flat when the lease was up, and he didn't show. I put his stuff back in storage, but not his personal things like phone and computer. I have been checking them both almost every day in the hope I'd find something out.'

'Is there anything else you can tell me?' I said.

'You were married when you guys met, right?'

I nodded. I didn't tell her I was still with Tom.

'I remember an odd comment Dan made. It was about six months before he vanished. He said some men didn't realize when they had a good thing. I didn't ask him to explain because I thought he was referring to some rich guy we saw getting out of a black limo. I thought it was just a throwaway comment.'

'Where was that?'

'Here. At this coffee shop actually. Dan was looking out the window and then we saw this limo. A man got out and he had a beautiful woman with him. You know the sort. Blonde, skinny.'

'Yes. I do.'

'I think he was talking about you, even then.'

'We never met before that day in Harrods,' I said.

'No? But did you come in this coffee shop before then?'

'A few times. It's close. I like to shop here.'

'Maybe you didn't know him, but it's possible he knew you. Or had seen you here. This place was one of his haunts,' Becki said.

I wondered if this was any different to being spied on by Tom's private detectives, and decided it was. Had Daniel seen me before Tom hired him? And if so, was this a contributing factor as to why he took the job? Without Daniel to explain, I knew I may never know the answer.

Chapter Thirty-Nine

I had to leave Becki because I wanted to be back in time for Tom. I didn't want him to know Tina had been with Melody all day as it would lead to all sorts of questions.

I agreed to meet Becki the next day to check out Daniel's computer.

My head was reeling as I caught the tube home and rushed back to the flat.

'Melody is bathed and ready for bed after her last feed and change,' Tina said. 'Are you okay? You seem ... upset.'

'I'm fine,' I said. 'The tube was packed and that always has me flustered. You go now. Oh, and the removal company is all arranged for tomorrow.'

Tina left and I was alone with my thoughts. Something kept nagging in the back of my mind. I recalled a particular day a couple of years ago when I had been to Harrods with Tom to meet Isadora. I wasn't sure if my mind was just making connections where there weren't any. But I wondered if it was Tom and me that Becki had seen arriving in a black limo. I was sure that a few days after that trip to the store I'd met Daniel – as Ewan – for the first time. I tried to recall if

I'd ever noticed him before then, perhaps in the coffee shop.

With only my memory to rely on I wasn't convinced that the picture I'd seen in Tom's office was of that first meeting.

What played through my head over and over was how Daniel had told his sister he was in love with me. That he *had* lost a wife, and that the flat – our potential new home – was all genuine and had happened. I was sure too that Daniel had been originally engaged to tempt me. It was probably a test: Tom had shown he was capable of that sort of thing.

I hadn't seen Daniel after Reykjavik for over a month. Then he appeared again as I returned the purple satin sheets that had upset Tom so much. At least, with Tom's revelations about Isadora, I understood why that was now. I put my hand to my cheek with the memory. He had never hit me before or since and there was no reason I could think of that would suggest he'd do it again. Even so, sick fear came into my stomach at the memory of Tom's enraged expression. I pushed the thought away and thought back to Daniel Evans.

He had told Tom I was faithful, but this didn't explain why I saw Daniel at Harrods again. At that time, Tom knew I was pregnant, and he was ecstatic. Why would he put Daniel under my nose when my pregnancy would ensure that I wouldn't stray?

If my memory served me, Daniel had been surprised to see me again. The meeting must have been accidental. I looked back over every detail of my relationship with him, remembering that it was a couple more months before he randomly texted to see how I was. That was after the miscarriage and I was annoyed with Isadora. Was that a coincidence? Or had it been planned to test me once more?

But none of that mattered: Daniel had been planning to start a new life with me. That much I knew from Becki. The pain of his failure to meet me was still raw, even after all those months. Knowing he had planned to be there eased it a little, making me feel I wasn't foolish after all: he had loved me.

But what had happened to him that prevented our meeting? Where was Daniel now?

I heard the keypad at the front door beep and a minute later Tom was in the corridor. He placed his briefcase by the door as usual and then he came into the kitchen where I was prepping dinner.

Melody was in her bouncy chair where I could watch her. She was growing rapidly and beginning to show signs of having a personality. As Tom came in she kicked her legs and waved her arms.

'Daddy's home!' he said, and he kneeled down before her. I watched him smiling and chatting to her – the normal behaviour of a loving father. I didn't find it uplifting. There was a knot in my stomach, and I couldn't stop thinking of Daniel. *Missing.*

The only connection with him I could think of was the man who shared my bed every night and now looked lovingly at our baby. For surely Tom knew something.

Then I remembered: Tom hadn't been home the night before I had planned to leave him. He had said he'd gone to see Isadora. It never occurred to me to ask her if this was true. Without her confirmation Tom had no alibi. The thought struck a dark terror in my heart. I'd never know for certain, but what if Tom had met with Daniel that night?

Chapter Forty

The investigation into Daniel's life continued the next day when I travelled with Melody to Becki's apartment. She lived over in Hammersmith, and I thought about the time I spent with Daniel at his flat during our affair. The taxi passed the building and I discovered that Becki didn't live far from there.

Becki opened the door, and I went inside carrying Melody in the carry car seat.

'You've had a baby?'

'When Ewan ... Daniel ... didn't show, my husband came and found me.'

Becki took this in. I felt the need to explain.

'I thought ... Daniel had abandoned me. That he'd deliberately ruined my life. You've got to understand, I was distraught. I had nowhere to go. I guess I just went back to what felt safe.'

'I understand. This way,' Becki said.

I followed her through the apartment and into a small living room. The apartment was clean but not salubriously decorated like mine was.

I saw a laptop on the coffee table. I put Melody's carrier down and took a seat in the chair next to it.

'It's already open in his emails. What you looking for?'

I took a deep breath, 'Emails from my husband engaging Daniel to seduce me.'

'*What?*'

Becki sat down on the sofa opposite.

'That's how I found his email address. I found an email in Tom's deleted box. It was from Daniel saying he'd had dinner with me in Reykjavik but nothing happened and so he should leave well alone.'

'What kind of man tries to entrap his wife like that?'

I met her eyes. Then shook my head. 'I need the whole facts. One email isn't enough to prove anything.'

'What will you do if you find the evidence?'

'Leave him,' I said.

Becki watched me as I began to search Daniel's emails. I searched first for Tom's email and it showed up as a contact. There were no other emails though.

'There's no other communication to Tom. But I'm going to do another search for my name.'

I did and three emails came up with my name in the subject line.

I opened the first one and found an introductory letter from a private detective called Jake Abbott. Abbott was based in Soho and it was a contract to engage Daniel's services. He was to contrive a meeting with me. They would tell him when and where. The contract also had an NDA attached for Daniel to sign.

'What's that mean?' asked Becki.

'Non-disclosure Agreement. Whatever happened between

him and me, and during his dealings with them, he couldn't discuss it with anyone. They'd sue if he did.'

The email quite clearly outlined that Daniel was to 'befriend' me and see if it led to 'more'.

The second email was a reply from Daniel accepting the job. He didn't ask many questions but said that he wanted to 'discuss' some of the terms.

The third email confirmed a payment had been sent to Daniel's bank. It also had the details of my trip to Reykjavik. Including where I was staying and that Tom wouldn't be there the first two days.

'That's your evidence,' Becki said.

'It's not enough,' I said. 'There was no mention that Tom was directly involved. This third-party company acted as a buffer. They would no doubt be working under their own NDA with Tom to keep it secret.'

'But surely the email you found previously does link him,' Becki said.

'Not if Tom didn't reply. He could have been set up.'

'Maybe you just don't want to accept that he's behind this,' Becki said.

'Believe me, I do. Things have been so wrong. All in ways I couldn't put my finger on. Daniel not showing up has never sat right with me. I *knew* him, Becki. Yes, maybe not enough because he *had* lied to me for certain. The last conversation we had in person he said something that jarred with me, and I've replayed it over and over in my head ever since. He said no matter what happened he really loved me. He also said he had lots to tell me, but at the time I'd thought it all ordinary stuff about the flat or our plans for the future. I didn't think it was some huge conspiracy that had been going on behind my back. I sort of forgot this, or thought it was part of the deceit. Especially when Tom showed me a Facebook page.'

I told her about CATFISHED.

'I know Dan wouldn't have hurt you deliberately. That has to be a coincidence. It couldn't be him.'

'I want to believe that too. But I need proof. I studied as a lawyer and I understand the law well enough to know that we don't have enough evidence that he was directly involved based on one email from Daniel. Someone could have been setting Tom up. That's how his people will play it.'

'You said, "protect" yourself. Are you worried about your safety?'

I didn't say anything but my cheeks burned.

'I'll take that as a "yes",' she said.

'This is a dead end at the moment,' I said. 'Let's flag these emails though. It will make them easier to find for the future. I think I have a lot more investigating to do.'

We went through Daniel's history and found that he had at some point googled the detective agency that had contacted him. From the search I learnt a bit about Jake Abbott, the main proprietor. He was a former police officer, as these people often are, and he had a team of people working for him. There were no faces of his crew online. I suspected this was because he wanted to keep their identities secret. There was, however, a short video of Abbott talking to camera and I was sure I recognized his voice.

'He could be the man Tom was talking to at the fundraiser,' I said.

'Look, it seems to me you already have enough evidence to doubt your husband. He's admitted to having you followed and to trying to set you up. Put that together with what we have.'

'It's my word against his. He'll deny it. And these guys aren't going to tell the truth, are they? You were right earlier. It is entrapment.'

'Show me that Facebook page,' Becki said.

I typed in the page name. A few similar pages with CATFISH came up, but not the one that Tom had shown me.

'It's not here,' I said.

'Where did Tom show it you?'

'On his home desktop,' I explained.

'And you haven't looked for it since?'

'No. I didn't want to be reminded.'

'Charlotte ... is it possible that Tom showed you a fake Facebook page?'

'Fake? But how could he manage that?'

'It's not as hard as you think. Hackers clone sites all the time to make people put in passwords and personal data. Tom has enough money to pay someone to design a page like that.'

I let this idea sink in. Was it possible?

I glanced at my watch.

'I have to go. I need to be home before Tom,' I said.

'You're going *back* there?'

'I have to. He can't suspect until I'm in a position to leave.'

I stood up.

'You don't know me,' she said, 'but if you need to, you

and your little girl can come here. Daniel would want me to help you.'

Becki hugged me and I hugged her back. She was the only thing I had to connect me with Daniel and, although I barely knew her, I was already sure I could trust her. For all my brave words about leaving Tom when I had enough evidence, I wasn't sure I still had the strength.

As I got into a black cab outside I looked down at my beautiful baby calmly playing with her booteed feet. My mind was full of 'what ifs': what if Daniel Evans was dead?

Chapter Forty-One

I made it home just in time. The rush-hour traffic had almost foiled my taxi driver and he'd had to take several detours. Hurrying into the apartment, I turned lights on and quickly removed Melody's outdoor clothing. Then I ran her a bath. When Tom came in I had wrapped her in a towel and was getting her ready for bed.

'You all right, darling?' Tom asked.

'Sure. Melody was sick on herself,' I lied. 'No chance to start dinner.'

'I'll get us a takeaway then,' Tom said.

I sighed as he went off to phone our local Chinese for a delivery. I carried Melody into the kitchen once she was ready for bed, and warmed up a bottle for her.

'Let me do that,' Tom said.

He took her from me and settled down in the living room with her and the bottle. It was hard for me to let her go. I pulled out some plates for the food and laid the table.

Tom winded Melody like an expert, and she vomited a little on his suit trousers.

'She *is* a bit sickly tonight,' he said.

I cleaned her up and then, as the doorbell rang with the food order, I put Melody to bed.

Tom answered the door and brought in the takeaway bag, placing it on the dining table. My nerves jangled. I ran my palms down my jeans to remove the clammy sweat I felt there.

We sat in our usual seats and I began to dish out the food.

'How's the house plans going?' he asked.

'Haven't heard anything from the kitchen company, but Tina has moved into your mother's flat today.'

'Oh good,' said Tom.

'In fact, she's coming tomorrow to look after Melody while I do some shopping.'

'Good,' said Tom.

'What are your plans tomorrow?' I asked trying to be casual. I wondered if I could contrive another visit to his offices. I had to search that filing cabinet. It was the only place I could think of that might contain the file.

'No meetings tomorrow. But lots to do.'

I had no appetite, but I forced myself to eat. Tom demolished a portion of chicken in black bean sauce and a whole pack of egg fried rice. I picked at some crispy seaweed and some sweet and sour chicken.

Melody began to cry, and I remembered I hadn't given her the colic drops.

'I'll see to her,' Tom said.

He went away and I cleared the table, putting the leftovers in the fridge. A few minutes later the baby monitor went silent. I shook it and listened, hoping it would come back to life, but nothing happened.

My heart thudded in my chest and I ran from the kitchen and down the corridor to Melody's room. I burst into the room and found Tom sitting in the rocker holding our daughter.

'What's wrong?' I asked.

'What d'you mean?'

'The monitor stopped working,' I said.

I took Melody from him and looked at her.

'It's probably the batteries,' he said. 'What's up with you?'

Tom stood and picked up the monitor. There were spare batteries kept in a drawer in the kitchen and he went off to change them. When he came back the monitor was working perfectly.

He frowned at me and I forced myself to smile, as I placed Melody back in her cot. I didn't know why but I had an overwhelming fear of Melody being alone with Tom.

'You're tense tonight,' he said.

'I'm just a bit stir crazy. And waiting for the move is annoying.'

'Just as well you'll have time alone tomorrow.'

He glanced at me and I began to regret mentioning Tina would be back to work the next day.

'I think I'll go to the gym,' I said. 'That'll make me feel better.'

Later I received a text from Becki checking in on me. She said she was worried and hoped I was okay.

All fine, I replied, *I'll be in touch soon*, and then I deleted both texts from my phone.

Tom went to his office to check his private emails. Left alone I began to process everything Becki and I had discovered that day. Then it occurred to me I hadn't asked her about the Hammersmith flat that Daniel had occupied.

I sent a text, but turned my phone to silent and stowed it in my jeans pocket. A short time later she asked:

What apartment? He used to live with me until he got the one you were both going to share.

I gave her the address

I'll look into it.

I erased the texts again and switched the television on to the news for Tom. He came in soon afterwards and sat down beside me.

I levelled my breathing out to appear relaxed, but my heart jumped in my chest when he came in the room. I imagined that he could feel the tension but didn't comment on it because he didn't understand what it was.

'I saw my therapist again today,' he said. 'She told me in order to deal with everything I need to apologize to you.'

'Apologize for what?' I said.

'For not trusting you. I also need to say, I forgive you for what happened.'

'Thank you,' I said.

His hand fell onto my leg.

'I need to make love to you,' he said.

I didn't say anything. Thankfully, Melody began to cry again, and I hurried away to take care of her.

Melody screamed for a few hours that night. Eventually Tom went to bed to try and get some sleep. I gave her colic drops, but even after she settled, I stayed with her.

It was midnight when, exhausted, I left the nursery. I

glanced down the corridor and noticed our bedroom door was closed. I began to walk towards it, then I saw Tom's briefcase.

I walked past it and stood by my bedroom listening.

Tom's breathing was level. I was sure he slept.

I went back to the hallway and picked up the case. Not wanting to make any noise that might reach the bedroom I took it into the kitchen, placed it down on the work surface and looked at the lock.

I pressed both sides of the locking mechanism, but it didn't open. This case was unusual in that it wasn't a combination but a key lock only. It was odd that Tom would lock the case at all though, especially considering it travelled to and from work in a private car, and then remained safe in our home. For this reason, I suspected he had something inside he didn't wish me to see.

I went back to the hallway and looked for Tom's keys. He didn't need them to get into the apartment, but I knew he carried some. They weren't by the door where I had seen him leave them in the past. I glanced into the living room. His suit jacket had been thrown over one chair, but the keys were nowhere to be seen. I was about to return to the kitchen when I thought about his jacket. I picked it up and felt the weight of something in the pocket.

I put my hand in. Tom's phone was there, and so were his keys.

Taking the keys into the kitchen, I found the one for the case then turned it in the lock. It clicked open with a loud *thunk*.

I glanced at the door then waited to see if the sound had echoed through the apartment. When there was no movement I opened the briefcase and looked inside.

I was right: the DANIELS/CHARLOTTE file lay on top of Tom's personal diary. It surprised me to find the file there and I just stared at it for a long time before I pulled it out.

I closed and locked the case. After that I returned it to the hallway and took the file into the living room with me and closed the door.

'Char?' said Tom.

I shoved the file under the seat cushions and sat down on it.

'Have you seen my phone? I forgot to put it on charge.'

I glanced at the jacket and then, remembering the keys, I reached for it, and stuffed them back in the pocket.

Tom opened the door and peered into the room at me. I had the main light on and it was bright in there compared to the hallway and so he blinked until his eyes adjusted. I held the jacket out to him.

'Is it in here?' I said, making a show of searching. I pulled the phone out and handed it to him.

'Thanks. Are you coming to bed?'

'Yes. Wasn't tired and so was going to make some chocolate.'

Tom rubbed his eyes. He looked exhausted.

'Go back to bed,' I said. 'I'll be in soon.'

I couldn't risk reading the file while Tom was potentially awake and might catch me. I hid it more thoroughly in the bottom of my sewing drawer. Then I went to bed. Tom appeared to be sleeping and I slipped in beside him trying not to wake him. I lay tense listening to him breathe and then I turned on my side and closed my eyes, trying to sleep.

Chapter Forty-Two

'It's almost nine!' Tom said.

'Whaa ...?' I jerked awake as Tom climbed out of bed.

'This is parenthood for you,' he said. 'Lack of sleep and late to work.'

He hurried into the shower and got washed and shaved in record time.

'No time to eat,' he said. 'I have texted Stefan and told him I overslept and he's downstairs waiting.'

Tom pulled on a clean shirt and suit from the wardrobe. Then he hurried down the corridor, picked up his case and left.

I lay dosing for a while and then I opened my eyes suddenly, remembering I'd taken the file from his case. He'd get to work and open it. Then he'd know I'd taken it.

I got out of bed and pulled on some clothes. Then I looked in on Melody. The little girl was still sleeping, and I didn't want to wake her.

'God. I hope this was worth it,' I said.

I hurried down the corridor and into the living room, then I pulled the file out of the sewing drawer and placed it on the coffee table.

I took a breath and opened it.

Daniel's face smiled back at me. It took a moment to recognize the place and the back of my own head. This was the sushi restaurant in Reykjavik.

My heart hurt, my head pounded. I waded through the photographs. All of them were date stamped and the file catalogued my entire affair with Daniel. There were even photographs of us in bed together at the Hammersmith apartment. Graphic images that horrified me. The pictures appeared to have been taken through a slit in the curtains in the bedroom.

We thought we had been careful, but Tom's detectives had recorded everything.

An awful thought occurred to me: Tom had this whole file and he obviously looked at it regularly. Why else would he have it in his case?

I spread the pictures out on the table. There was even a photograph of me entering the room at The Savoy.

I had a flash of memory then. The man with the brogues had obviously been watching me, or Daniel. He must have snapped the picture while he pretended to enter the room next door.

I gathered the photographs up into the file and then I hurried back to Melody's room. I had to get her up, feed her and get away before Tom realized the file was missing.

A short time later I returned to the living room with Melody, now dressed, and a small case packed with a few essentials. I grabbed a pack of nappies and placed them under her pram and then fed Melody. After she was fed and content, I put my daughter in her pram.

I looked around the apartment for anything essential. Then picked up the file and began to stuff it into Melody's changing bag because it was the only thing big enough to carry it. My hands were shaking and some of the photos tumbled out onto the floor in the hallway. I bent down to collect them and then the door beeped as the passcode was entered from outside.

I stood up, holding the pictures, my hand shaking, not knowing where to hide them as the door opened. Sweat trickled down my spine but I was frozen to the spot.

'Forgot my keys,' Tom said.

He stopped moving. His eyes fell on the pictures in my hands and then he saw the suitcase beside the pram.

'What's going on?' he said coldly.

'I'm taking Melody and we're leaving,' I said. 'You can't stop me.'

The truth was, Tom was much taller and stronger than me. I couldn't barge past him if I wanted to and he was now blocking my exit.

'Charlotte,' his voice was calm and almost a whisper, 'I know what you have there. Give me chance to explain. This isn't what it seems.'

'Get out of my way,' I said. I dropped the pictures I was holding and placed my hands on Melody's pram.

'Hear me out. That's all I ask. Then if you aren't happy, I won't do anything to stop you leaving.'

He moved into the hallway and closed the door. Locking us both in.

I backed up, scared.

'I'm not going to hurt you. Look I'm going to go in the living room and sit down and you can stay there, near the door.'

I was trembling as he passed me, but he made no effort to touch me.

True to his word he sat down on the sofa and looked at me.

'I want to tell you everything,' he said.

I remained by the door ready to grab Melody and run.

Tom put his head in his hands and sighed.

'This isn't how it looks.'

'What is it then?'

Tom's explanation went like this.

'I don't know what's the matter with her,' Tom had said to Isadora. 'We're happy but she's not interested in having children.'

'What is she interested in?' Isadora asked.

'The gym. Her friends ...'

'What about you, Tom? Have you noticed any cooling off?'

'No. Don't be silly. We're happy. I'm just ready to do this now. She isn't.'

Isadora formed a plan then.

'It's just a little thing,' she had said. 'To test how settled Charlotte is. It's possible she's feeling curious.'

'Curious about what?'

'Other men.'

Tom went quiet. He couldn't conceive of me being unfaithful to him, but Isadora sowed the seed, and with his mother's past history, he didn't doubt that any woman could be unfaithful.

'Not Charlotte,' he had said.

'Well you'll soon know. I have a number for someone. A private detective. If nothing else it will put your mind at rest.'

Tom agreed because once the idea had been planted in his head he had to prove to his mother that I was nothing like her.

It started at Harrods. Isadora had arranged for Daniel to see me with them. And, when Tom was occupied elsewhere, she had pointed out the purple satin bedding to me.

Sheets that Ewan bought, and we later made love in.

The experiment ended as far as Tom was concerned when I didn't take any great interest in Daniel.

Tom admitted receiving the email saying that nothing improper had happened. But, when he came to join me on our trip, and I didn't mention meeting Daniel, it had worried him and made Isadora more suspicious.

Isadora continued to have me trailed but when I fell pregnant, she told Tom the truth.

They had an argument about it. Isadora said she'd cancel the detective, but he was still following me when I returned the bedding and bumped into Daniel again. This time quite by accident.

The PI watched us talk and took pictures of us in the café. He even sat near us and listened to the conversation. All of it was relayed back to Tom's mother.

When I tripped and the bus hit me. Tom said it was the PI who called an ambulance. He didn't talk to the police though. The PI told them he thought I'd thrown myself down deliberately. The man had heard me say to Daniel that I didn't want to be pregnant, and although he hadn't seen exactly what happened, only that I was injured, he had made this assumption.

'We wanted to make sure you didn't try anything again,' Tom said. 'That's why you were kept in the private hospital so long. I had to make sure your state of mind was good. When you lost the baby anyway, I felt guilty. I shouldn't have listened to Mother's suggestion in the first place.'

Tom was sincere but I just didn't know what to say to him. I had the evidence of what he'd done in my hands.

'Mother kept paying to have you watched though. I guess she recognized the signs even as I buried my head in the sand. The result is there. In that folder.'

'It's disgusting,' I said.

'That man was paid to be with you, Charlotte. It was all a lie. He never loved you.'

I didn't want to reveal that I knew his real name, and now Daniel's sister.

'I don't believe you. I think you are behind this whole thing. Why else would you have this with you?'

'After your affair came out and I took you back in, Mother kept what the detectives had found. Perhaps it was her idea of a sick joke. She left this for me to find after she died. It was in an envelope in her office at the London flat. I found it the week after the funeral when I went there alone.'

I hadn't been to the flat, afterwards. Tom had sorted it all out himself. Everything he said was plausible, but my heart didn't stop racing.

'I ... opened it and saw ... all of this. I sat and cried Charlotte. I saw you. With that man. *In those sheets*. I've tried to put it behind me. You know I have. I've tried to forgive you. And then, there were the same sheets in Mother's room. And your face … you were remembering being with him and I knew it! All those horrible memories came back and I lost it.

'You don't know this, but Isadora tried to split us up before the wedding too. She came to my room … she called you a gold digger. I threw her out and told her I loved you. She went cold, Charlotte. She said one day I'd regret not listening to her. But we got married and she started to accept you. *I thought.* Really she was lulling me into a false sense of security. Waiting to deliver a hurtful blow. *That.*'

He pointed at the pictures.

Melody made a gurgling sound in her pram. I looked at her and my mouth felt dry. If Tom was to be believed, Isadora was a cold and spiteful woman as well as an abuser. She'd hid this side from me very well. She had always seemed such a good mother, caring only for what Tom needed. I'd found her overbearing and controlling but not psychotic.

'If this is true, why did you keep these?' I murmured.

'I wanted to remind myself what you were capable of. That's why I pulled those detectives back in and had them check on you. I suppose the jealousy sent me insane. I was going to shred them all last night, but the evening got away with me, and with Melody having a bad night I thought it could wait.'

I stared at him and then my strength left me and I sank down onto the chair opposite him.

'Let me take them, Char,' he said. 'Let me destroy it all and let's never look back.'

I had heard these fresh start speeches once too often.

'No. I have questions. And you're going to answer them, or I'm taking Melody now and I'm leaving.'

I don't think I had ever spoken to him so firmly before. At that point though I was strong. I had the evidence I needed against him and my doubts and fears were all justified. He had been involved with this. I knew it.

Chapter Forty-Three

Tom sank back into the sofa like a drowning man. He looked haggard and distraught. I took in his every action, his every expression. Even the best actor couldn't pull a performance off like that. I had him where I wanted him. I was shocked at how good it was to have the upper hand for once. It was infuriating to always be the weak one who was in the wrong no matter what. But the tide had turned and now I'd be calling the shots.

'If Ewan was all a set-up, I want to know how Isadora arranged it.'

'I don't know,' he said. 'He more than likely told them every time you made plans.'

'You're telling me that all that time you knew nothing?'

'I swear,' he said. 'I couldn't have been normal with you. You know how upset I was when you told me you were leaving.'

'What's Ewan's real name?'

'Daniel Evans,' he admitted. 'I learnt that when I had him investigated afterwards.'

'Where is he now?'

Tom's face dropped. 'What does it matter?'

'I want to know.'

'I think Mother paid him money to ... disappear,' he said. 'A lot of money because I've seen it gone from what should have been there in her estate.'

'And you're assuming it went to him.'

Tom wiped his hand over his mouth and looked at me with sad eyes. 'She told me she had paid him. That night in the hospital. She admitted it all. That was what the row was about really, and I know you heard some of it. I saw it in your face.'

I blinked. I didn't deny or admit that I had heard anything. I was cold to Tom. It was the only emotion I was capable of right then.

'If she paid him off, she had to know where he'd gone. The payment must be traceable.'

'Swiss account,' Tom said. 'I've already had my people on it. We can't find out who owns it. You don't understand, Char. I wanted to find that bastard too! I can't bear what he did to you. How he broke your heart like that. How he made you break mine. All I could think about afterwards was how I wanted to beat the shit out of him.'

My head started spinning and I couldn't take anymore. Melody began to cry and so I picked her up. She needed changing again. I left Tom and took her into the nursery.

When I returned Tom wasn't in the living room. Then I heard the shredder in the office, and I knew it was too late. All the evidence was gone before I reached him. How could I be so stupid to leave him alone in the room with it?

'There,' he said. 'It's over.'

An overwhelming sense of loss consumed me. I didn't know

what it was. Maybe it was because those pictures were all I'd had of Daniel and now they too had 'vanished'. Or perhaps it was because the fleeting power I'd had was now gone.

I burst into tears and locked myself and Melody in the nursery. I couldn't explain how I felt. I had seen freedom for a few moments and now it was pulled away from me again.

'Come out, Char,' Tom said. 'This is silly. Today you're shocked by finding this, but we've been through worse. We'll be okay. Everything I've done has been because—'

The doorbell rang.

I pressed my ear against the door and then I heard Tina's voice.

'Are we all set for the move?'

'The kitchen isn't done yet. But nearly,' Tom said. I couldn't believe how normal and unruffled he sounded.

'Where's Charlotte?' Tina asked.

'She's not feeling that well; Melody had one of her screaming sessions last night.'

I heard Tina approach the nursery.

'Charlotte? Let me take over. You go back to bed and get some sleep.'

I opened the door because I didn't want to make a scene and then I fell into Tina's arms and cried.

'There, there. It's not easy being a new mother. Come on, this is nothing that some sleep won't cure.'

I let Tina bundle me back to our bedroom and she put me to bed as though I were her charge not Melody.

She closed the bedroom curtains and then left me with the instruction to sleep.

I heard her reassuring Tom and a short time later he left and went to work.

I was drained and shaken, and so I closed my eyes and gave in to the much-needed sleep.

When I woke I was groggy and confused, but I made my way into the living room where Tina was playing with Melody.

'Sit down, you poor thing,' she said. 'I'll get you a drink of tea.'

Tina got me a drink and a sandwich, and she fussed over me until she saw me eating.

'Right, tomorrow you're getting time out,' she said. 'Go to the gym, get your hair done, whatever you need. Take all day. Melody will be fine.'

I toyed with the idea of telling her everything, but I didn't have the strength. I couldn't bring myself to share it. The shame I felt as I recalled the contents of the file was enough to make my cheeks burn. I hid it from Tina as best as I could.

I had never been more alone.

Tina left at five after bathing Melody. Then my mobile rang, and it was Tom.

'I spoke to my therapist and told her what happened. I think it best I don't come home tonight. She said you might be scared and, although I would never hurt you, Charlotte, I don't want you to be afraid of me.'

'Fine,' I said.

'I don't want to lose you—'

I hung up before he could say anymore. I sighed with relief.

I was grateful that his therapist told him to stay away though. The thought that he had been looking at those photographs made me want to vomit. I didn't think I could ever get past his excuses.

I went to the front door and double bolted it. Tom couldn't get back in now, even if he changed his mind.

I picked up my phone and dialled Becki. It rang out for a while and just as I was about to hang up she answered.

'Charlotte?'

'Hi. It's been a pretty fraught day. I found a folder in Tom's case. Full of photographs of Daniel and me. Even ... in bed.'

'Oh God!'

I told her about Tom destroying them.

'So my evidence is gone,' I said.

'Are you safe?' she asked.

'For tonight. I've locked him out.'

'Maybe you should come over here.'

'I'm okay,' I said. 'I think I ought to engage a solicitor though and start proceedings for a divorce. I'm sure I have enough now to show unreasonable behaviour.'

'Sounds wise,' Becki said. 'My friend is a divorce lawyer. I'll ring him for you.'

'I'd appreciate that. Thank you. Did you learn anything about the flat Daniel used to take me to?'

'Interesting you mention that. I went there today and from a distance I saw the woman you talked about and I know who she is. She told you no one else had lived in her place, right?'

'That's right.'

'Well, she was in the local press recently. She's going off

to Africa to help teach underprivileged children. The article says she's been before. Two years ago: she went away for six months. The dates fall in completely with the time that you and Daniel were using the place. It's possible her boyfriend sublet to Daniel during the day for your meetings, but she didn't know about it.'

'How do we find out?' I asked.

'Bull in a china shop perhaps?'

'Huh?' I said.

'We can just confront the boyfriend and ask him outright. I got some pictures of him today with her on my phone.'

'Can you send me those?'

'Sure.'

I hung up and went into the kitchen. I put a jug of milk in the microwave. I was too upset to eat but I made a hot chocolate to help settle me for the night.

My phone beeped as I stirred the chocolate into the milk.

The photos had arrived from Becki. The first picture was of the girl I'd seen eighteen months ago. The second was a photograph of the article Becki had told me about. The third was the girl with a man. The picture was blurred but he looked familiar. A fourth picture came into view. A long shot of the guy. He was wearing jeans and brogues.

I expelled a breath. This man, I'd now seen him three times. Once in The Savoy. It was the same man who'd been outside the Italian restaurant the night Tom had taken me to dinner, and I'd also seen him leaving Tom's building earlier that same day. It didn't take a genius to work out why he was connected to Tom.

I rang Becki again.

'You're sure this is her boyfriend?' I said.

'Yes.'

'It's not the same man she showed me on her phone when I spoke to her: I think this guy works for the detective agency.'

'So. He used her flat with Daniel for your trysts.'

'Yes. And ... Daniel probably knew we were being watched and photographed.'

'I can't believe he'd do that!' Becki said.

I sighed. 'I don't want to believe it. But what else can it mean?'

Becki had to agree that if the woman was telling the truth and she hadn't known someone was using her flat, then the boyfriend was behind it. Even so, it was suspicious that she had shown another man's photo to me, and not this one. Either way, it still looked as though Daniel had willingly set me up.

'It doesn't mean that he didn't fall in love with you and regret it though,' Becki said.

I didn't answer.

'Tell me more about Tom's pictures.'

'It was everything we did. Our first meeting. The restaurant in Reykjavik. The time we bumped into each other again. Then Hammersmith ... There's pictures of me going in and out of the apartment block and of us ... together.'

'What about Milan?' Becki asked.

'Milan? No. There weren't *any*.'

'Then, even if Dan had been in on this to begin with, he didn't tell them you were going away with him. Maybe he didn't tell them about most of your meetings. Charlotte, he did love you. He told me, remember?'

I thought back to the pictures. It was difficult to remember them all. But I was certain I was right: there had been none in Milan. Maybe it had been a scam at the beginning and Daniel had gone along with it. Maybe he had fallen for me. I wasn't certain we'd ever find out. Daniel was missing, and I was convinced we'd never find him.

'I want to believe that,' I said.

I went to bed and lay there unsleeping. It was a relief that Tom wasn't home. Even so, every little noise in the apartment jerked me from my shallow sleep with the fear he had returned and somehow got inside.

In the middle of the night I remembered something. A phone call Tom had answered. I hadn't heard who had called but I know it was someone enquiring about my trip to Milan. Tom wouldn't tell me what the call was about, but he had been shocked and angry. It was one of those times when I had sensed violence bubbling inside him. Had he been angry because Daniel had taken me away and hadn't passed the information on, not because he suspected me for the first time of having an affair?

I turned over in bed and squeezed my eyes shut, but sleep wouldn't come. I just kept going over that night again and again.

At six in the morning, I repacked my suitcase with Melody's crucial things. Tom had unpacked it, presuming I supposed that his story about Isadora being behind everything would sway me back to his side. It hadn't. There were too many unanswered questions. I didn't believe or trust him. I wanted out. No matter what, I was leaving.

I rang Tina on the way to Isadora's flat and told her I was bringing Melody.

'What's wrong?' she asked.

'Tom and I. Things aren't going well with us and I need to get away for a while. If I bring Melody to you and he calls, please don't tell him she's with you.'

'Of course I won't.'

'So the tears weren't just tiredness yesterday?' she said when she let me in the apartment.

'It's a long story. I don't want to involve you in it. Listen this doesn't change anything regarding your employment. Isadora left me a lot of money and this flat, so I can stand on my own two feet without Tom. I'm going to try and find us a big enough place to all stay in, probably outside of London, but it will take time.'

'Take all the time you need.'

'I'm sorry. This changes the move to Surrey.'

'Don't worry. I'm on your side.'

I reassured her that her salary would continue and because I owned the flat, she could remain. Even so, I couldn't stay myself, because I thought it might bring Tina more trouble and, although Becki had offered, I wasn't sure I could impose on her either.

'I'll pick Melody up at five,' I said.

'Where are you going to go?' she asked.

'A hotel probably. It'll be safer I think. More public.'

'Charlotte? Are you *afraid* of Tom?'

'I ...'

'That bruise on your cheek?'

My eyes watered. 'It was just the once.'

'Oh my god. That *bastard*! You're doing the right thing. Any guy that hits you, whatever the excuse, isn't worth it.'

Tina hugged me and promised to keep Melody safe then I left.

'Let me know if he contacts you. If he calls me, I'll say Melody is with you so it should be all okay.'

I sent Tom a text telling him I'd taken Melody and left. I said we were staying with a friend and I'd be in touch. I finished the message with:

Please leave me alone. I have to think long and hard about what you've done.

A response came back almost immediately:

I love you Char. I don't want to lose you. Please let me explain.

He tried to call me, but I put the phone on silent and stowed it in my handbag.

Chapter Forty-Four

I took the tube to Hammersmith to meet Becki and her friend the divorce lawyer. The man was already at her apartment when I arrived.

'Colin Craig.' He held out his hand.

'It's kind of you to meet me,' I said. 'Especially out of your office.'

'We'll do the formalities another time. Becki said this was urgent,' Colin said.

I sat down in Becki's living room with Colin and I gave a huge sigh.

'I just don't know what to do,' I said.

'Well, let's first deal with facts. Your marriage has broken down. It's not really relevant at the moment why. But the law is that there is a fifty-fifty split of all assets and debts. Becki tells me you have a daughter?'

'Melody. She's just nine weeks old.'

'He may go after custody. Or joint custody. It's easier if you both agree on this beforehand, so it might be good if you can keep some line of communication going. The best divorces happen for those who try to be reasonable.'

'I don't know if I can. I'm not sure Tom will agree to anything. He wants me to stay. I've told him I need time to think.'

'Is divorce what you want? Or are you exploring options?' Colin asked.

'I can't go on the way things are.'

Colin gave me all of the facts based on the information. I wasn't really interested in Tom's money, but he pointed out that it was important for me to get everything I could straight, because even if I agreed to settle for less than I was entitled to all divorces had to be made in 'full and final settlement', which meant I couldn't ask for more from Tom afterwards. My head was reeling by the time he left.

The truth was, faced with the idea of going down this route, I wasn't sure what I wanted to do. I needed to think and process everything. The lawyer was right that we had to try to be amicable at first. If that didn't work then I'd cut all communication with him and just go down the legal route and let the lawyers deal with it.

'I'm so confused,' I said to Becki when Colin left. 'I'm torn between being horrified and feeling sorry for Tom. His mother was behind all this.'

'So *he* says,' Becki said. 'This situation is weird. What kind of man keeps pictures of his wife having sex with another man? That's fucked up.'

I knew she was right. Her words helped strengthen my resolve again.

'And my brother is still missing, and we don't know why,' she said.

In my heart I believed that Daniel was dead. Perhaps it was the only thing I could accept, since he hadn't come back for me. But I didn't say this to her as she placed a cup of tea in front of me.

'You look fragile,' she said. 'And you've lost weight.'

I couldn't remember when I'd last eaten.

'I'm sorry,' I said. 'I wanted evidence against Tom; I found it and now I'm wavering. This is a huge decision. I'm scared.'

'This man has made you like this, Charlotte, don't you see? How many decisions in your life has he allowed you to make? It may be that he's not that violent, but he is abusive. Spying on you! Introducing you to a guy and having pictures taken of you having sex with the guy. There's a word for that.'

'He says Isadora did all that, and what if she did? Then he's a victim in this too.'

'I don't believe him,' Becki said. 'But then, I don't know him. I know my brother, and if he was involved, it wasn't because he was getting paid. There's just something else we don't know. Another piece of this puzzle.'

'I don't know how we are going to find it without Daniel,' I said.

'Do you really want to?'

I didn't answer and Becki went into the kitchen to make me a sandwich. I slumped back into the sofa, feeling drained and more than a little broken. Becki was right. I could see it was all true: Tom *was* domineering. He always controlled what we did, and I hadn't known how to stand up for myself. On those rare occasions when I did, he mentally wore me down with his reasoning – it was always manipulative – and I found it hard to argue back. Recently it had been with stories of how awful Isadora was. There was nothing in my life they hadn't both somehow had a hand in.

'I must frustrate you,' I said to Becki when she placed the plate down on the coffee table. 'I'm frustrating myself. I was never this weak.'

'It's easy for someone to make judgements. I may be wrong about Tom. You obviously saw something in him or you wouldn't have lasted this long. But things don't add up. You know it or you wouldn't be running scared. What will it take to tip you over that edge?' she said.

'The whole truth. I need real evidence that Tom *is* the bad guy. I need to prove it to myself without any doubt so that I have the strength to get the hell away from him for good.'

'You've had legal training, so I get that. You need facts. But Charlotte, what are your instincts telling you?'

I took a bite out of the sandwich to avoid having to answer. If I listened to my instincts they were telling me to run and get as far away from Tom and Carlisle Corp as I could. But Becki was right, my logical brain couldn't let my instincts rule everything. Not without evidence.

'I've got an idea. It's risky, but it might work.'

'I'm listening,' I said.

'Eat up. You're going to need your strength.'

Chapter Forty-Five

W e reached the exterior of the familiar Hammersmith apartment block and watched the entrance from the bus stop across the road. Becki had given me a hoodie top to wear so that if the woman's PI boyfriend saw us, he wouldn't recognize me. I wasn't convinced, but I put the top on and hid my hair.

We sat on the bus shelter bench and watched the entrance. After an hour we saw no movement. The boyfriend didn't appear and neither did the girl.

'I would bet he's already left for work,' Becki said.

A bus pulled in at the stop obscuring our view, and a woman got off laden with shopping. As the bus moved away, we saw the back of a man as he walked from the apartment.

'That's him! Good,' said Becki. 'The last thing you want is him to see us. Because he's obviously seen a lot of you in the past.'

The colour drained from my face. It was such a horrible thought that someone else had been watching the private moments I had with Daniel. I gave Becki a sideways glance: she didn't notice how uncomfortable I was; she never took her eyes from the entrance of the apartment block. I brought my mind back to the moment.

'What now?' I said.

'We tackle her head on. Faced with the two of us, she might crack and tell us the truth.'

'And then?'

'The thing is you need more than what we have. And I need something to take to the police to encourage them to investigate Daniel's disappearance again,' she said. 'They won't do anything without more information, so the case has just gone cold. We know it's all connected though, don't we?'

'What do you mean?' I said even though I knew what she meant.

'Daniel's dead. Someone killed him. He wouldn't have disappeared like this. He wouldn't have let me worry. We need evidence that will make the police look into it again. No matter where it leads.'

I squeezed my eyes shut. Becki's words were a blow to my heart. Daniel's death was the only thing that could have stopped him from contacting her. Now that it was spoken between us, I could no longer speculate that it 'might' be the case. Daniel was dead. He had to be. I tried not to think about who his death might lead back to.

We had to try to get the girl in the Hammersmith flat to talk. If we found out Tom was lying about Isadora, then he might well be guilty of worse. If that evidence was there, then I'd take Melody away from him for good. I didn't know how, but I'd disappear as surely as Daniel had. But not before I helped put that evidence in the hands of the police.

'Let's go,' said Becki.

I followed her, my heart racing. I couldn't believe the thoughts that had slipped so easily into my conscious mind. Was Tom behind Daniel's disappearance? Did I really believe my husband was capable of 'making someone disappear', whatever that might mean?

I followed Becki into the lift and tried not to think about it too hard.

On the third floor both of us took a breath before we approached the door. I felt nauseous as Becki knocked.

'Just a minute!' called the woman behind the door.

I stepped aside from the spy hole in case she remembered me, but Becki stood there looking benign.

The door opened.

'Can I help you?' she said.

She looked at us both but gave a jolt when she saw me.

'What d'you want?'

'We have evidence that my brother spent time in this apartment, with my friend here. You said you didn't know him. We aren't leaving until you tell us what you know, and if you refuse, I'm going to call the police and show them the pictures taken in your bedroom.'

The woman flushed. 'I don't know what—'

'Don't lie to us, Paula' I said.

'How do you know my name?'

'We know a lot about you. Particularly your trip to Africa. And, the fact that you sublet this place to my brother while you were gone,' said Becki.

Paula looked down the hallway as though she feared

someone had heard. She stepped back from the door then. 'You'd better come in.'

She closed the door and we stood in the hallway of the apartment. It hadn't changed much, though it was newly painted.

'Look I didn't know,' she said. 'That creep sublet it while I was away.'

'You need to tell us what you do know,' said Becki.

'He works at an agency. They don't do anything illegal. They just follow people to prove when they are unfaithful. That kind of thing.'

'Entrapment is illegal,' I said, even though I knew that my use of the word wasn't strictly accurate. I wanted to scare Paula into talking.

Paula swallowed. 'I only saw the pictures a few days ago. I had a major row with him but he says he's keeping them for insurance.'

I glanced at Becki.

'Let us see them,' she said.

'I can't. Troy took them away.'

'Where were they?'

'Hidden under one of the floorboards in the bedroom. I was cleaning and found it loose. When I looked inside there was an envelope. There were loads of pictures.' Paula glanced at me. 'Of you ... and a man.'

'Who was the agency working for? Who hired him to take the photos?'

'He didn't say.'

'I want to see this hidey hole,' I said.

'All right, but I told you, he took everything!'

We went into the bedroom and it was the same except for the bedding: there were no purple satin sheets. Even so, I was overwhelmed by memories of my time there, and it took a huge effort for me to cross the threshold and pass into the room behind Becki and Paula.

Becki was determined though and she ripped up the floorboard and looked down into the hole.

'I need a torch,' she said.

I pulled my phone out of my handbag and turned on the light, then I moved into the room. I held the light over the hole and Becki reached in.

'There's something there.'

Becki pulled up a partially torn photo. It was of me and Daniel sitting on the bed. She looked at the picture and around the room then back at Paula.

I turned off the light and stuffed my phone into my pocket. My heart began to regulate. I had proof!

'Listen, you're going to help us. I want you to ask him who paid for his services. And if you don't, I'm coming back here with the police.'

'The police won't be interested,' Paula said. 'You got what you wanted, now leave.'

'My brother is missing,' Becki said. 'And your boyfriend is somehow connected. That's enough for them to investigate.'

'Look, I don't want any trouble. I'm just about to go away again—'

'Do you own this flat?' I asked as a legal element came into my head.

'Rented.'

'And subletting is against your rental contract I'm sure,' I said.

Paula crumpled. 'All right. I'll ask. But he won't tell me.'

'Ring him. Let's find out,' I said.

Troy didn't pick up but he did text Paula back.

Working. What is it?

Who is the woman in the pictures? I think you're lying to me.

I haven't got time for this. It was a work thing. I told you.

Who for?

You know I can't tell you that.

'Tell him that the police came by looking for the man because he's missing,' Becki said.

'Isn't that playing our hand?' I said.

'How about I say I'm locking him out unless he tells me? He needs me and my flat. He can't get his own place – he's got a terrible credit history, and no one will lease to him,' Paula said surprising us both.

'Try,' I said. She sent the text and we all waited. After a moment, his response arrived.

I don't know the name but it was a woman. The girl's mother-in-law I think. She was probably trying to break them up.

We all looked at the text then Troy sent another.

Baby, are we good? I promise it's all I know. I kept the photos, cos, you never know in the future …

'Tell him you're good,' I said.

I felt the colour drain from me once more. It was the answer I hadn't expected. It meant that Tom was telling the truth about Isadora.

'None of this explains where Daniel went,' Becki said as we left Paula with the promise to keep her out of it in future if she kept our visit a secret to her boyfriend.

I had one picture though. Evidence of a sort. It was Daniel looking at me lovingly following a kiss. I put it in my pocket. I remembered the moment as clearly as if it had just happened. My heart was sore.

'Tom told me she paid him to disappear. Maybe he rented the flat and involved you just to make that disappearance more believable,' I said.

'My brother wouldn't—'

'I'm exhausted,' I said. 'I have to get Melody.'

'Charlotte. Don't go back to Tom. We still don't know everything ...'

'Thanks for helping Becki,' I said. 'I'll stay in touch. I want to get to the bottom of this just as much as you do. And I have no intention of going home right now.'

I made my way to Isadora's flat in a taxi. All the way there I looked through hotel booking sites on my phone in order to find one for the next few days.

The taxi pulled in front of the apartment building right behind a black limo.

My heart leapt in my chest as I realized Stefan was standing beside it. I paid the taxi driver and got out.

'What are you doing here?' I said to Stefan.

'Mr C said he had to collect something,' Stefan told me.

I hurried into the building and pressed the lift call. It was on the top floor, Isadora's flat was only on the second, so I took the stairs two at a time and reached the landing just in time to see Tom entering the apartment.

I raced down the corridor after him.

'What are you doing here?' I yelled. 'You have no right!'

Tom turned around and looked at me. 'Charlotte. I've been trying to call you.'

'I don't want to speak to you right now—'

'Will you stop shouting and listen ... Melody's ill. Tina took her to hospital but she couldn't reach you. She had to call me to give permission for the tests to be done.'

I took my phone out of my pocket and looked at it. There were several missed calls from Tina and many from Tom.

I pressed the voicemail and heard Tina's panic as she described Melody's symptoms.

'Where've you been?' he asked.

I stared at him. 'I have to get to the hospital.'

'I'm just getting Melody's things and then I'm heading there,' he said. 'Come on.'

Stefan broke a few laws getting us to Great Ormond Street in record time. I leapt out of the limo and ran inside, searching frantically for the ward. My heart hurt so much. I was trembling with shock and fear. My only wish to see my baby. I'd been so concerned that Tom wouldn't reach me it hadn't occurred to me that Tina might need to.

After several discussions with reception staff, and a helpful intern taking me to the right place, I eventually arrived at the ICU. There I found Tina talking to a doctor as he examined Melody who was lying in a hospital cot.

'Here's Mrs Carlisle now!' said Tina. 'Thank God. I had to phone Tom ...'

She was pale with worry. Then she saw Tom behind me.

'What's happened?' I asked.

'They suspect that Melody has viral meningitis.'

'Oh my god!'

Tina put her arm around me; I think she knew I was about to collapse. My little girl was hooked up to a heart monitor and had an intravenous drip in her tiny arm. She was unconscious and the doctor said she would need a 'percutaneous indwelling catheter' if she didn't improve quickly.

Tina helped me to a chair beside Melody's cot. I was shaking. I felt the colour drain from my face.

'She's unconscious but we are doing everything we can,' the doctor said.

'How?' I said. 'How did this happen?'

'Melody was premature, not fully developed when she was born. There are so many things that a prem baby can be susceptible to. You're lucky that your nanny acted so quickly. She's now in the best place.'

Tom stood back, looking helpless while a nurse went to fetch me a glass of water.

'You can go,' I snapped. 'I'm here now.'

'I'm not going anywhere. You need me as much as Melody does.'

'I *don't*,' I said.

'Let me help,' he said. Then he stroked my hair and kissed my forehead. 'Melody is my child and you're my wife. I'm not leaving.'

I knocked his hand away. 'Don't touch me!'

Tom's hand dropped to his side. I turned away so that I couldn't see his hurt expression.

Tina went home but Tom wouldn't leave. We kept vigil all night. Finally, after a few hours, our poor little girl began to come around. It was a massive relief. When I knew she was out of immediate danger I let the exhaustion take me and I slept in the chair beside her cot.

I woke as the nurses clanged around tending to the children in the ICU ward.

I looked at my baby still sleeping soundly and wondered how I would have forgiven myself if anything had happened to her.

Tina returned to the hospital a short time later.

'Tom asked me to come and take over for you both. He's talking to the doctor now. Go home and rest. She won't know you're not here, and I promise I won't leave until you get back.'

'My phone will be on. Tina, I'm sorry. He kept ringing and I ...'

'Look. He's very worried about you both. Maybe you guys could ... sort things out.'

I thanked her again. I didn't want to think about my marital troubles with Melody sick. I was too tired to make any decisions about anything, let alone assimilate the information I'd gleaned the day before.

Tom met me at the ward door.

'The doctor says she's out of danger. They want to monitor her for a day or two and make sure she's recovering. She's come around quickly, so there shouldn't be any permanent damage.'

'What type of damage?'

'There could be a problem with her hearing. But it's likely she will make a full recovery with no ill effects. They are going to do all the tests. Come home and rest.'

'Tom, I don't want to—'

'What don't you want? I won't touch you. I won't talk to you. I certainly won't hurt you. Don't you *know* that?'

I shook my head. I didn't know it. But I did know he'd told the truth about Isadora's part in hiring the private detectives that had set me up with Daniel Evans.

'Let me take care of you, Char.'

I was too tired to argue and so I let him lead me out of the hospital and we waited outside as Stefan fought traffic once again to reach us. Then, when the limo finally arrived, I sank back into the leather seats and closed my eyes.

True to his word, Tom left me alone. But I watched him through the slit of my eyes.

We entered the apartment and I went inside the bathroom and locked the door. I looked at myself in the mirror. Dark circles were under my eyes and I was overly thin and very drawn. Every ounce of the strain I'd been under was showing on my face and figure.

'I've put the kettle on,' Tom said through the door. 'Are you okay?'

I didn't answer.

'Charlotte?' he said trying the door.

'I'm fine. I'm going to take a bath.'

I heard him go away. It was a relief. I wanted him to just leave me alone.

I ran the cold tap into the sink and reached for my toothbrush with trembling hands. I was halfway through brushing my teeth before I realized my toothbrush should have been in the case I left at Tina's not back in the glass on the sink top.

I dropped it into the basin and came out of the bathroom. My case was at the bottom of the bed. Unpacked.

Tom came in the room.

'I got Stefan to fetch everything back last night while we were at the hospital. Let's stop this nonsense, Char. We love each other, why can't we just put the past behind us?'

'You dick,' I said. 'How dare you keep making decisions for me!'

'What? I don't—'

'Yes you do. You and your bloody mother. I'm sick of it, Tom. So sick that I can't eat, or think, and all I want to do is run away.'

Tom sank down onto the bed as though the wind had been knocked from his lungs.

He was stunned into silence. I went back into the bathroom and started running the bath.

'I think I've just realized exactly what my mother meant when she said this is all my fault,' Tom said on the other side of the door. 'I *have* been controlling. But it was all because I wanted to make you happy. Charlotte, will you talk to my therapist? Let her explain what I've been dealing with and then, if you can't see past everything, I'll let you go. I won't fight any divorce settlement you want and I won't go after custody of Melody. As long as you let me see her.'

His voice was reasonable, and even though I questioned if he was manipulating me again, the fight went out of me.

'Is that okay?' he asked.

'I'll think about it. I'm tired.'

'I know, darling. And I'm sorry. Sorry about everything, more than you could ever know.'

Chapter Forty-Six

The doctor discharged Melody a few days later.

'Why did you opt not to breastfeed?' he asked me as he was signing the release papers.

'We were advised against it,' Tom interjected before I could respond.

'Anyway, she seems fine and healthy now. Carry on as normal but monitor her. If you have any concerns bring her straight in.'

We took Melody home and life resumed as normal, on the outside. I wouldn't let Tom near me though, and even though we slept in the same bed he kept to his side.

'I'm not willing to move to Surrey right now,' I told him.

'It's on hold until you're ready,' he said. 'Whatever you want. Tina is happy in Moth— the apartment and says she'll help anyway she can. I'll give you time, Char.'

A few nights later, going through the motions of everyday life, I cooked us dinner. Melody had recovered but we still monitored her. There hadn't been any problems but I was terrified to leave her alone. I remained cold to Tom. I couldn't change how I felt overnight. Our life had got too weird and it was difficult to forget all that had happened.

'Thank you for cooking,' Tom said after we ate dinner in silence. 'I've arranged for you to meet Louise Clark tomorrow.'

'Who?'

'My therapist.'

'I didn't know her name,' I said.

'You never asked.'

I couldn't argue with his comment: it was true. I hadn't shown much interest at all in Tom's progress as he attempted to deal with the aftermath of his mother's death and her previous abuse. I realized how selfish that was as I looked at him across the table.

The guilt came again. Also, I was curious about his therapist.

'Okay,' I said. 'I'll meet her.'

Tom leapt out of his chair and rushed to me.

'Thank you, darling. Thank you. I know this will help us both.'

I let him hug me but didn't respond. I had no emotion to give him, but I was willing to hear what his therapist said. It might help me understand why he had behaved as he had. After that Tom chattered away over the dinner table as though there was nothing wrong between us. I barely answered above a yes or a no.

'I have permission to speak to you about your husband's state of mind,' said Louise Clark. 'But not reveal everything he's told me.'

Louise Clark was a clinical psychologist and her accreditation was displayed on the wall in an expensive frame.

'I understand.'

'Perhaps we should start with exploring how you are feeling?' she said. 'Anything you say to me will be confidential unless you give me permission to share it with Tom.'

I didn't know what to say.

'When did your problems start?' she prompted.

'I'm sure he told you I had an affair.'

Louise nodded.

'I was unhappy before that. I felt like ... I didn't have any say in my own life. Even the sheets. Those goddamn purple sheets.'

'Tom told me about it and why he was angry. He says he shared the details of his relationship with his mother with you,' Louise said. 'That you know about, but don't understand, some of the things he's done. That you struggle to get past them even though he wants to try.'

'Obviously, it's all *my* fault to him,' I said. 'Do you accept his behaviour was okay?' I asked.

'What matters is, do you?'

'He frightens me.'

'What can he do to make you feel more secure?' Louise asked.

'I don't know.'

'I can see that this will not be easy for either of you. It's obvious to me that you are suffering from depression. That you've struggled ever since this man you met abandoned you.'

I looked at Louise, surprised by her words.

'In your current state of mind, it's impossible for you to make any rational decisions. You can't forgive Tom, because emotionally you aren't in the right place. Equally you can't make a final decision as to whether the marriage is over.'

'I thought I came here to talk about Tom.'

'You both need help,' Louise said. 'Tom's recognized that, which is why he asked me to see you.'

'So, this is a medical intervention,' I half-laughed.

'Charlotte, I'm here to help you both, that's all. I can do that if you open up to me.'

'I feel ... tired. Drained all the time. Scared. And sometimes as though I can't feel anything.'

'All of these could be symptoms of depression,' she said. 'Or anxiety.'

All sorts of responses tumbled through my mind and I couldn't express any of them. So, I was depressed and anxious – not surprising really ...

I had to come to terms with Daniel's abandonment. No shit, Sherlock.

I couldn't decide whether my marriage was worth saving – that was true.

'Did Tom tell you his mother set me up to meet Daniel?' I said.

'Yes. He told me about it. He was very upset with the extent of how far she went. But he tells me he doesn't hold you responsible.'

'You believe that?'

'I do, yes.'

'Daniel is missing. What do you make of that? He vanished

the night before he was supposed to start a new life with me. Tom told me Isadora paid him off.'

'But you don't believe him?'

'I don't know what to believe. I just know Daniel had other people in his life that he would have made contact with.'

Louise's eyes narrowed. I stopped talking.

'Who?'

'I ... well ... he must have had ... you'd think,' I blustered. For some reason I didn't want to tell her about Becki or all the things we'd learnt together. Or the picture of Daniel that was hidden away in the bottom of my jewellery box.

'Charlotte do you know if there is any history of mental illness in your family?'

I didn't answer immediately, then I asked, 'Why would that have any bearing on how I feel?'

'Sometimes depression can be hereditary.'

'I don't know,' I said. But I recalled my mother had suffered from something. Post-natal perhaps. I just didn't want to tell her.

Louise studied me for a second as though she didn't quite believe me.

'I have to speak to Tom after this,' Louise said when our conversation dried up. 'What do you want me to tell him?'

I didn't know why but my paranoid side kicked in again. Could I trust Louise? After all she was Tom's therapist. This was a private practice. Tom was used to paying for anything he wanted.

The anxiety was back inside me and I was afraid of giving the 'wrong' answer even to someone who was supposedly impartial.

'Tell him ... I'll *try*,' I said. 'I can't promise more. But he needs to give me time.'

Louise smiled. 'I'm so relieved to hear that. I do think, and I'm not supposed to give my own opinion, that he deserves the benefit of the doubt. He's been through so much. In the meantime, I'll ask our practice doctor to prescribe you something. It will help to calm your nerves.'

'No. I don't want any pills.'

'It's just temporary and they are very mild. To see if it helps. You've been through a great deal and on top of it you have a new baby. All of these things can contribute to a range of emotions that can make it difficult sometimes to see straight. Wait here and I'll get the prescription for you.'

She left me in her office but returned very quickly with a prescription.

'One a day. That's all and they'll help you sleep better. Everyone feels stronger when they get enough sleep.'

I couldn't see any harm in trying the pills and so I took the prescription. It would be a relief to feel less stressed, and if these worked then it might clear my head enough to figure out what I wanted to do.

'Give it a week before you make a decision on whether they are helping. Then come back and see me and we'll talk again.'

Chapter Forty-Seven

Tom rang me when I left Louise's office. 'How did it go?' he asked.

'She gave me some pills. She says I'm depressed.'

'Oh my god, darling! I'm so not surprised. All of this ... shit ... we've both had to deal with. All because of my mother. It's just horrendous.'

'Yes,' I said.

'I've asked Tina to babysit tonight,' Tom said. 'I thought we could go to dinner. Talk.'

The thought of it made me feel anxious again but I had promised to try and so I agreed.

'Great,' said Tom. 'A date night. We haven't had one for ages.'

I went to the pharmacy and had the prescription made up. I was still unsure about taking anything but I was miserable and thought it worth a shot. I decided I'd at least give it the week as Louise suggested. If there was no improvement in how I was feeling I'd stop taking them.

I was on the way home when Tina called.

'Tom told me about your date tonight. I've booked you a hair appointment so that you can feel nice.'

'Tina that's really nice of you but—'

'They only have the one slot in forty-five minutes. Can you get there in time?'

I said I could but didn't really want the fuss. Then it occurred to me I'd let myself go a bit recently. Improving my outward appearance might have an impact on how I was inside. I put the phone down and I changed direction and went to see my hairdresser.

'You look nice,' Tina said when I got back to the apartment.

'It was a good suggestion,' I said. 'It has made me feel a little better.'

'Well you have to make an effort for date night,' she said.

I didn't correct her because she was happy with the thought that Tom and I were working things out. I spent time with Melody to give Tina a break because she'd be staying later that night.

At five o'clock she took Melody away to bathe her. 'You go and get yourself done up for tonight,' she said. 'Stefan's calling for you at six.'

'Isn't Tom coming home?' I said.

'No. He's meeting you at the restaurant.'

'I'll keep my phone on,' I said.

'Stop worrying now, Melody is fine. She's over it and the doctor's said there's no permanent harm done.'

'I know but ...'

'Stop blaming yourself. It would have still happened, even if you'd been with her.'

I got ready without much enthusiasm and the decision of

what to wear was harder than it should have been. I didn't want to look dowdy, but I also didn't want to look too available and give Tom the wrong impression. I wasn't ready for that part of our relationship to resume and wasn't sure if I ever would be.

Stefan rang upstairs from the reception to let me know he'd arrived, and so I pulled on a simple black dress and some casual jewellery to liven it up.

At the restaurant Tom was already at the table and waiting. He'd brought me back to the Italian but we had a quiet little booth near the front this time not the usual table.

He stood up when he saw me and kissed my cheek.

'Neutral environment,' he said as I took my seat in the booth opposite him. 'Is it okay for me to say you look beautiful?'

I smiled at him. 'Thank you.'

He'd ordered champagne and a waiter appeared to fill our glasses.

'We're celebrating?' I said.

'Louise told me you said you'd try. That's all I needed to hear, darling. And so, even though I get it – she stressed it's not a fix all at this stage – it feels like a major step forward for us.'

The champagne made me relax and we had a pleasant evening. I found myself chatting with him about Louise and the possibility of things improving between us. I think I was susceptible for a number of reasons that the alcohol aided. Louise had made me realize that the way I was feeling all the time wasn't normal and I could improve it. Also, I couldn't deny that Tom was at least trying to alter his behaviour by seeing the therapist in the first place.

'I'm so happy!' he said again and smiled at me, reaching over to stroke my hand. I pulled back from his touch though. I wasn't ready for even the smallest intimacy.

'But don't rush me, please,' I said. 'I'm just not ready right now to make any serious decisions.'

'Okay,' he said. 'I understand. But I know we'll get through this.'

Tom was smiling. He sat back in his chair and ordered another bottle of wine. I let the waiter refill my glass, then swigged down too quickly to hide my nerves. Was I doing the right thing? Or should I just get away from Tom as fast as possible.

When we got home, I took the first pill and then got ready for bed. Before I finished brushing my teeth, I was feeling groggy.

I climbed into bed and closed my eyes. My head was spinning with the excess of wine I'd drunk.

'You're mine,' Tom said.

I could feel him climbing into the bed beside me but couldn't move. I tried to open my eyes and look at him but I couldn't rouse myself at all. I slipped down into the dark depths of drug-induced sleep and didn't wake until morning.

'How do you feel?' Tom said the next day. 'You were sound asleep when I came to bed.'

'Was I? I thought you spoke to me.'

'Nope, you were unconscious when I came in. I was watching Melody sleep for ages – she's so beautiful and I'm so grateful she's better now.'

'Those pills worked their magic on me ... I don't feel too bad actually. A little groggy though.'

'Louise said that passes after a couple of days. Naturally, I asked her about them.'

I made breakfast. Tom didn't seem to be in a rush to go to work and then I realized it was Saturday.

'What should we do today?' he asked.

I didn't know what to answer. Then Tom's phone rang. He spoke for a moment and then hung up. He turned to me smiling.

'Good news! It was the builders. The work in the nursery and Tina's quarters is finished. Would you like a trip to the Manor? We could stay overnight. Check out the work and come back tomorrow.'

'I don't know.'

'Come on. It'll be a change of scenery.'

'I'm curious to see the renovations.'

'Then that's settled,' he said. 'Don't worry, all the rules between us still apply!'

With Tom's reassurance that he wouldn't push things and we were still taking it slow, I couldn't think of a sufficient argument against going to the Manor. I did want to see the finished work and so I got Melody dressed and packed an overnight case with all the things we'd need for a short stay.

Tom got the Range Rover out of the parking lot under the building and we set off out of London.

We reached the house just after one and were greeted by Sara, the housemaid who'd been taking care of things in our absence.

'The baby's grown so much!' she said. 'Are you sure you don't need me, Mr Carlisle? I could do with taking a trip home to make sure my mum's okay.'

'Yes, that's fine, Sara.'

Tom took our case inside, but the thought that Sara wasn't staying and we'd be alone made me very nervous. This was ridiculous, of course, because we were always alone in the flat in London and being alone here changed nothing.

'Will you be back tonight?' I said to her.

'No, Mr C gave me the day and night. Is that okay Mrs C?'

'Of course it is,' said Tom coming out again. He took Melody from me and went inside.

'I'll see you in the morning,' Sara said.

Sara left and I entered the manor house for the first time in weeks with a great deal of trepidation.

'She needed a break,' Tom explained. 'Please don't get paranoid. I want us to have a nice visit. See how it feels to be here again.'

I forced a smile. 'I know. Let's go and see the renovations.'

The nursery was finished with white cupboards from floor to cciling and lavender walls. There was a new cot for Melody and a pretty mobile attached to help her sleep. Tina's quarters were expensively furnished. I hadn't seen the choices she'd agreed with Tom, so it was a surprise to see the rooms so bright and cheerful. Her kitchen and bathroom were nice too.

'I have a surprise for you,' he said.

He placed Melody in her cot and set the mobile going. The

little girl gurgled at the moving animals as they lit up and flashed light around the room.

'That's nice,' I said.

'Oh, not that.'

He took my hand and led me away from the nursery back to the main landing. We were outside Isadora's room.

'Ta Da!' he said opening the door.

The room had been transformed. The bed removed and a new, luxurious bed stood in its place. There was a large dressing table in antiqued glass and it had all of the perfume and creams that I used already on it.

'I brought some of your things over a few weeks ago. Stuff I knew you wouldn't miss. Look in the wardrobe.'

'Tom ... I.' I frowned.

'Please, darling, you said you'd try.'

I was feeling bulldozed again but I opened the walk-in wardrobe and discovered it had also been rearranged. Gone were the heaps of shoe racks.

'You're not a shoe obsessed girl. Not like ...' he stopped himself. 'Anyway, I found this in your wardrobe. Darling, I don't think you've ever worn it.'

Tom pulled out the purple velvet dress that I'd wanted to wear two years earlier at the charity fundraiser, when Isadora had different ideas.

Tom's hand ran over the dress.

'Will you wear it for me?'

I didn't see how I could refuse without being accused again of not trying. 'Maybe later,' I said. 'Let's look at the rest of the work. I'm sure you have other surprises.'

'I do,' he said. 'Let's go for a walk.'

We collected Melody, and Tom got the pram out of the car. Then I placed her inside. We took a walk around the house and there, near the woods, at the back of the kitchen was the beginnings of a small play area.

'This will have a swing, slide, seesaw. Everything. And the ground will be surfaced with this soft substance that looks like tarmac but is actually spongey. If she falls it will be hard to hurt herself.'

'It's lovely!' I said genuinely impressed.

'Pick her up. Let me get a photo of you both as a before and after picture with the play area behind you.'

I let him take the picture and then found myself enjoying both his company and being back at the Manor. It was the most relaxed I'd felt in a long time.

'We can be happy here, Char,' he said noticing my change of mood. Then he kissed me on the lips for the first time in a while.

I let him be the one to pull away. He was happy and smiling after that and was delighted to be out in the open air.

'This is what we can't have in the city,' he said.

'I know. It's lovely here,' I said. Then I bit my lip.

'It's okay to relax with me,' he said. 'I want us to get back to being normal. I can't stand how distant we are these days. Please. Please ...'

His eyes filled with tears, and I had to hug him.

'We'll be okay? Won't we?' he said.

'I am relaxed,' I said. 'I'm having fun. This is a good start.' Melody was worn out with the fresh air and we put her to bed in her new room. Tom had thought of everything. He had even had a baby monitor wired in that had a portable console we could carry around the house with us. It was such a big house I don't think either of us would have relaxed otherwise.

'I'll make dinner. Why don't you try out the new bathroom and change?'

I didn't object because Tom was like his old self. Stress-free and happy and I did enjoy seeing him this way. It was so exhausting being unhappy all the time and so it was a relief to feel better, even if it was only temporary. I went upstairs and ran a bath. When I came out into the bedroom to remove my clothes I found the purple dress laid out on the bed and thought, *why not?*

'You look ... stunning,' said Tom as I came downstairs to the formal dining room.

I hadn't tried the dress on since that night and I had forgotten how it clung to me; I'd lost weight recently but the dress made my slender frame look curvy.

Tom handed me a glass of champagne. 'To us,' he said and he chinked my glass.

I sipped the wine and felt very calm. There was no anxiety or panic and I was happy to feel attractive. Tom's admiration wasn't so repellent either. Maybe the pills were working to soothe my nerves after all.

'Dinner is almost ready,' he said. Then he pulled me into his arms and delivered a warm, gentle kiss to my lips. He held me for a while, stroking his hand down my back until it rested on the top of my waist. Then it slipped lower and he cupped my bottom.

I pulled away and reached for my glass again.

Tom came up behind me and wrapped his arms around me.

'Sorry. You look amazing and ...'

His hand cupped my breast. The champagne was doing its job and I felt a surge of lust, but also a rush of nerves

'What about dinner?' I said trying to distract him.

He let me go and I was both relieved and slightly disappointed. There was a nervous sexual tension between us. It was confusing. I liked it and feared it.

'I'll go and get dinner,' he said. 'Sit down.'

He came back with two bowls of a beef casserole.

'You didn't make this,' I laughed.

'You got me.' he smiled. 'Sara put it on for us before she left. It's been stewing all day.'

I shook my head. 'Well, thank you for serving it!' I said.

Earlier, Tom had brought an expensive bottle of red wine up from the cellar and decanted it. He poured us both a glass to have with the casserole.

He brought in a plate of warmed crusty rolls and butter as well.

The food was delicious and I found myself relaxing more as the wine went down too easily.

After dinner Tom attached his iPod to the stereo and put some music through the speakers in the room. Then he pulled me to my feet and into his arms for a slow dance.

'It's okay,' he said when I tried to pull away. 'You're like a frightened little bird. I won't force anything. Can't we just enjoy this? Touch each other a little? It's been so long, Char?'

I tried to relax in his arms and accepted the groping.

'Your arse looks and feels wonderful in this dress.'

He kissed me again, more insistent but not forceful. Then, just like that, he stopped.

'Okay. I guess we need some sleep.'

I was relieved that he hadn't pursued things as we went upstairs. But a little confused as he went from being aroused by me, to completely shutting down. He was either pretending or had developed a great deal of self-control.

'Are you okay?' I said as we went upstairs.

'Yes. I'm doing as I'm supposed to,' he said.

'What do you mean?'

'Louise told me I had to keep my hands off you if I hoped to keep you.'

I was surprised to hear him say this and that he took so much notice of his therapist. It was a good thing though.

'Thank you,' I said and then I kissed him on the lips.

'I'll get you some water so that you can take your meds,' he said.

I checked on Melody and found her sound asleep. She was settling well at night and sleeping right through.

'You're such a good girl,' I said to her.

Back in the bedroom I found the water and pill by my side of the bed. Tom wasn't there and so I took the pill and then went into the bathroom. This time I couldn't finish brushing my teeth; I became overwhelmed with exhaustion.

'Char?' said Tom as I staggered towards the bed.

He caught me before I went completely unconscious. He picked me up and carried me to the bed.

'The pills work so fast ...' I said.

His eyes looked down at me, I was still wearing the purple dress, and they became filled with excitement. His hands stroked over the velvet again.

I tried to fight the sleep as it overtook me.

'I want you so much,' he said.

Chapter Forty-Eight

Tom was leaning on his arm watching me when I woke. He was smiling and flirty.

'Are you okay?' he said.

'Groggy.'

I lay back and stretched. I was still very sleepy and I hadn't much enjoyed the feeling of completely blacking out fully clothed.

My eyes fell on the purple dress, now lying across my dressing table stool. I lifted the covers and found I was wearing one of my nightgowns. I squeezed my eyes shut. I tried not to think about Tom stripping and changing me while I didn't know what he was doing.

I opened my eyes and found Tom still looking at me.

'Did you ...?'

'Of course I didn't. You were unconscious.'

I sighed then rubbed the sleep from my eyes trying to ignore the intense way he was studying me.

'Char?' he said.

I glanced at him and then away. I wished he'd stop looking

at me like that. So needy. So ... He pulled me to him and kissed me. I didn't resist, or respond.

'Please,' he begged between kisses. 'Please, Char. I love you so much!'

The situation was as it was. And so, I let him. I knew I was falling back into my old submissive patterns again but I couldn't help it. He was so intense it made me feel vulnerable: I didn't know what would happen if I refused.

After breakfast I went up to our room and started to pack the overnight case while Melody lay on our bed. Then I heard something outside. I picked up Melody, left the bedroom and traipsed downstairs.

'Another surprise, darling,' Tom said. 'We're moving in today!'

I had no opportunity to object as he opened the door and there was Tina and a removal van.

'Hey!' Tina said. '*Surprise!*'

Tina's smile dropped when she saw my expression. I couldn't hold the disappointment and shock from showing on my face even as I stepped back and watched the movers bringing in all of my personal things. I watched them taking boxes upstairs to Isadora's old room under Tom's direction. A sick, sinking feeling consumed me. I hurried into the downstairs bathroom and vomited.

'You should have warned me he was planning this,' I said. 'I wouldn't have come. I don't like to be tricked and I'm not ready.'

'I'm so sorry, Charlotte. He told me things were okay with you two!' Tina said.

She was distraught that not only had I been tricked but so had she.

I shook my head. I was trapped and very scared. I didn't know what to do. All the time I fought the rising panic that wanted to take hold of me. The urge to flee was so strong that all I could think of was what Becki would say about it: *follow your instinct not your head.*

Tina put her hand on my arm. It broke the spell my dread had me under.

'I'm really sorry. I know things have been ... difficult ... but I'm here as well. You aren't alone. Let's see how things settle. If it doesn't work out then we'll leave with Melody. I'm on your side, Charlotte.'

I took a breath and forced myself to calm down. She was right. Having her and the residential staff did guarantee that Tom and I were never really on our own. Perhaps this would be better than being in the flat with him where it was just him, me and Melody. At least the house was big and I could always find somewhere to be away from Tom if I wanted.

I regretted giving in to Tom that morning though. I was uneasy because I knew this meant I'd agreed to our relationship normalizing sexually. A situation I wasn't a hundred per cent ready for. With everything that had happened in recent months it was difficult to reconcile all of my emotions against all of the revelations. This meant that, typically, I had fallen back into my role of capitulation. It frustrated me. It angered me too.

I left Tina and went off to find Tom to give him a piece of my mind. I had to stand up for myself, and insist on those boundaries. Maybe I'd even move into one of the other bedrooms. At least here there was a choice.

Tom was in the garden looking at the groundwork of the mini-playground again. He was smiling as he looked over the ground and the thin grove that had once been Isadora's spring flower beds.

'You shouldn't have done this,' I said behind him. 'You've taken control from me again. It's bang out of order!'

His expression went dark, he looked angry, then his features smoothed and he smiled again.

'Your therapist won't be impressed by how you've pushed things.' I was angry and I let him know it.

'Sweetheart,' he said, 'I don't know why I did it. I should have consulted you. It was impulsive … Look, I'm heading back to the flat this afternoon and you will have all the time you want here. You're right. But I know we can make it work. I just thought here, we might have a fresh start. Thank you for this morning. It was wonderful to feel close to you again.'

The wind was taken out of my sails again. He was an expert at doing that. Tom kissed me on the head and hugged me.

The anxiety washed away from me with the thought of him gone.

'I'll leave you the Range Rover so that you can go out with Melody and Tina,' he continued. 'Let's go and unpack. My suits and some personal stuff are still at the flat, but I've had everything of yours brought here. I thought you'd be upset otherwise.'

Everything of mine had been brought here … Had every trace of me and Melody been removed from the London flat? I tried not to think too much about what that meant.

I went up to Isadora's bedroom – I still couldn't think of it as ours – and waded through the boxes, hanging up my clothes and storing my jewellery and toiletries, while Tom unpacked all of his more casual clothes onto the other side of the walk-in. I didn't speak to him while we worked, pretending to be concentrating on the task. But each time I took out a personal item I weighed up whether I would need it if I took Melody and left. I was even more ready to flee than I'd been before. And I felt, instead of anxiety, a burgeoning rage.

A few hours later Stefan turned up in the limo, and Tom returned to London with a small bag containing his toiletries.

'I'll need two sets. Some there and some here,' he had said. 'I've left you a list of things to buy for me this week. It's on the dressing table.'

I didn't answer. He kissed me on the head and left.

Sara made a roast dinner for Tina and me that night.

'Mr C said you both had to be looked after,' she said.

It wouldn't be usual that Tina would eat with us as the plan was she had her own space in the house just as we did. It was difficult for me to know how to behave in this situation ultimately. Whenever we'd visited Isadora, the help had never joined us for dinner. But Tina had become closer to me than that. This was someone I trusted to care for my child and we had a growing friendship too. Equally, it would be just as weird to have her around us all the time.

After dinner we retired to our rooms. I took Melody's monitor with me, even though Tina was in the room next door. We'd agreed certain days and nights when she wouldn't be working just as we had in London. That night was one of Tina's but I was finding it difficult to relax and leave Melody to her if she woke.

Although I knew I didn't need to worry, I wasn't sure I wanted to take another of the pills – they were making me too sleepy too quickly and I needed to be more alert for Melody on my 'on' nights.

I relaxed and watched some television instead and I let the day's stresses wash away.

Tom's absence relieved a huge amount of pressure. I didn't have to talk, or be polite, or 'try' to make things work. I didn't have to do anything. It was the most relaxed I'd felt in a long time.

I heard Melody stirring a little on the monitor. Tina was on the ball and she hurried into the room.

'There's a good girl,' she cooed.

Melody settled down and all went quiet, then Tina's phone rang. Tina answered it in hushed tones.

'Hi Tom,' she said.

I sat up and picked up the monitor, turning up the volume.

'All is okay ... No, Melody is fine ... Charlotte was angry with me for not warning her.'

There was a long pause as Tom obviously replied at length.

'Paranoid?' said Tina then. 'Yes. She is. You're right. But don't worry, things will improve.'

The call ended and I didn't know how to react. My brain was overloading again. Could it be that Tina was conspiring with Tom?

I got up out of the bed and paced. I felt betrayed and scared again. That dark anxiety was back with a vengeance. Was Tina now Tom's spy instead of the detective agency?

I couldn't sleep after that, and in the end, out of desperation, I took one of the pills Louise had given me. I lay in bed afterwards waiting for that blackness to consume me again. But this time the pill didn't work so quickly.

Perhaps I was getting used to them after all. Then a suspicion reasserted itself. Maybe it wasn't the pills that had been making me sleep. Perhaps it was something else entirely?

Consumed with doubt again I sat up in bed. Why wasn't the pill working? Then I remembered – Tom had left me water on each occasion I had taken a tablet. Perhaps he had added something else?

Panic surged up inside me along with that sickening nausea that accompanied it. I was unsure what to do. I couldn't trust anyone. Tom could be very persuasive and I had no doubt he had given Tina a very reasoned argument as to why we had problems. Maybe he'd even laid all the blame my way in order to ensure her help. It didn't matter either way. I now couldn't confide in her.

The urge to run was strong. But I knew I couldn't go anywhere that night, just in case the medication did suddenly kick in.

I got out of bed and crossed the room to the dressing table. There I picked up my mobile phone and looked at it. Who could I call? I had to tell someone how I was feeling. I thought about Valentina, but realized that was impossible. Rufus's loyalty was to Tom and so would hers be. I'd have to tell her everything or she would think I was losing my mind. The twists and turns of my life went back too far and I couldn't share that shame with anyone.

Then I thought of Becki. I hadn't spoken to her since we had been at Paula's flat, though I'd sent her a text telling her about Melody being ill.

I dialled her number as I sat down at the dresser.

'Hey,' she said. 'Hadn't heard from you in a while. How's Melody now?'

'She's better ... Becki I ...'

'What's wrong?' she asked.

I told her about Tom's 'surprise'.

'And now he's gone, suddenly my pills aren't making me sleepy.'

'Charlotte,' she said, 'Tom can't be trusted. What if he's been slipping you Rohypnol?'

'No. It couldn't be that, I just crashed asleep each time.'

'No memory loss?'

'Just sleep. Waking groggy. That's all.'

'I can't believe he tricked you into moving there,' she said. 'Every move he makes is just ... creepy.'

I couldn't disagree. Even groping me in the purple dress had been too intense.

'I'm feeling a little tired now,' I said. 'Maybe the meds are working.'

'Try and sleep. But call me tomorrow,' she said.

I hung up but brought the phone to the bedside. Then I climbed back into bed. I was sleepy now, but nothing near the dramatic 'blacking out' of the previous few nights.

I closed my eyes and drifted down.

Then, I thought I heard a movement. Someone was in the bedroom. I tried to open my eyes, but the medication was doing its job now. I fell into an anxious dream, where I was convinced Tom had come back to the Manor, late at night, and was standing over the bed watching me. In the dream I yelled at him to leave me alone. But Tom remained silent, frowning, intense and utterly terrifying.

Chapter Forty-Nine

The next day I woke feeling more clearheaded than other mornings. The residue of the dream left me with a vague discomfort and phobia. But I knew it was just stress and was all in my imagination.

I texted Becki to say I was okay.

If you have any doubts, you should leave, she replied. *Glad you're OK xx*

I pulled on my robe and went into Melody's room. She was awake but playing with her hands. I stared down at her. My beautiful girl was so sweet and innocent, so oblivious to all the turmoil in her mother's life. I could tear her away from her home but on what basis? Had Tom drugged me? If so, why? There was no motive. He had me there, sleeping beside him. I'd even had sex with him.

Perhaps I was paranoid and just reading into things. In the cold light of day my panic the night before seemed ridiculous. As for the antidepressants it was more than likely that my body was just getting used to the medication.

Tina came in the room, fully dressed and ready to work.

'She never woke,' she said. 'She's such a good baby.'

'I guess now her illness is settled she's catching up on sleep,' I said.

'Did you sleep well?' she asked.

'Yes. Took a while.'

'I expect you're missing Tom,' she said.

I nodded then picked Melody up and held her close.

'My beautiful girl,' I whispered, kissing her forehead.

I looked up to see Tina smiling at me.

'Everything's going to be okay, Charlotte,' she said. 'You already seem so much happier here.'

I didn't correct her, but I let her take Melody and left them, while I returned to my room to shower and change.

Tom rang me later and I had to ask, 'Did you come back here? Late last night?'

'No, of course not,' he said. 'What's this all about? Are you okay?'

I didn't answer his question and found an excuse to hang up instead. It had to have been a dream, but it was so vivid: I'd been certain someone had been in my room.

The days passed quickly as we all settled into a routine at the Manor. I registered at a local gym. I went out shopping locally with Tina and Melody and we bought Tom's toiletries for the Manor. Then on Friday, I took the train into London and made my way to Louise Clark's office for our agreed meeting.

At her offices I was hurried in ahead of schedule.

'I had a cancellation,' she said. 'How are you? How have the pills been?'

'Tom surprised me with a sudden move to Surrey,' I said. I was blunt because I wanted to see how she reacted.

'He *what?*'

I told her how the week had panned out.

'I suppose you didn't know he planned this?' I said.

She was frowning. 'I would have advised against such a sudden change. Especially going back to the Manor. With his history there.'

I was quiet for a moment, then I said, 'The pills have been okay. They made me very tired at first but that's settled down.'

'That can happen. What about your anxiety?' she asked.

'Tom's been in London all week. He comes back for the weekend this evening. I haven't been anxious much in his absence.'

'Oh good. Then the medication is working,' she said ignoring the obvious reason for my lack of anxiety. 'I'd like to keep you on them a little longer.'

I took the next prescription and waited for her to ask another question.

'So how are you and Tom getting along now?'

'He's been in touch every day, obviously. I'm a little nervous about his return. We had sex last weekend. I ... couldn't say no.'

'Charlotte, you must say no if you don't want to. That's important for his therapy and for yours. Tom recognizes that he is ... controlling at times. It's important that you fight your corner with him. *Do you understand?*'

It could have been my imagination, but I wondered if Louise was trying to tell me something else. I studied her face, but her expression was blank and gave nothing away.

'I can't see you again,' she said. 'But I'll recommend someone to you.'

'Why?' I said.

'It's okay for me to help a couple in *joint* therapy but in this case, I feel you should both have separate treatment.'

'Okay,' I said. 'I only came because Tom wanted me to speak to you.'

'That's what I mean, Charlotte. You have to start doing what you want. Not just what Tom does.'

I left her offices and made my way out onto the street. There I found Stefan and Tom waiting with the limo.

'I thought I'd surprise you, darling,' Tom said.

Of course – he had known I would be here.

'Stefan will drive us home together and we'll be back in time for afternoon tea.'

'Good morning, Stefan,' I said.

'Mrs C ...' he nodded.

Tom's chauffeur no longer met my eyes; instead, he kept them turned down as though he had to examine his shoes for blemishes. I don't know why but his refusal to look at me made me wonder if Tom talked to him about our problems. It didn't seem likely but the thought made me uncomfortable.

Tina was already packed for her weekend in London when we arrived home.

'Stefan's heading back now,' Tom said. 'He'll drop you at the flat.'

'See you Sunday, Charlotte,' she said as I took Melody from her.

'Have a nice break,' I said.

I put Melody in her pram for her afternoon nap, and then I wheeled her through the hallway and down to the kitchen. The house was huge to me still and I wondered if I would ever get used to being there. Despite the years of living in a two-bedroom apartment in London, Tom was perfectly at home there. I supposed that was because I had never been brought up in such ostentatious surroundings and didn't take them for granted as Tom did. Beyond being pleased with the new decor, I doubt he even noticed the splendour of his childhood home.

Afternoon tea was waiting for us both as we entered the kitchen. We sat down at the large rustic table and Sara served us hot tea, smoked salmon sandwiches, scones with butter, jam and thick whipped cream and there was also a selection of cakes to choose from. It was an overwhelming amount of food.

Sara left us alone, and Tom reached across the table to hold my hand.

'I missed you,' he said.

I smiled at him but didn't respond.

'Melody's grown too!'

'She's much more alert now,' I said, 'and I think the smiles aren't just wind anymore.'

Tom laughed. 'She changes by the week at the moment.'

Sara came back into the kitchen.

'I'm going now if there's nothing else?'

'That's fine,' said Tom. 'We'll see you Sunday evening.'

I'd expected Tina to go away for the weekend but not Sara, even if she was off duty.

I tensed up when I realized that Tom and I would be alone for two nights again.

'Just think,' he said as though reading my mind, 'we'll have this place all to ourselves.'

'What about the groundskeeper?' I said.

'Old Freddie has gone to visit a friend. He does take the occasional weekend off, and we rarely see him even if he's around.'

'Oh,' I said.

'How did it go with Louise?' he asked.

'Fine.'

'More pills?' he asked.

'She did give me another prescription.'

'Another week's worth until she sees you again no doubt,' said Tom.

'I'm not seeing her again.'

Tom put down his sandwich and sat back in his chair. 'Charlotte, I thought we agreed to give this a shot.'

'You don't understand. She said *she* can't see me again as she's treating you.'

Tom frowned. 'But I agreed with her that it was okay.'

'She has obviously changed her mind. She thinks it would be unethical.'

Tom sipped his tea and nibbled his sandwich. He was very quiet.

'Darling, just excuse me a moment, I have just remembered I have some work to do. A couple of phone calls to make. Then I'm all yours for the weekend.'

He kissed me, then went off to the Manor office in the west wing. It occurred to me then that I'd been in the house a week and hadn't even looked in the office. Or thought about tending to the expenses.

The Manor's expenses had been shifted temporarily to the finance office at Carlisle Corp while we hadn't been there. Yet, if I was living in the house, I knew I should be taking on the duties that Mrs Tanner had taught me. At least until we found a new housekeeper. Instead I'd been leaving most of the running of the estate to Sara without thinking. No wonder she wanted to get out of there for the weekend! She must have been exhausted.

I tidied up the plates, putting the cakes and scones away and covering the remaining sandwiches with foil. I put them in the fridge with the intention that we'd eat them later.

Pushing Melody's pram I made my way over to the office to see if Tom was finished and to take a look at the estate emails, just in case there was something I needed to attend to.

As I approached, I saw that the office door was open and I could hear Tom having a heated debate with someone on the phone.

'I told you what I wanted, and this does not help me in the slightest!'

The call ended as I reached the office door.

'I need to check the emails,' I said.

'Leave it,' he said abruptly. 'It'll still be there in the morning. Let's go for a walk.'

He took over pushing Melody's pram and we went back towards the kitchen and into the grounds through the back door while I followed.

*

Tom was a little distant that evening. I was sure it was my fault. I must have said or done something wrong, but couldn't pinpoint what it was. He cheered up when he spent time with Melody though, and enjoyed feeding her before her final change.

'She's adorable, Char,' he said. 'I love her so much.'

'Me too,' I said.

Our daughter was delightful. It was the only thing I was certain we both agreed on.

Eventually I took Melody upstairs, bathed and changed her, and sat in the nursery until she drifted off to sleep with the musical, animal mobile slowly spinning above her cot. Then I went downstairs and joined Tom in the huge lounge.

He was sitting in one of the chairs by the fire. As I passed his chair in order to go to the one next to him, he pulled me onto his lap and wrapped his arms around me. Then he cuddled me to him. I rested my head on his shoulder and tried to relax.

'Are you hungry?' I asked after a while. 'I can fetch the sandwiches and some cake.'

'Okay. I'll find us something nice to drink,' said Tom heading towards the wine cellar.

I went off to the kitchen, returning shortly with the tray of food, which I placed on the coffee table.

Tom had already uncorked the wine and he held out a glass to me.

I took it and sat down, opposite him now.

We ate, and then finished the bottle of wine. After that Tom took my hand and led me upstairs to our room.

'I need you, Char,' he said. 'But Louise told me to let you lead everything.'

I was trembling as I went into the bathroom to brush my teeth. It was ridiculous that the thought of having sex with my husband of twelve years would strike such terror in my heart. When I came out of the bathroom, I found a glass of water and my jar of pills by the bed.

'I think we should just cuddle,' Tom said. He was already in bed.

I went into the walk-in wardrobe and pulled a nightgown from one of the drawers. Then I took my clothes off in there and changed.

I came into the bedroom and got into bed. Tom held out the water and pill to me. I couldn't really refuse without revealing that I was nervous of drinking water he'd brought me.

I took the pill, swallowing it with the least amount of water I could.

Then Tom pulled me to him and wrapped his arms around me. Within moments I was feeling woozy, unlike every time I'd taken the medication when Tom wasn't around.

'No ... you've ...' My words were slurring.

'Sleep, Charlotte,' Tom said. 'I'll watch over you.'

He's definitely drugging me!

I woke with this thought in my head, even as I stumbled blearily from the bed and into the bathroom. I was nauseous too. I splashed water on my face, then came back into the bedroom. Then I noticed Tom wasn't in the bed.

I picked up my phone and checked the time. It was 6.30 in

the morning and the room was still quite dark, with no light peeping around the curtains. I turned on the bedside lamp, and then I noticed that Tom's side of the bed didn't appear to have been slept in.

I glanced back to my side, and saw that Melody's monitor wasn't there.

I pulled on a robe and left the room, hurrying down to the nursery.

I opened the door and found Tom fast asleep in a chair with a blanket thrown over his legs. I checked in the cot and found Melody asleep and well.

I put my hand on Tom's shoulder and shook him gently. He jerked awake.

'Charlotte?'

'Why are you here?'

'She was restless. I was worried. And you were so fast asleep ...'

'Tom. What did you put in my water?'

'Your water? What do you mean?'

'Every evening when you weren't here, the pills only made me a little drowsy and not straight away. You drugged me, didn't you?'

'Good God! Why would I do that?'

'I don't know, but you did it.'

'Charlotte. Have you heard yourself? That's insane?'

'So is drugging your wife.'

'I swear to you I didn't!'

Melody began to cry a little. I glanced in at her. It was half-hearted and her eyes were screwed up in sleep.

Tom was on his feet when I looked back at him.

'Charlotte ...' he reached for me.

'Don't touch me.'

Tom went away and left me in the nursery with Melody. A few moments later he came back holding his mobile phone out to me.

'It's Louise. She wants to talk to you.'

I took the phone.

'Hello? Charlotte?'

'Yes,' I said.

'What's wrong? Tom says you're having a meltdown.'

'He's been drugging me,' I said.

'Charlotte, explain why you think this?'

I told her about the way the medication had been affecting me, but only when Tom was around.

'Is there anything you were doing differently just because he's home?' she asked.

'No. Of course not. Though ... he might not be putting it in the water, it could be the wine he gave me—'

'*Wine?* Charlotte have you taken the pills after alcohol?'

'Erm ...'

'Didn't you read the instructions? You're not supposed to have these with any alcohol.'

I handed the phone back to Tom. He spoke to Louise a little longer then he hung up.

'I take it you haven't drunk anything alcoholic while I was away?'

'No. You know I barely drink.'

'Sweetheart, I just don't know what I can do to regain your

trust. This is breaking my heart. All I want to do is have my wife back. A normal life. Is that too much to ask for?'

Tom was in tears so I went to him. I choked out an apology, but it just didn't seem enough. When Tom kissed me, I knew what would make things right. And even though my heart and mind fought a battle with my insecurities, I had to smooth things out.

It was true that I had become paranoid but was I losing my mind too?

Chapter Fifty

I was sick of myself. So tired of fighting against what appeared to be inevitable. I promised Tom I would make an appointment with Louise's colleague who was based in Surrey. In the meantime, I forced myself to have as normal a weekend with him as possible. I didn't have any wine and afterwards, when I took my pills, I wasn't blacking out, or groggy and sickly in the morning. The pill just soothed me into a normal sleep.

When Tina and Sara returned on Sunday we had fallen back into our old patterns before all of the troubles. I went through the motions of appearing to be happy. I let it be natural to reach for his hand, and allowed him to hold mine without being awkward about it.

'Look at you two lovebirds!' Tina said after Tom kissed me goodbye just before he left again with Stefan. 'You had a nice time together then?'

I smiled at her words. By the end of the weekend our time together had been sort of nice. I'd forced myself to stop analysing everything Tom did.

It was easier to enjoy Tom's company when I didn't 'think',

and he had loved spending time with Melody. I told myself that all it took was for me to chill and stop looking for problems where there weren't any.

'You're gonna be all right,' Tina smirked. 'I can tell!'

Tom sent me a text when he reached the London flat.

Missing you already xxx

He phoned me before bed that night too and chatted about Melody and his plans for work that week. He kept in regular touch that week, texting, phoning and sending me silly selfies. There was something romantic about the amount of energy and attention he spent thinking about me instead of the company, even though he was there all week.

By the next weekend I was actually looking forward to Tom's return and we began a process of healing again that I hoped would be the end to all of our troubles, as Tina had predicted.

The weeks went by. And then, as Melody turned four months old, Tom decided he could work from the Manor.

'I'm missing you both too much,' he said.

By then I was pleased to have him around. I was no longer behaving like I expected a blow any minute, and for this reason Tom started to appear less threatening. Perhaps my behaviour had brought this constant tension into our lives. I didn't blame myself for everything, instead I began to accept that we had both made mistakes and we could rectify it if we tried.

Life normalized. It was what I wanted more than anything else. Tom was a great father and I knew he could be a wonderful husband. Especially as he was trying so much to make me happy. I stopped feeling guilty about everything, trying to focus on the present and future only.

Despite Isadora's role in ruining Tom's life, I still remembered her words about 'choosing to be happy' and I did. Perhaps it was easier than the alternative of living with paranoia. Some might say I'd rolled over and offered my belly as sure as a docile cat would. But, living in a state of flux and unhappiness had made us all miserable. This was the best and only way forward.

Tom stopped seeing Louise, and because I was now fine, I dropped the pills and didn't, in the end, take up her recommendation to see someone she knew. Now the anxiety had receded there didn't appear to be any need. I was convincing myself that all was well. It wasn't that difficult to do in the end, once I'd made up my mind to improve things.

I woke one morning with a good lift in my mood and I knew then that the depression was gone. I'd turned a corner. There was no longer any fear or anxiety and Tom was being thoughtful and loving all of the time. His behaviour showed me there was nothing to panic about.

I was lulled, but then, on our fifth week in the house, everything changed.

It was a Friday afternoon. Tina and Sara had both gone for the weekend. Tom and I were alone. This was the usual routine and I was very comfortable with it.

Work had continued on the mini-playground at the back of the house, even though Melody was years away from using it, and Tom was outside overseeing this as his own personal project.

By then I was in a regular routine of running all of the estate's finances and payroll. Every day I checked the Manor emails and on Fridays, when Melody was safely in her cot having her afternoon nap, I did the paperwork associated with salaries. That Friday, while Tom was outside, I entered the office as usual.

It was huge, but it only had one main desk. Tom had ordered another one that he would set up to work on when he was at home; however that day he was still using the antique mahogany desk, which stretched six feet wide in the corner. The Manor desktop stood on it and so now did Tom's laptop.

I sat down at the desk and turned on the computer. The laptop lid was open but the screen was dark. I picked it up, moving it aside so that I could pull the desktop keyboard and mouse closer. My finger nudged the mouse pad on the laptop and the screen lit up. I glanced at it.

It was open on Tom's work emails. Nothing unusual in that. I placed it down at the other side of the desk, then I looked back at the desktop monitor.

The running software was still loading. I'd mentioned to Tom how slow it was, and we were planning to update the machine. Then I heard a ping from Tom's laptop and I glanced back at the screen.

An email had arrived. I glanced at Tom's laptop in reflex. I froze.

The email was from Abbott's detective agency.

I told myself it was probably nothing, but the subject header said 'Charlotte'.

The suspicion returned in a rush of apprehension. I felt my face flush and my heart jolted in my chest. My trembling hand reached out with a mind of its own and before I could stop myself, I was operating the mouse pad and double-clicking on the email. My mind screamed at me not to look, but I couldn't stop myself.

The message opened up with the note, 'Copies attached as requested'.

There was a zip file attached and I clicked 'download'. It took a moment and then a box came up asking if I wanted to 'open' or 'save'. I clicked 'open'. Inside the folder were hundreds of jpeg files. I hesitated for a split second and then I opened the first one.

It was a picture of me with Daniel Evans.

The blood rushed harder into my face. Flustered, I rifled through the other images: this was a digital version of the folder of photographs that Tom had previously destroyed.

But why? Why did he want them?

Outside I heard the builders' trucks leaving and I knew that Tom would come in at any moment. I took a deep breath and quelled my nerves. The best course of action was not to run away scared, but to face this and learn what it meant. We'd had such bad communication and it had led me several times down the road of misunderstanding. I'd never asked Tom why he had done anything before I reacted – often rashly. This was a perfect opportunity to show some maturity and to confront my phobias at the same time.

Tom came into the room.

I stayed in the chair, behind his laptop and I looked up at him. He was smiling.

'Builders have gone now for the weekend, but we have a delivery of stuff coming in the morning.

Tom glanced at me, and then his laptop and his face changed.

'What are you doing?'

'I came in to do the accounts. As usual.' I was calm. 'Your laptop was open ...'

'I need to get some more work done. I'm afraid our evening can't start just yet.'

He walked around the desk and then he saw what I was looking at.

'Why do you want copies?' I asked, my voice as neutral and calm as possible.

I looked up at my husband standing beside me. What I expected to see wasn't there. Gone was the loving husband. Instead I saw the man that had hit me after Isadora's funeral.

He walked back towards the office door and closed it, turning the key in the lock. He turned to face me. Tension oozed from him even as his face went blank. Calm.

'Charlotte,' he said, 'why have you been looking at my laptop?'

'I ... didn't intend to. It was open, Tom. Then this came in. Just tell me why? That's all I ask. Look, I'm not going to make a fuss ... I just want to understand.'

His voice was cold; his eyes flint hard.

Despite my determination to show no fear my body reacted

and I stood up as he walked towards me, knocking the chair over. It tipped to the floor.

I backed away until my body pressed against the wall.

'I'm trying to be reasonable. Giving you the benefit of the doubt.'

'Then why are afraid?' he said.

The hairs stood up on the back of my neck and arms as he studied me. He was so cold it was terrifying.

'No!' I said. 'Don't. Please. Just stay there. Let's talk.'

He continued walking towards me. Like a cat playing with a mouse. My fear intensified with the realization that he *enjoyed* seeing my terror.

'Don't ...' I said again.

'Don't what?'

'Don't touch me.'

'I'm going to touch you, Charlotte. I'm going to touch you anytime I like.'

'Tom!' I held my hand out before me trying to ward him off. But he caught hold of it and yanked me to him.

I had a flash of a scene from a film we had watched together. Jack Nicholson in *The Shining*, approaching poor Shelley Duvall with a baseball bat and promising that he didn't want to hurt her.

'Get off me!' I yelled.

'You're mine, Charlotte,' he said. 'I'm sick of this game we play where you think you have any say over that at all. It's time you learnt the truth.'

He caught hold of me. I struggled, turning my face away as he tried to kiss my lips. But Tom was strong and so much bigger than me. He was able to hold me around the waist with one hand while his other grabbed my hair, yanking it painfully as he forced me to face him. He pressed his lips hard on mine, tongue probing my mouth open. I struggled, lashing out with my feet and hitting him with closed fists, but I was like a fly trying to swat a giant. His tongue was suffocating me. I turned my head, and bit his lip.

Tom yelped, pushed me away and wiped his hand across his mouth. It came back covered in blood.

He smiled coldly when he saw the blood. I knew then I had to get away from him and no amount of therapy would ever make me believe again that Tom was sane. He wasn't.

'You little bitch,' he said. 'I'm so going to enjoy cowing you once and for all.'

All that time I'd known there was something wrong. I'd tried to deny my instinct to run. Now Tom had shown his hand, I had to get away, or I never would.

Tom was grinning and the blood dripping from his mouth only served to make him appear even more terrifying: and absolutely psychotic.

I threw my body weight towards him, he stumbled back and I dashed around him and the desk heading to the door. But Tom was too quick for me and he grabbed at my arm, yanking me backwards. He pinned me in his arms, holding me tight around the waist. He glared in my face with an expression of maniacal hatred. I lashed out with my free hand, long fingernails raked his grinning cheeks. Tom yelped again.

He pushed me away and then his hand moved, backhanding me in the face. The full force of his rage sent pain shooting through my right cheek. I fell back, arms flailing unable to stop my crash to the floor.

My head cracked against wood. I was aware of the dull crunch of my skull connecting with the mahogany desk and then blackness swooped in around my eyes.

Chapter Fifty-One

Damp grit hit me in the face. I twitched. I was lying at an odd angle; one arm trapped and numb under my body. I was confused, dreaming. There was a blur of sound. Scraping somewhere above me. Metal hitting stone. Birds? The rustle of leaves.

My head hurt as I tried to remember where I was. I floated above consciousness. Had I drunk too much the night before? Had the pills reacted with the alcohol ... but no. I wasn't taking the pills and I hadn't drunk anything.

A vision of Tom smiling pushed its way behind my eyes. Then the smiling façade fell away and he appeared to grow in size like some comic book villain I'd once dreamed him to be.

Another smack of dirt fell over me. A drop of a pebble that hit my ankle, shocking me awake.

And then my half-conscious mind knew where I was. The dream warped into a nightmare. I was in a grave and someone was throwing dirt over me.

My survival instinct kicked in as my mind forced me to wake.

I opened my eyes. My vision was blurred and I blinked until it cleared. Then I turned my head and looked up.

I was in a pit of damp soil. I could see a canopy of trees overhead and then I realized I was in the wood at the back of the Manor, just beside Melody's playground.

My arm below my body had gone to sleep; I shifted, freeing it, then stretched my numb fingers out.

Another shovelful of soil hit me. The shadow of my husband towered over the hole.

'Tom?' My voice cracked.

Tom stopped moving and even though I couldn't make out his features I felt his eyes on me.

'So, you are still alive,' he said.

Did he think he had accidentally killed me, then panicked and tried to hide the evidence? If so, then there was a possibility I could survive this. I glanced around and then back up. The hole wasn't that deep. I could climb out myself, but it would be easier with help.

'You should have listened to me. We could have had a life together.'

I struggled into a sitting position. My hands grasped at damp dirt and soil. More fell over me.

My god! He's really going to bury me alive!

'Tom. I'm your wife ...' I stuttered.

Tom raised the spade, and I knew my end was about to come.

'Time to sleep, Charlotte,' he said.

'Wait! At least tell me why.'

'I'm not going to hurt you, Charlotte. You left me. You tried to take Melody but I wouldn't let you. So, you left *alone*.'

'Think about this, Tom. No one will believe that.'

'Oh, but they will. Tina knew you were irrational. Paranoid. Then there is Louise. How you accused me of drugging you. You've been displaying signs of insanity for quite some time.'

'You planned this. All along. But why?' I was terrified but had to keep him talking while I tried to think of a way out.

'You're mine,' he said.

'I am, Tom. I am.'

'I told Mother you'd betray me. But she said you wouldn't. Oh, at first it seemed she'd won, and I was about to call my spies off and then ... you met him again and went for coffee.'

'You were behind it all ... with Isadora.'

Tom laughed. 'She didn't want to do it. Tried to convince me it was wrong. But I had to see what you would be capable of. And I wasn't disappointed.'

'But, I thought this was all behind us, Tom. I thought you'd forgiven me.'

Tom laughed harshly.

'That's just the point. I *loved* watching someone else fucking you, knowing you're mine and no one but me can keep you ... oh how you screamed in his arms.'

Nausea. I put my hand to my head and felt dried and crusted blood. I must have been out for a while. At the very least I had concussion, but I had to keep my wits about me. Had to talk my way out of this hole.

Think Charlotte!

I forced myself to be as calm as possible. I had to sound reasonable and placid. I had to appear to be pliable.

'Okay. You liked it. I get it ...'

338

'Yes.'

'What do you want me to do?'

'Do?'

'I'll do whatever you want, Tom. We can still be a family. You want that, don't you? You can keep the photos. I won't ever look at your laptop again.'

'You're mine.'

'I am. I really am. But if you ... *kill* me ... I *won't* be yours anymore. Is that what you want? Me gone, *forever*.'

Tom raised the shovel above his head. I covered my head with my arms waiting for the blow.

Then his hand reached down and grasped my arm.

'Come on,' he said.

My other hand dropped and scrabbled at the earth as I tried to climb to my feet. And then I touched something else. Something cold and hard and round. I looked down at my hand and even though I couldn't see clearly my eyes had adjusted enough to make out the shape of a skull.

A muffled cry came from my lips. My calm crumbled. There was a body in the grave with me and I was certain that wasn't a coincidence. Ignoring Tom's outstretched hand, I looked up again, trying to get my bearings. This spot, near the trees, was already a grave. Tom had known that all along. I had a flash memory of the selfies he'd taken here. Realizing this was his own private sick joke. But why? Who was down here? There could only be one explanation.

'What have you done?' I said.

His hand dropped. Tom lifted the shovel again.

'Oh my god,' I said. 'You killed him. You really did it.'

I lost my composure then. Tears leaked from my eyes and I knew this was the end. I couldn't talk Tom down. I wasn't getting out of this grave now that I knew Daniel Evans's body was in it. It was over and with the confirmation that Daniel was dead my will to fight dissolved.

Images from the past few months flashed behind my eyes. The selfie taken in this very spot. The obsession with building Melody's playground here. Was it really about our daughter or was Tom building a permanent monument over the body of the man he killed? And now I'd be under it too.

There was a loud *thunk* above. I flinched, then glanced back upwards. The spade dropped from Tom's hand onto the ground above me and he crumpled.

Then he fell head first into the pit beside me.

I scrambled to my feet and up out of the hole. A hand reached for me and pulled me up.

'I couldn't wait any longer,' said a voice. 'I rang the police but they were going to take too long.'

It was a woman and she was wearing a hoodie. I couldn't see her face until she turned to glance back at the house and the rear security lights lit up her face.

'*Mrs Tanner?*' I said.

'I promised I'd protect you,' she said.

She hugged me then, dropping the spade she'd been carrying to the ground beside Tom's.

'I don't understand,' I said.

'I hit him. He won't be dead, but he'll have one hell of a headache.'

'What are you doing here?' I asked.

'I've been watching over you ... I couldn't just leave ... knowing what I know.'

It started to rain. The damp earth on my clothing turned to mud. I glanced into the pitch-black hole. Tom didn't move.

'Oh my god! Daniel Evans's body is in there. Tom killed him.'

In the distance I heard an approaching siren.

'I have to go,' Mrs Tanner said. Then she picked up the spade. 'You fought him off. He was trying to kill you. *I was never here.*'

She pushed the spade into my hand and then she hurried away, back towards the house.

'Wait!' I called.

'I'll be in touch!' she said. 'There's loads to tell you.'

She passed into the house and disappeared.

The rain fell in big fat droplets and poured down into my eyes. My hair was plastered to my head – blonde turned into dirty wet streaks that clung to my cheeks. I'd been here before, another time, another moment of betrayal and sadness. *Déjà vu.* Fear sank down into the pit of my stomach. I was drowning in the endless possibilities of 'future'. What about my daughter? So small, so helpless, so alone.

Oh God! *Melody.* She was in the house ...

I wanted to run, make sure Melody was all right, but I couldn't move. My limbs were frozen, my whole body weak. I might have been suffering from shock – and no surprise.

I ran my hand over my face, clearing the water from my eyes. And then my fingers touched the sore sticky wound on my forehead and I found myself staring at the red stain on my palm. The rain eroded the blood, as though it could wash away the evidence of my crime.

One minute later, a dark shape climbed from the pit behind me and strong arms grabbed me from behind. I was thrown to the ground and then I saw Tom, once more looming over me. His face was a mask of madness. In his hand was the spade. The blade of it was turned down as though to cut right through me. He pulled back his arm ready to finish what he'd started and then a shot rang out.

The spade fell from his fingers as a bud of dark liquid blossomed on his chest. He fell to his knees.

I back-pedalled away from him to the edge of the hole. I think I was screaming. And then I was surrounded by my uniformed rescuers and among them, Old Freddie, hunting rifle still in his hands.

'He was trying to kill her,' Freddie said.

Chapter Fifty-Two

I was in the Manor office when the phone rang.

'Mrs Carlisle? This is Detective Walker. We have some news finally on the body found in the grave. I thought you'd like to know.'

Six months had passed since Tom had tried to murder me, and I saw Mrs Tanner again. Old Freddie's witness statement declared that I was alone with Tom – the old man intervened when he realized Tom was going to kill me. The police told me that a woman rang. The call was anonymous, but it came from our house. I didn't tell them, even though I knew it was true, that Isadora's former housekeeper was there and she had saved me. I kept her secret – yet she hadn't contacted me as promised and I didn't think she ever would.

Tom had died in surgery. Freddie was a good shot and he'd aimed to kill. I never asked him why he hadn't gone to incapacitate, because deep down I knew ... Freddie had been watching out for me too. I guess the old man already understood what my husband was, just as Mrs Tanner had.

'The man we found was identified as Peter Derbyshire. He'd been missing for seventeen years,' Detective Walker told me.

'We now know he met with foul play. We interviewed your mother-in-law about his disappearance at the time. Witnesses implied she was having an affair with the man.'

'Who killed him?' I asked.

'Maybe your mother-in-law and perhaps your husband helped her hide the body. It might explain his instability. We've spoken to his therapist as you suggested. An abusive mother. It all adds up.'

I put the phone down. It didn't add up. Even though I had no proof, I knew the abusive mother story had been another of Tom's lies.

I walked from the office to the kitchen and looked through the back window to the land beyond. For the time being the work had halted: Daniel Evans had not been found but I had to make sure there were no other bodies out there.

'Charlotte?'

I turned to see Sara standing behind me.

'There's a man here to see you. He says it's important.'

I took the card she was holding and read the name: 'Colin Craig. Attorney'. *Becki's divorce lawyer friend.* I was surprised he was there but curious enough to invite him inside.

'Bring him in,' I said.

I put the kettle on and pulled two cups out of the cupboard.

Colin Craig was exactly how I remembered him. Tall, smartly dressed – every bit the lawyer.

'Sit down,' I said.

I offered him a drink.

'No thank you. I'm just here to deliver something to you.'

He sat opposite me at the rustic kitchen table.

'Becki probably hasn't told you, but I'm no longer in need of a divorce lawyer.'

'I know about your husband's death,' he said. 'I'm acting in a somewhat alien capacity for me, though. A third party contacted me and asked me to deliver this to you.'

He opened his briefcase and held out a bulky envelope.

'I asked what was in it. For obvious reasons I didn't want to deliver something offensive. But I've been assured that it is a letter with some information in it that you'll need.'

Colin left when I took the envelope. He'd done his duty and I needed to be alone to read the contents. I didn't need to ask him how he knew about Tom's death; the circumstances and the following inquiry had filled several pages in the nationals for a while.

'Aren't you curious?' I asked him before letting him out the front door.

'I was paid not to be.'

I took the letter into the office.

The room had been significantly changed. As well as new decor, there was a play pen, and a new modern desk on which stood a new computer system that linked me both to the estate and to Carlisle Corp – for which I was the acting CEO until such a time as Melody was old enough to take over. I'd taken to corporate life like the proverbial duck to water. All of my education and recent experiences came to the fore. I was finally a grown-up.

The antique desk, with the stain of my blood on the corner, was no longer in the house. I didn't ask Sara or Old Freddie where they put it. Everything that reminded me of that night had been removed.

I was still having therapy, trying to come to terms with the madness of my husband. It was the thing that delayed my healing. It would probably be the question I'd always ask.

I sat at my new desk. For once Tina and Melody weren't in the room with me. Melody was in a baby walker, racing around the house followed by her devoted nanny. She was ten months old, not that far from walking and was a beautiful happy child.

The office was quiet and I stared at the envelope, recognizing the swirl of perfect handwriting. It was from Isadora.

The thought that my dead mother-in-law had sent me a letter beyond the grave might have sent me into screaming panic months ago, but now any stress was replaced by curiosity.

I took the envelope knife I kept in my desk drawer and I cut a neat line through the top. Then I removed the handwritten note. It was several pages long.

Dear Charlotte

If you are holding this letter then I am no longer with you.

I cannot tell you how sorry I am that things went the way they did. I have always tried to protect you even when you believed I was interfering.

And now for some truths that I couldn't give you before. You have no idea how difficult it is for me to say this: I've recently come to believe that Tom has serious mental problems.

They may have begun in his teens. Perhaps it was the onslaught of puberty, and maybe I was somehow to blame because I was unhappy and looked outside of my marriage for affection. At this time, I met a man called Peter Derbyshire and we started an affair. But it wasn't just the usual fling for me. Peter was the love of my life.

Tom's father, Conrad, was indifferent as a husband. I never intended to divorce him, but as my relationship with Peter grew, I couldn't carry on the way things were. We met frequently at the Manor when Tom was at school, the staff were off duty, and Conrad was in London. I was discreet but it wasn't enough for either of us and so we began to plan my leaving. Like you and Ewan Daniels – I wanted to be with Peter. We made plans to start a life together. I had every intention of taking Tom with me though. I love my son, and have only ever wanted the best for him.

But it wasn't such an easy decision to make. I put it off many times, until at one meeting, Peter raised the question again. He was naturally growing impatient. So, we agreed I would end things that week with Conrad and I'd move out.

On hearing this Tom burst from my wardrobe revealing he'd been there all along watching and listening. I was horrified to realize my son had been watching us have sex. I didn't know it at the time, but it'd been going on for months.

Tom was insane with rage. He was yelling at Peter to get out. Telling him he couldn't take me away. We both tried to reason with him but he attacked Peter. There was a struggle and Peter tried to avoid hurting Tom, but things got out of hand and when Tom knocked me down during the tousle, Peter swung for him.

I was mortified. I couldn't accept that he tried to hit Tom. Tom was only 15 and a child. He couldn't be responsible for his fear of losing me.

I sent Tom to his room, and Peter and I had our first and last argument.

He left. I never saw him again. You see, Tom is everything to me and I couldn't forgive Peter's behaviour easily. So I'd told him it was over.

Over the next few months I was distressed by what had happened. Tom tried to talk to me, but I refused to discuss it with him. I regretted my anger at Peter and decided to call him, but he wouldn't return my calls. After a few weeks, when he didn't contact me, I knew it was really over.

At first Tom, feeling guilty I suppose for what he'd done, tried to comfort me. I told him I'd have taken him with me. He was sorry for interfering. But it didn't make me feel any better. Then his words turned from kindness to a sort of blackmail.

'You can't leave Father,' Tom had said to me. 'Think of the scandal. And that man wasn't worth it, Mother.'

A few months later a detective called to the house and told me Peter had been reported missing by his mother. I couldn't help because I hadn't had any contact with him since that night. But it worried me. I had a private detective look for him too.

The next part of the story is the hardest for me to admit. As I recovered from the loss of Peter, Tom would often find *his way into my room. He'd beg me to be happy again and then he's say, 'You're mine, Mother.'*

I grew concerned about his overzealous interest in me. It made me feel uncomfortable. So, I managed to persuade Conrad to send him away to a residential college when he was 16. It was both difficult and a relief to be away from him. I sent him letters and care packages like any other mother would, and I locked what had happened away deep inside myself, trying never to think about it. When he came back, he was behaving normally. Ultimately, I blamed myself. If I hadn't had the affair none of this would have happened, Tom would never have seen me with Peter, and I wouldn't have hurt my own child without realizing it. I guess I put his odd obsessive behaviour down to the thought that he might lose me as his mother and it had made him insecure.

After his return, Tom had a variety of girlfriends that he didn't treat very well. I tried to ignore his behaviour, telling myself it was part of growing up. But his cruelty made me feel uncomfortable. There was one particular girl that stopped seeing him. I overheard Tom on the phone to her. He called her a 'slag'. When I asked him about it, he said it didn't matter – she was nothing to him. But I met up with the girl's mother some weeks later. 'Will you ask him to stop calling?' the mother said. 'She's getting scared now, and I'll call the police.' I asked her to explain and she told me Tom and Izzy – yes that was her name – had broken up because Tom had hit her. I denied that he'd do that, but Izzy's mother was insistent. She said it happened after Tom had a jealous rage when she smiled at another boy.

I talked to Tom and he denied the whole thing. He said the girl was not what he thought she was, and then refused to discuss her again.

When Tom went to Oxford and began talking about you, I was relieved. Then, when Conrad and I met you, I realized you were a sweet girl and I was happy to see Tom in love. It was a good thing he'd broken up with Izzy, and I began to believe that had all been a lie on the girl's part after all

It didn't occur to me how similar you and I were until much later. I was just so pleased Tom was happy.

At your engagement party I overheard one of the wives of Conrad's colleagues commenting on how Tom was 'marrying his mother'. You'll remember we held the party at the Manor? I caught the woman looking at the painting of me at the top of the staircase. I looked up and I could see what she meant. You were a younger, prettier version of me.

I left the party and went to my bedroom to think. I tried to convince myself I was imagining it, and it was a silly remark for the other wife to come out with anyway. After half an hour I decided I couldn't hide away any longer and I returned to the party to see you both dancing together. You looked so happy, that I decided I was worrying unduly.

Oh Charlotte, I know you thought I was interfering, but my plan was never to offend but to help you. I don't think I did this as well as I could have. If only I could have seen a little into the future.

The first time I began to suspect that things weren't right was the night before your wedding. I came upstairs after overseeing the decorations in the marquee. Everything was prepped and I'd taken care of every single detail.

By then Conrad was sick and he was in the hospital having chemotherapy. You know how that was, Charlotte, and how he just managed to hold on long enough to see you both married?

So, I was sleeping alone. I hadn't looked for any other comfort elsewhere. I knew Conrad wouldn't be around much longer and felt that one day in the future, at some point, I might find companionship again. Maybe even the same depth of feelings I'd had for Peter. I was thinking all of this when I entered my bedroom and found Tom in my room.

'What are you doing here?' I asked.

I was immediately uncomfortable, though I didn't know why. He put his hand down on the sheet then snatched it back as if a snake had bitten him.

'I hate satin,' he said.

I blinked. I didn't know how to respond. His face became a mask of fury and I knew he was remembering that day and my affair with Peter. I experienced a burst of fear of him for the very first time. But no sooner had the rage appeared than his face smoothed out and he smiled at me.

'Goodnight, Mother,' he said. 'Get some sleep. We have a big day tomorrow.'

Then he stood up and strolled from the room.

Do you remember my warning the next day? I said to you: 'Are you sure you want to be a part of this family?

The world of Carlisle is not what it seems.'

I should have warned you better, I know. But how could I without appearing like an overprotective mother who thought you weren't good enough for her son?

After the wedding though, you were both so happy that I stopped worrying. I'd never seen Tom behave with anyone the way he did with you. He was a gentleman. Not the arrogant boy I knew he could be. He treated you so well. Declared over and over to me how he wanted to make you happy.

When Conrad died, Tom stepped up and became the man of the family. I let him do that because I thought it was good for him, even though I knew Carlisle Corp would possibly become more important to him than his marriage. It was always the case in the Carlisle relationships: the Corporation was a demanding mistress. But I soon realized that this was not a problem. Tom was on the surface always a devoted husband.

I watched for signs of unhappiness in you. There didn't appear to be anything to worry about. Although I guessed that someone of your intelligence was bored at times. Hence why I suggested having a child to you so often.

Finally, I was able to put all of my concerns to rest. As the years went on, Tom was just ... normal. Happy. I didn't think his childhood trauma mattered at all.

This brings me to more recent events of which you are more familiar.

Outwardly Tom was only concerned about the company: his days were spent wheeling and dealing, and he barely gave you a thought beyond what you might make for supper.

But the truth was Tom showed very little interest in the company. This didn't matter because Conrad had all of the right executives in place. Tom was always going to have an easy job, as Carlisle Corp ran itself.

But it gave him too much time to think, and Tom was obsessed with you, Charlotte. I just didn't know how much.

The idea that he wanted to see what you did with your day presented itself when one of his executives made a comment about wives, and their easy life. Days of lunching, beauty appointments and gym visits. Tom listened to the chat and decided to have you followed – just to gain insight into what he believed you were really like.

The detective agency soon told him that you were a very good wife. There was nothing out of the ordinary.

'I thought Charlotte would be more interesting than that,' he said to me. 'I wonder what she would do if presented with an interesting new friend.'

Remember Harrods, Charlotte?

At Harrods, Tom mentioned he liked them. I knew those sheets had a different connotation to Tom and reminded him of an unhappy time in his teenage life. Later you bought them. He then got angry with you. This upset you but like the good girl you are, you took them back to please him. Tom knew you'd do that.

He was there. Waiting, watching.

The thing he didn't plan on was your accidental meeting again with Daniel. Daniel hadn't been paid to be there, you see. He believed you were no longer being followed.

When he invited you to coffee, it was because he wanted to. It all played perfectly into the little scenario that Tom wanted to create.

I don't know this for sure but I've pieced together the events of that afternoon and I now believe it was Tom who pushed you when you fell into the bus lane.

There. I've said it. It pains me but God help me I think this to be true.

I paused taking this in. I thought about everything that Isadora's letter told me but it was hard to read and for a time I couldn't take anymore. I remembered the accident, of course, even that feeling of a hand in the small of my back. Oh God! Could it be true?

I heard laughter outside the office. I placed the letter in the top drawer of my desk and then I went out into the corridor and saw my lovely baby girl racing along in her baby walker, legs strong enough already to support her, while Tina chased after her. It reminded me that the terror had ended. It grounded me. I could do this because I needed to know it all, no matter how painful it was.

I went back into the office and sat once more at the desk. I took a breath and then I removed the letter again. I was ready.

Charlotte, dear, you must be thinking now about how I failed you. In my defence I can only say that I didn't always know what Tom was doing. It was much later that pieces of this puzzle came together. You see, when I questioned him, Tom always had a reasonable answer. And he was so good at switching the blame elsewhere.

When you miscarried with the first baby, I came to the flat to let in the mattress company while Tom was at the hospital with you. The bed was ruined, and I pulled strings to get the mattress removed and replaced as quickly as possible. While I was there, I found packaging stuffed under the bed. There were two boxes, both empty, in a paper pharmacy bag.

I thought you'd done this yourself at first because Tom had put the idea in my mind that you might have deliberately walked in front of the bus. That you didn't want to have a baby because you'd been so resistant to motherhood.

You see, I googled what the drug was and discovered it was the morning after pill. Only supposed to be effective three to five days after unprotected sex, but I thought you'd taken two and brought about the miscarriage yourself.

Tom was so distraught about the miscarriage that it never occurred to me the bag was hidden under his side of the bed.

I took it and kept it though. I did it to stop Tom learning what I thought you'd done. But I found the bag recently when I was going through my things – trying to make my departure easier for my son – and I looked inside and discovered that there was also a till receipt. The last four digits on the paper were from Tom's card number, not yours. I knew then that he had somehow fed them to you.

I hate to believe this but the pain you suffered may have pleased Tom. He said something to me later, about you being 'cleansed' by suffering.

I noticed Tom's change after the ball. He became very happy and relaxed all of a sudden. He was behaving like everything was going wonderfully well with you both.

I don't need to rehash anything else here, except for Daniel Evans. You see, I didn't know you had been seeing him. Or that you had begun an affair, but I later learnt that Tom did. You, and Daniel, had fallen completely into his trap. Without knowing it, you were giving Tom everything he wanted.

I got involved when I learnt what Tom was doing. I had a tremendous feeling of guilt. Tom was a voyeur and I was sure this had something to do with what he'd witnessed growing up because of me.

Looking back, I should have seen the signs, but I didn't, and for that I'm sorry.

You are probably wondering why I'm sending you this letter, after my death. If you and Tom are happy it is not my aim to spoil that.

But other things have happened that lead me to say – I'm worried, Charlotte – and as my end approaches, I know there is nothing I can do to help him anymore.

Isadora

Chapter Fifty-Three

I turned the paper over, hoping for some continuation, wanting more, but knowing there wasn't any. I was left feeling frustrated by Isadora's letter. While confirming that Tom had set me up with Daniel, it was also hinting at something else. And that was the only door I needed to close. I still had no idea what had happened to him. The abrupt ending of the letter made me nervous. There was something she wasn't telling me.

I stuffed the letter away into the top drawer and paced the office. It was heartbreaking that I couldn't finish this chapter in my life. I was sure that Isadora knew for certain what had happened and where Daniel's body was. But as always, even in death and compelled to send me – this – she still covered up for Tom.

I left the office and returned to the kitchen where I filled the kettle and switched it on. I always made tea when I had to think. It was as though the kettle was a timer and the solution would present itself as the hot steam poured from it at boiling point.

My mobile phone rang in my pocket.

I answered the call even though the number was not one I recognized.

'Charlotte?'

'Yes?'

'It's Audrey Tanner here.'

'Mrs Tanner. I've been waiting a long time for your explanation,' I said.

'You read Isadora's letter?' she said.

'Yes.'

'Do you have a paper and a pen?'

'I have questions,' I said.

'I have a lot to tell you. But I need you to write down this address first.'

I headed back to the office and wrote down the address she gave me. It was not far from the Manor.

'Meet me there in an hour,' she said.

The sat nav in the Range Rover took me to a large country estate. The house, once owned by wealthy landowners, had been turned into a private hospital. I parked in the car park at the front and then went into the building through the main entrance.

I could tell as I entered the building that this had once been a home as grand as the Manor. Now it pandered to the needs of the wealthy.

There were signs up around the clinic offering plastic surgery deals of all kinds. I was sure that this was the type of place that some of the other executives' wives would attend to hold onto their looks.

The reception was empty though, and Mrs Tanner was nowhere to be seen. I walked to the desk and without looking up the receptionist asked my name.

'Charlotte Carlisle,' I said.

'Ah yes. You're here to see a patient,' she replied.

I didn't ask any questions but followed as she led me into a small, glass-panelled room that overlooked a therapy pool and exercise area, the likes of which any exclusive gym would be proud to own. This room could be used as an observation area for doctors, visitors and patients. It was a small area with a few tables and chairs, and a vending machine for hot drinks in the corner.

It was in there that I realized this hospital offered more than cosmetic services. Several patients beyond the class were participating in recovery therapy for other surgeries. I saw one man helped from a wheelchair and placed on his feet between two wooden frames, and there was a woman lifted into the pool, with a nurse in the water to assistance her with her therapy.

'Wait here,' said the receptionist.

I looked around the space then chose a table overlooking the pool. There was no one else in the small room. The door behind me opened. I looked over my shoulder. Mrs Tanner walked in, she closed and locked the door and came towards me with the confidence of someone who knew the place well.

'Hello, Charlotte,' she said.

'What the hell is going on?' I asked.

'I brought you here, because this is the best place to tell

you what you need to know,' she said. 'At the end, Isadora told me a lot of things.'

'She gave you the letter for me?'

She nodded.

'Why did you use Colin Craig and not the family lawyer to deliver it?'

'I wanted someone who didn't know Isadora and therefore had no vested interest in anything she might have said. I needed anonymity. Also after her funeral, knowing what I knew, I thought I'd better wait to give it to you.'

'What do you mean?'

'Isadora didn't seal the envelope. I read the contents and I knew she was still trying to protect Tom. You see I think she knew what he was all along, but she was in denial.'

'But how did you *choose* Colin Craig? You see I'd met him before,' I said.

'I found his card at the manor. It was torn in half, cast into the bin in the office. I noticed he was a divorce lawyer and realised you must have spoken to him. I wanted someone you trusted to bring you the letter.'

I processed this information. I hadn't thought about the business card Craig had given me all those months ago. Tom must have found it and destroyed it. It was sheer luck that Audrey Tanner had found it.

'You know what happened with Daniel, don't you?'

'Isadora told me the story. I doubt she even knew she was doing it. At the end she was so full of drugs and her guilt came to the surface. I suppose I was her confessional.'

'Tom told me she was a terrible mother.'

Mrs Tanner laughed, 'Tom, my dear, was a sociopath. I doubt he ever said a true word to you. He couldn't help himself, even as a child. He lied all the time.'

'But why? What happened to make him like that?'

'Nothing traumatic.'

'He saw Isadora with her lover,' I pointed out, knowing she'd read the letter.

'He was always ... watching her. Following her around. Sometimes he hid and jumped out to surprise her. She thought it was funny – and I suspect he'd hidden in the wardrobe that day for this very reason. He was possessive of her. I think his possessiveness was something he was born with but she indulged him, encouraged it almost.'

'You'd better tell me what happened. I'm rapidly losing my patience,' I said.

'I like this change in you. You're stronger now. You've become everything you should have been,' she paused before saying, 'I heard the board tried to replace you as CEO and failed.'

'Melody's future had to be protected. They wanted to sell off the company because of the scandal. Good job I got that first in corporate law.'

'I'm so proud of you. And I suppose that's why I knew I could trust you with this final secret. I can trust you, can't I, Charlotte?'

I wanted answers and so I nodded. Then she told me Isadora's final secret.

'I found out about your affair for the first time when Tom rang Isadora to tell her you were leaving him. She later told me he admitted that he had known all along. Tom loved knowing another man was sleeping with you, Charlotte, but he didn't want to lose you, that was never his plan. He thought the affair would fizzle out and he'd have the photos and video footage to enjoy when he wanted. He didn't disclose this to Isadora, but she'd suspected that this was his fetish. The game he played with you, where he nagged about having a baby, was just that. He wasn't really bothered about fatherhood. He was having too much fun watching his wife's secret life. His own personal reality TV.

'Isadora rang Daniel when she learnt what had happened and she invited him to the Manor. I was around but I was discrete and they sat and talked in the kitchen. He told her he loved you and wanted to take care of you. Apparently, following his wife's terminal illness the insurance company had paid out. He had money, not what you were used to with Tom, but he believed he could look after you: Daniel was the real deal and he loved you. I had never really thought Tom was worthy of you and after what he'd done, setting you up like that, I think Isadora found it hard to ignore that Tom had problems too.

'They were still talking and drinking in the kitchen when Tom arrived. Before that though, Isadora had tried to buy Daniel off. He wasn't interested.

'When Tom saw Daniel there, he flipped. He picked up a breakfast bar stool and smashed Daniel over the head with it before he could react. Daniel fell to the floor. His skull was cracked open and there was blood all over the tiles.'

'Oh my god,' I said.

'Isadora screamed at Tom. "You've killed him!"'

'Tom went white. His game had gone too far and he knew it. "You've got to help me, Mother," he said. "This is all your fault. You made me what I am. I love Charlotte, I can't lose her."

'I was afraid to be seen and stayed hidden. The rage returned to Tom's expression and I knew Isadora was in danger if she didn't help him. But by helping him she was implicating herself in a murder. So, she did what she always did when Tom scared her, she took charge. Forcing him to revert to a child. She told him she knew people that could make Daniel Evans's body disappear, that she'd take care of everything. The rage went out of him. He was like a child, crying one minute, blaming her the next..

'She sent him away. Warned him to stay away from you that night because I think she was afraid he'd hurt you too. She told him she would be his alibi if anything led back to them. He listened to her eventually and, after calming down, he went off to find a hotel for the night.

'After Tom left, I revealed my presence to Isadora. I checked on Daniel and then I discovered that he was still alive—'

'*He was alive?*' I said.

Mrs Tanner paused.

'Alive, yes. But badly hurt. I told her she had to call an ambulance. But she couldn't do that; there would be too many questions and the police would definitely be called.

'She felt guilty but very scared. I've always been loyal to Isadora. I should have called the police and an ambulance myself, but I couldn't do that to her. It would have destroyed her to see Tom arrested. So, I knew what I had to do. I phoned the manager of the clinic. He is a friend of mine, and with

Isadora's agreement, he arranged to send an unmarked ambulance. They took Daniel away. Each of the medics involved in bringing him in was paid a large sum of money for their discretion. Isadora had to protect Tom, Charlotte. But I couldn't keep a murder secret, no matter what, and so she agreed to pay for any treatment he'd need. I suppose she thought this cleansed Tom for his actions.'

'Daniel ... is he ...?'

'Isadora had the best brain surgeon shipped in and they operated. Daniel wouldn't wake though, Charlotte. He was in a coma.'

I felt sick, scared. I wanted her to continue but was afraid to listen.

'Then Tom rang Isadora and told her he'd brought you home. That you were broken and believed that Daniel had abandoned you. Tom loved that he was now the knight in shining armour who had come to rescue you. He knew he could bring you back and keep you. That was what he wanted above all else. He asked Isadora again for her help. They had a row. She told him it was all his fault and she didn't want to lie to you about it. But his tone changed and he said, "If you don't help, then you're in my way, Mother. I can't have anyone in my way."

'It was the first time he'd voiced the threat that I knew was there. I saw then that Isadora was genuinely afraid of Tom. She had to play along or she'd be in danger too. We all did. I'd seen what Tom was capable of and the last thing I needed was him finding out about how we'd helped Daniel Evans. Eventually, to keep the peace, Isadora agreed to meet up with you at the restaurant and lie about her "many" affairs. There'd been only Peter, you see.

'Because you were now back in Tom's clutches, I felt responsible for you. But I didn't know how I was going to help you. I thought of telling you what I knew – but that would only bring trouble to Isadora and those medical professionals we'd enlisted and paid off. It would impact everyone and so I was trapped with my knowledge. Then, when you came to the Manor with Tom, you both seemed to be getting along and happy. I thought maybe Tom did deserve a second chance after all. You didn't seem in any danger and so I thought I'd better let sleeping dogs lie.

'Soon after that, Isadora learnt she had cancer. The life had gone out of her after Tom had attacked Daniel. To ensure my silence she changed her will leaving me a large sum on her death. But I told her I'd still talk unless she left you the bulk of her estate. I wanted to make sure that, when the time came, you too had the money to be free of Tom.'

'I overheard you talking to Old Freddie,' I said. 'I knew neither of you liked him, just not the reason.'

'I had wanted to tell you – but I was afraid. I knew the cover-up could get me in serious trouble and others too as I've said. But I was … scared of Tom too. He was a powerful man. He had the means to pay someone to seduce his wife, so why not to make someone disappear? At the time, I feared if I revealed what I knew, then I'd be in serious danger and so would Isadora.'

She fell silent again and glanced through the glass to the therapy room beyond.

'When you fell pregnant, Tom was indisputably happy. He swore he'd be a good husband and father. He was so genuine that, despite all she knew about him, Isadora hoped this was the turnaround he needed. No Mother wants to believe her son is irredeemable, and she was no different. But you were both settled then and happy, so I kept the end of my bargain until Isadora was gone.'

'You said Isadora talked while she was on meds?' I asked. 'What else did you learn?'

'When she first learnt she was ill, Isadora went to Tom's office to see him. There she discovered that Tom's PA, Gillian, had left. She queried Tom about the suddenness of her departure, but he wouldn't talk about it. He was so circumspect that she became suspicious. She didn't think he was having an affair with her. Nothing like that, but she knew something had happened to end her long career with the company. So, she brought in her own detective and she tracked her down.

'At first Gillian wouldn't talk. She said she didn't know anything. Isadora had to tell her she had concerns for you in order for her to open up. Then she told her that Tom had made her pretend to be Isadora on phone calls with Abbot's detective agency all the time they had been following you. She gave them their instructions and dealt with all their emails. Once you became pregnant for the second time, Tom decided to cut ties with them. He wanted a clean slate so he paid Gillian for her silence and she retired early.

'But that wasn't all she told Isadora. She said she'd become scared. Tom had a folder full of pictures of you and Daniel. She said he liked looking at them.

'That was the only thing Isadora's letter was clear about. And, he admitted he *liked* looking at them,' I said.

'Isadora found out that he was still having you followed periodically. It was an obsession. They had another row about it and she told him he had to start trusting you or he would lose you. That's when he demanded a paternity test for Melody. He had no doubt at all that she was his. He knew where you were all the time because the detectives reported it. But it was another way to upset and frighten you. To make you more insecure. Isadora, as you know, got involved and I arranged the test. Because Charlotte, if by some miracle Melody hadn't been Tom's, my people would have said she was anyway.'

'She was his!' I said.

'I know. But I'd have had it proven either way.'

'Why?'

'I had begun to believe that you were in real danger and if Tom had any doubt that Melody wasn't his, he would hurt you.'

I was stunned by this revelation.

'You ... should have told me sooner.'

'It was wrong of me, I know. But that's why I was there that night. I'd been returning regularly. No one knows that house like I do, or how to not be seen in it. And I was afraid for you – especially after he hit you.'

I felt my face flush with shame.

'Yes. I knew. Freddie did too.'

Mrs Tanner closed her eyes as though she couldn't bear to see the blame on my face.

'I have been wracked with guilt. I blame myself every day for not helping you more, or sooner. Old Freddie was a different kettle of fish. He too suspected Tom was dangerous. I'm glad he didn't hesitate in the end when you needed him.'

'Freddie won't discuss it with me. But how did he know?'

'The bones in the garden.'

'My god! He knew they were there?'

'Not right away. But one night, he found Isadora digging there. She had pulled the monitors off and staggered outside and was scraping at the soil. I came out and we both helped her back to her room. "He's dead," she said. "Tom killed him. That picture in their house ... it's just like one I had taken with Peter."

'She was mostly incoherent but I managed to ascertain that Tom had taken a selfie of you. She'd seen it and it was playing on her mind. After that Freddie went digging and he found something. I told him to cover it back up and we never spoke about it again.'

I tried to process everything she told me. It all made sense now. Isadora's distress when she saw the picture Tom had taken of us. Right on the spot where Peter's body was found and where Tom tried to dispose of me.

'What did you do with Daniel's body in the end?' I asked.

'Body?'

'His sister deserves to know where he ended up.'

'Charlotte, Isadora paid for him to be taken care of. Even though the doctors said it was pointless. He was in a coma and showed no sign of coming round. Even so, we kept him safe and hidden from Tom.'

'What? He's ... *alive?*'

'Yes. It's why I brought you here. A few weeks ago he woke. The doctors couldn't explain it. It shouldn't have been possible, but somehow while he slept, he healed enough.'

'Oh my god. I want to see him.'

'Charlotte ... he's not what he was. He's weak. Atrophy wasted his muscles. It's going to take months of therapy. And his mind was damaged. He doesn't remember things.'

Tears sprang into my eyes at the thought of Daniel being anything but what he had been.

'He'll be given treatment for as long as he needs it,' Mrs Tanner said. 'Isadora covered it all. Turn around. Take a look.'

I froze. 'He's here?'

I looked in the direction she pointed, into the therapy room and now it all made sense. I saw the man walking between two frames, legs weakened, barely moving. His once fair hair had a tinge of grey, but the hollow cheeks still bore his always familiar expression. He smiled as he reached the end of the frames and his face lit up. It was the man I had once known as Ewan Daniels, but had come to call Daniel Evans.

I had thought I had no more tears left, but they flowed freely as I watched his slow struggle to walk. Why hadn't I recognized him? How many times after he vanished had I searched faces in the crowd, expecting to see him any time?

'I have to go to him,' I said.

'He may not recognize you.'

'I don't care.'

'He doesn't even remember Tom attacking him.'

I shook my head to show her that nothing she could say would dissuade me from seeing Daniel.

She led me from the observation room out to the door that led into the therapy room.

I wiped my eyes and then pushed the door open.

'I'll say goodbye now,' Mrs Tanner said. 'If you speak to the authorities about this ... I'll deny everything I've said.'

'You know I won't do that,' I said. 'It would serve no useful purpose, since both Isadora and Tom can't be held account-able.'

When she walked away, I knew that would be the last time I'd ever see her. I considered that I should have thanked her, after all. Despite the secrets she'd been hiding, she and Old Freddie had saved my life.

I stood and watched Daniel make his way back through the frames. Then, as he turned for his triumphant third round, his eyes met mine.

He faltered, and I hurried forward. He was changed and ravaged by his injury and the effects of a long-term coma, but I had changed too and I knew I was not the same woman that was left waiting for him in the rain.

He held onto the frames as I approached and he stared at me as though it was he who had seen a ghost and not me.

'Daniel?' I said.

'Oh Charlotte,' he gasped and then he staggered towards me between the frames. I was there before he reached the end.

I knew as I hugged him that I should ring Becki and finally reunite them but I wanted this moment to last before I broke the spell. The pain of our journey washed over me. I was no longer standing in the rain. As the tears flowed down my cheeks, and I held the man that was once the love of my life,

I could see the brightest future coming from the darkest of pasts. Nothing else mattered in that moment.

I held Daniel tight, and I promised myself I'd never let him go.

THE END

Don't miss *The House of Killers*, an absolutely gripping new thriller series by Samantha Lee Howe…

Serial killer Neva has been conditioned not to ask questions of the mysterious Network, to remain perfectly incurious and perennially cold-blooded. She must simply execute the targets they text her and live to bury the tale.

But then she's tasked with terminating a fellow assassin and glimpses her own future in her colleague's fate. When she leaves flowers on the gravesite, someone notices.

Agent Michael Kensington knows he'll have his work cut out for him when he's recruited by MI5 onto operation Archive to piece together patterns in cold cases. Nothing could ever have prepared him for Neva…

An assassin obsessed with hell, a fugitive tortured by the secrets of her past, a woman destined to unthread him.

**'One of the deadliest female assassins
I've ever encountered in fiction'**

**Brendan DuBois, *New York Times*-bestselling
author of *The End* with James Patterson**